Their Cc

Promɪꜱe

STAND-ALONE NOVEL

A Western Historical Romance Book

by

Ava Winters

RUBEDIA
PUBLISHING

Disclaimer & Copyright

Table of Contents

Let's connect!.

Did you know *you* can help shape my stories?

The title, the cover, even the soul of the book you're holding were all inspired by my wonderful reader family.

I'm so grateful for the encouragement and ideas you've shared—and this book is for you!

If you're not part of my reader circle yet, I'd *love* to welcome you in! Plus, you'll get a special gift: my novella **"The Cowboys' Wounded Lady"**!

FREE EXCLUSIVE GIFT
(available only to my subscribers)

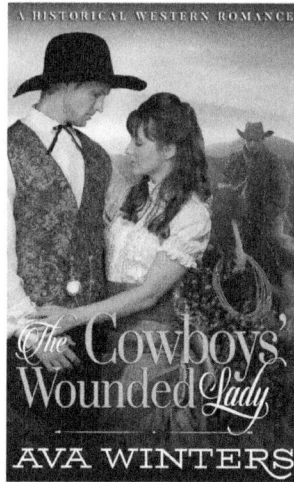

Follow this link:
https://avawinters.com/novella-amazon

Letter from Ava Winters

"Here is a lifelong bookworm, a devoted teacher, and a mother of two boys. I also make mean sandwiches."

If someone wanted to describe me in one sentence, that would be it. There has never been a greater joy in my life than spending time with children and seeing them grow up - all my children, including the 23 little 9-year-olds that I currently teach. And I have not known such bliss as that of reading a good book.

As a Western Historical Romance writer, my passion has always been reading and writing romance novels. The historical part came after my studies as a teacher - I was mesmerized by the stories I heard, so much so that I wanted to visit every place I learned about. And so, I did, finding the love of my life along the way as I walked the paths of my characters.

Now, I'm a full-time elementary school teacher, a full-time mother of two wonderful boys, and a full-time writer. Wondering how I manage all of them? I did too, at first, but then I realized it's because everything I do, I love, and I have the chance to share it with all of you.

And I would love to see you again in this small adventure of mine!

Until next time,

Ava Winters

Prologue

Poughkeepsie, New York, 1871

When does a person fail? Is it when they miss the mark? Break a promise? When a day ends in silence instead of song, the hearth gone cold and no laughter left to echo off the walls? If the effort was honest—if the hands come back empty but bleeding—does that count?

Maisie Ward had failed many times, but in her twenty-two years, she had never failed like tonight.

Ivy—her precious elder sister—lay in their iron-framed bed, fever burning hot enough to set the cotton bedding on fire. Maisie had tried all she could, but money was scarce, and what little they'd managed to collect this week went toward little Junie's needs. Maisie's niece was only a year old, and she needed much.

The night felt hollow, the silence stretched long and thin like a taut thread ready to snap. A single oil lamp—their only one—waited in the kitchen, casting a dim halo that barely softened the chill crawling up from the floorboards. Its flame flickered, light snagging in the crevices of the pale paint peeling from the walls.

Her reflection wavered in the water heating inside the enamel pot. Hazel eyes, sun-kissed skin, dark-blond hair—features that were usually familiar—looked ghostly and wrong. Her chest tightened, as if even her reflection knew she was failing.

"Maisie."

Ivy's voice, once musical, sounded cracked and rough from the bedroom. Had Maisie not been listening—ever alert for her sister's call or Junie's cry—she might have missed it.

She carried the oil lamp and the fresh bowl of heated water back to the room. Every step drew a groan from the aged wood, the sound mixing with Ivy's shallow inhales.

"I'm here," Maisie said.

The lamp found a place on the bedside table, next to a delicate porcelain cup. Inside lay a herbal infusion she'd prepared for Ivy mere minutes ago.

Maisie dipped a cloth in the water. The basin smelled faintly of mint and rust. The liquid felt warmer than her heart, its steam soft against her cheeks. With trembling fingers and a sharp twist of her hands, the excess water noisily fell back into the bowl, leaving behind a damp but heated cloth. She wished, as she delicately cleaned the sweat from Ivy's exposed skin, that the warmth which felt so comforting against her fingers could heal her sister by magic, but Maisie was not foolish enough to believe that.

"Maisie."

"Yes," she answered the fevered call.

"Maisie. Junie...?"

Instinctively, Maisie looked to the corner where Junie slept, unaware of what was happening to her mother and too young to understand even if she were awake.

"Sleeping. She was a good girl today."

Ivy smiled. "Good..." Her voice drifted, lashes fluttering with the effort of staying awake. "Junie is such a precious girl."

"I know."

"Need to... need to keep her safe."

Maisie brushed a hand through her sister's deep, golden-blond hair. The vibrant locks she'd always envied were damp and matted against Ivy's skin, their luster gone—like Ivy's strength.

"We will," Maisie promised.

She helped Ivy sit, needing to feed her the infusion—peppermint and chamomile to coax a fever sweat, a small measure of white willow for the aches. "From Zeke," Ivy rasped, panic fraying the words.

"He'll take her. Maisie! He'll... he'll..."

"Hush." Maisie steadied the cup at Ivy's lips.

Ivy's coffee-dark eyes, dulled and glassy, begged where words failed.

"Swear it." Her hand trembled as it reached for Maisie's, veins stark beneath parchment-thin skin. "You'll protect Junie. Hide her from Zeke."

Maisie grabbed her sister's hand to keep it still, but Ivy dragged her closer and squeezed it with more strength than Maisie thought she could have.

Maisie let Ivy pull her closer and squeezed back, surprised by the flash of strength. "I swear."

"He can't have her, can't hurt her. Please," Ivy sobbed out, the sheen of tears beginning to gather in her eyes and carve a path down her cheeks.

Maisie hummed the lullaby their mother once sang, her voice barely a whisper, until Ivy faded off to sleep. Standing, she left to fetch more cold water. Basil and mint were soaked in the liquid before she returned with it to her sister's bedside.

Once more, she left a few cloths to soak before gently applying them as compresses to Ivy's forehead and limbs.

The night grew long as Maisie sat next to the bed. It was small, barely able to squeeze two, and Ivy needed the comfort more. Maisie would not be sleeping regardless. Her tiny home had never been meant for two people and a baby, but when her sister arrived, breathless and desperate, scarcely a month past, Maisie hadn't hesitated to welcome her.

They spoke of getting someplace bigger, but there were no funds for such a thing when Maisie alone worked. An apothecary assistant only earned a meager sum, not enough for grand dreams.

Maisie only left once more to get herself some tea. In the kitchen, the clock ticked away. It was nearly two in the morning. She sighed and returned to the bedroom with a warm cup of chamomile. Hours dripped by as she continued to work and watch as her sister's breath slowed.

By sunrise, Ivy Blackwell, née Ward, was gone.

Maisie could not say how long she sat there. Time had lost meaning. Her lips gently rested against Ivy's knuckles as she willed herself to control her breathing and hold back the burn in her throat.

If she'd studied more—learned more—would she have known how to save her?

Junie's cry lifted her from the chair. Her legs were stiff and tingling, as if half asleep. She lifted her sweet little niece and rocked her, murmuring gentle words of comfort. Junie was too young to understand; part of Maisie knew the words were more for herself than the baby.

As she started the morning's small rituals—cleaning and feeding Junie—she kept bumping into things that reminded her of Ivy. One month had been enough for the house to feel like *theirs*. It felt cold now, silent in a way she hadn't known it could be.

They needed to leave.

Maisie could not stay where every creak of the floor and shadow on the wall whispered of her failure. The rag doll Ivy had sewn for Junie lay beside the cradle. The chipped teacup Ivy favored still sat on the table, half full of cold infusion. Zeke would find her here easily as well.

Zeke would find her here easily as well.

She packed a small bag with what she could carry: a couple of blankets, a few bottles, some rations, the last of her herbs. Beneath the bedroom floorboard, she pulled out a tin with money Ivy had stolen from Zeke—"a rainy-day fund," Ivy had called it. There wasn't much—not even enough to afford the medicine that would have helped—but it would do.

Grabbing the warmest shawl she owned, Maisie wrapped Junie as tightly as she could. She didn't look around, didn't dare step back into that room to look upon Ivy's face one last time. A silent apology went to the landlord, who would likely be the one to find her sister's body—she had no time for a burial. Ivy had asked her for one last thing, and Maisie would be damned if she didn't do it.

She stepped into the street, where the world was waking. Milk carts rattled over cobblestones, a rooster crowed somewhere down the lane, and smoke curled lazily from chimney tops. Life went on, oblivious to the ache she carried in her chest. Where she would go was a mystery, but she needed to be gone before anyone asked questions—or Zeke finally realized where Ivy had run.

Chapter One

Twin Forks, Colorado Territory, 1871

Maisie's mother had taught her and Ivy that lying was a sin. If they were ever caught in a lie, they were immediately belted. It was never a harsh belting; Maisie was certain it hurt her mother more than it hurt them, but it was enough to make the lesson stick. She still respected her mother's teachings. She both loved and missed the woman dearly, despite how young she'd been when her mother passed of a fever. It was why each lie she spoke tasted of bitter tea brewed with weeds.

And still, she drank it down. Maisie forced each word past her tongue like poison meant to save a life. Junie's life. Nine weeks after losing her sister, she found herself telling lies each day.

The residents of Twin Forks were curious, and each question they asked was met with a lie in response. With every introduction, she used the new last name she'd chosen. It wasn't too bad; she rarely left the little house she had managed to get. There were only two reasons she stepped outside: the few odd apothecary jobs she managed to scrounge up, and the times she needed to collect supplies or payments.

The only thing she cared about was protecting Junie. She did not need a social life, did not need people to tell her to find a husband. She'd already swallowed many sideways glances, many hushed whispers behind handkerchiefs back in New York. She wore judgment like an old coat now; patched, heavy, familiar. This was fine. She would survive.

"Gahh!" Junie cried, her arms flinging up as Maisie came closer.

She grabbed the one-year-old, tossed her lightly—loud, shrieking laughter bouncing off the walls—then caught her and settled her on her hip.

"Is little Junie ready to go to the market?" Maisie asked the clapping child.

She knew to avoid the markets when they were busy. She'd gone once during a peak hour and had been bombarded with too many prying eyes and even more prying questions. By late morning, most locals would be tending fields, with only a few women and children too young for schooling left to wander. That was the best time for shopping.

Twin Forks was a rural town surrounded by ranches. Dirt roads were rutted deep with wagon tracks, and the smell of livestock clung to the air. Dust rose in lazy spirals with every hoofbeat. Wooden storefronts lined the main strip, leaning ever so slightly—as if the buildings were tired of standing straight against the wind. A blacksmith's hammer rang in the distance, the clang bouncing off the foothills, and a dog barked somewhere near the livery.

After seven weeks in Twin Forks, Maisie had a system. She knew where each stall she needed was, how long it would take to get there, and what she needed to buy. She moved quickly, hoping to be home before Junie grew fussy.

She kept her head down and her shoulders stiff as she walked. Her ears strained for any change in tone, any hush that might mean her name spoken behind her back. Her boots crunched over straw, and the hem of her cotton skirt caught on a splinter jutting from a warped boardwalk plank. She stopped, pulled it loose, and glanced around the market.

Barrels of dried beans and root vegetables stood beneath hand-lettered signs. The crisp bite of vinegar mingled with the scent of fresh apples, their skins still taut from the lingering chill of spring mornings. A woman with stains on her apron barked prices to a young boy wrangling a goat on a rope. Within half an hour, Maisie had gathered almost everything she needed. Her last stop was the baker's.

"Back for your usual, Miss Maisie?" the baker asked.

He was a grizzled man with blond hair that reminded her of Ivy and a scratchy beard his wife would soon make him shave.

"Yes, sir," Maisie replied.

Her eyes flicked around the market, uneasy. She didn't like being outside the protection of the house for so long. She felt eyes on her, though she knew none were truly there. This was the last errand; after this, she could avoid coming out again for a week—unless someone sought her out for apothecary work.

"Oh, if it isn't Maisie West!"

The cheerful call came from a bright-eyed woman with a hearty build and hair almost as blond as her husband's.

"Ma'am," Maisie greeted politely, forcing a small smile despite not welcoming the attention.

"I've told you, dear, call me Cissy." She ambled up, but not before flicking her husband a look that sent more of this and that into Maisie's order.

Maisie hated the pity, wanted to tell her that it wasn't needed, but it was. She needed every bit she could get, and she wouldn't be selfish enough to take food from Junie because of pride.

"Now, I have some news..." Cissy glanced around before leaning in to whisper. "A gentleman came by the market—a wealthy one, too. Had a hired driver, and I haven't seen clothes that fine in all my years."

Maisie nodded and leaned closer to catch every word. She wouldn't risk Junie on coincidence. A wealthy man was coming for her, and if this was Zeke, she needed to be ready. She knew—after watching her sister suffer in marriage to him—that he wasn't as kind as he liked to pretend.

"He was asking a lot of questions, said he was looking for family, the poor thing." The baker's wife locked gazes with Maisie, her smile still sweet, but her eyes sharp, and Maisie was struck with the thought that the woman might not be as naive as she thought. "He had a pretty picture of his family—looked sweet. His daughter looked near the age of this precious little tyke."

Cissy pinched Junie's cheeks, and Maisie's heart stuttered. Her throat clenched, and the world narrowed. Market sounds blurred, as if dunked in water. Her fingers tightened on Junie's back.

"Your order, Miss Maisie."

The baker's call snapped her out of it. She smiled, nodded thanks, and took the parcel. Cissy caught her trembling hand and gave it a reassuring squeeze.

"I told him I'd seen that sweet family, but they weren't here long. Pointed him in a direction I figured they'd taken, and he lit out of town. If he's found them, I can't say. I reckon he'll be back soon if he doesn't."

She let go of Maisie, who stared at the woman in shock or thankfulness. Maisie couldn't tell which she was feeling.

Maisie forced another smile, gave a too-stiff nod, and made her way home on shaky legs. Once inside, she barred the door, her heartbeat trying to punch through her ribs. Her hands moved on instinct—folding, wrapping, stuffing bags—while her thoughts howled behind her eyes.

Should she leave now? Wait? Both choices felt like stepping off a cliff. If Zeke had already left Twin Forks, she could vanish like smoke. If he hadn't, she might walk straight into his waiting jaws. The not-knowing was its own torment.

She waited through two searing days and three bone-rattling nights. The air grew thick with dust and heat, and every creak of the porch boards made her stomach twist. The bags sat like silent accusations by the door, a reminder of every minute she hesitated. She didn't dare crack the door—not even to fetch water, not even when she knew she needed to work for money. What if he was out there, waiting for her to blink?

When Zeke Blackwell finally appeared, striding down the hard-packed path, she spotted him through the grimy kitchen window as easily as if she'd conjured him.

She recognized him instantly: the confident stride of a man who'd never had to chase what he wanted. Clothing pressed clean. Jaw sharp as a blade. He used to turn heads—hers included, once. Now all she saw was a man wrapped in control and cruelty like a tailor-made coat. His auburn hair was slicked back, and though she couldn't make out the finer details of his face, she knew those shrewd blue eyes would be hiding anger.

Maisie jerked back from the window, breath trapped. Her knees scraped the splintery boards as she dropped low, crawling over grit toward the corner where Junie sat with her doll. The planks bit her palms; the stale scent of hearth ash and old stew filled her nose.

The house was no bigger than a chicken coop and just as noisy, and every slam of Zeke's fist on the door boomed through the walls like rifle fire, rattling the few dishes left in the cupboard.

"I know you're in there, you little tart!"

Perhaps the tone would have scared her if this were the first time she'd heard him yell with that furious growl—but it wasn't. He raised his voice as easily as he'd raised his fists toward Ivy, and Maisie had seen it, heard it, too many times to be surprised.

"Where is Juniper? Give me my daughter!"

Junie's wide eyes shimmered. Her tiny chest fluttered with shallow, fast breaths. She shrank as if she were trying to make herself disappear into Maisie's arms. The sight nearly broke Maisie in half.

She reached into the bag and fumbled out a dry biscuit, which crumbled in her fingers—anything to plug the terror in her niece's throat. She pressed it into Junie's hands, whispering a hush without words. Her gaze darted around the room like a trapped animal's. She scrabbled for the bags, pulling them close like a lifeline. Every move felt too loud. She prayed the floor wouldn't betray her with a creak as she crept toward the back door.

Did he know it was there? Would he notice her escaping? She didn't know, but she couldn't risk staying. He would break the door down; she was certain of it.

"You have no right to keep her. She's mine! Bring her to me, Maisie Ward, or so help me, I'll make you regret this for the rest of your pathetic life!"

Behind the back door was a narrow path with deep shadows that led to an alley. Maisie had scouted it the day she moved in and mapped every cross-way over the weeks.

She moved on instinct, body numb but obedient, shoes slapping dry dirt and stones that jabbed through the soles. The path carried her to the town's edge. She passed the wooden sign, its blue letters softened by the mist of early spring rains: Welcome to Twin Forks.

17

Junie fell asleep in her arms after an hour. Maisie's muscles ached and burned the longer she walked, but she didn't stop. She couldn't. When a lone carriage passed, she realized the road was too open; he'd see her. She cut away into the fields, shoes soaking as she trudged through the wet.

The air carried a cool sharpness, tinged with the scent of thawing earth and the first timid buds fighting their way into the light. The rustle of wheat brushing her skirt whispered to her as if they had voices. Somewhere far off, a lark called out, a high, sweet trill slicing through the silence.

As the sky lightened from black to deep blue and softened with each passing minute, she reached the edge of a ranch. She heaved the bags over a fence, then climbed after, holding Junie carefully. She didn't care if anyone saw; she didn't even look. She gathered the bags and kept walking.

Her legs quivered with each step, joints grinding like rusted wheels, but she didn't stop. Couldn't. Every step was a refusal to give up. Every breath was a rebellion. She'd carry Junie to the ends of the earth on bloodied knees if she had to.

Finally, when she got close to a corral, her knees gave way and she crumpled into the dust, her skirts soaking up the morning dew from the grass. Her muscles screamed, her lungs burned, but she clung to Junie like she was the last bit of grace God might grant.

Her spine met the fence with a dull thunk, rough slats digging into her shoulder blades. She wrapped Junie in two threadbare blankets, fingers stiff and shaking, and tucked the child close. The baby's soft breath warmed her neck. It was proof that she'd done something right today.

Just a moment, she told herself. Just a breath's rest, then up and on.

Maisie was out before the sun had truly risen.

Chapter Two

Twin Forks, Colorado Territory, 1871

The Calder Spread—some ten thousand acres of rolling sagebrush and corrals—demanded daylight drudgery from dawn's first birdcall to the lantern's last flicker. Wes Calder had been forced to take up the task at the meager age of twenty-one. Seven years later, despite men trying to buy it out from under them or sabotage what the brothers had built, the ranch stood strong.

The pre-dawn sky lay dark as bruised juniper. Cattle lowed in distant pens, and the wind carried the sharp tang of pine, damp sage, and manure warmed by yesterday's sun. Each breath on Wes's tongue was heavy with loam and the lingering musk of half-awake cattle.

Residual warmth from the cast-iron cookstove drifted into the chill air as Wes pushed through the kitchen door. His boot heels clicked and rang across worn flagstone. Broad-shouldered, he filled the doorway; his dark-brown hair brushed the collar of a threadbare work shirt. A pile of unbranded hides lay in the corner—tomorrow's chore, if luck held and weather didn't turn.

Eli's laughter rang sharp as pine needles on the wind while Rhett pursued him with the heavy scowl of a man chasing a runaway colt. For a moment, Wes felt the old ache of a boy who might have chased, too—before the weight of ten thousand acres settled over him again with the same inevitability as morning.

Jesse—average height, lean-muscled, hair the color of autumn wheat—stood by the stove, the picture of calm amid his brothers' racket. His gaze met Wes's with a steady appraisal.

"Looks like Zeke Blackwell's tryin' to buy his way back into the world's good graces."

In Jesse's hands was the *Rocky Mountain News*. He flicked his eyes back to the column. The twist in his mouth—half purse, half grimace—told Wes worry and annoyance were sharing space behind those cool, gray eyes.

"He's been buying out other ranches and properties around Twin Forks," Jesse said.

Eli skidded to a stop by the stove, chestnut hair flopping over yellow-brown eyes. "Jesse! The eggs!" He snatched the skillet just as little curls of steam rose.

Rhett—shorter than the others but stocky as an ox— launched himself into Eli's side. Lighter-brown hair caught the stove's glow as the eggs teetered at the skillet's lip. Jesse reached and plucked the pan free with a long-suffering sigh while the two youngest Calder men fell into a tangle of elbows and boots. He handed the newspaper to Wes and started plating breakfast with the practiced care of a man saving eggs and brothers both.

Wes scanned the article. It was tucked in a corner of the paper—near the end, like it wasn't news fit to wag tongues. There was a time Zeke Blackwell's name would have ridden bold on the front. That shine had dulled the day the man's wife and daughter "vanished," or so the city papers told it. Folks closer to the matter had their own version.

"If he comes sniffing around, you tell him to ride on," Wes said.

He and Jesse co-ran the ranch, but Jesse had the steady hand for people, the patience for accounts. Wes did best with land, stock, and work that bit back.

Passing the rolling duo on the floor, Wes nudged a boot into a fleshy side—firm enough to be felt, not cruel. "Off."

"Seriously?" Eli rolled away, clutching his ribs, while Rhett grinned like a fox with a hen feather in his teeth.

"Off the floor," Wes repeated.

"You didn't have to kick me," Eli muttered.

"Neither of you would've heard if we asked nice," Jesse called, already seated at the table with the coffee poured and plates set.

Wes slid into his chair. Eli and Rhett dropped into theirs a beat later. Jesse reclaimed the newspaper, folded it small, and set it aside.

"What are the chores for the day?" he asked.

"Inspection order," Wes said, leaning his tall frame over a pine scarred by years of fists, knives, and elbows. "Eli, you're point on the pasture. Ride the high ridges, mark any grass gone ragged. If it's thin, drop seed in those gullies by sundown." Eli raised a tin cup of bitter coffee in salute. "After that, check health on the herd. If you've got daylight left, trim hooves for the ones that can't wait."

"Will do, boss man," Eli said, gulping, then grimacing at the bite. He peered around for mercy. Jesse tilted his chin toward the honey pot, and Eli made the barest show of gratitude before dumping in a spoonful too many.

"Rhett—"

Rhett crossed his arms hard enough to creak leather. "You better not be putting me on fence duty again. I'll quit and go to Hurlock's place."

Wes leveled him a look that didn't need words. Rhett fidgeted, scowl deepening before he glanced away.

"Rhett's on trough detail," Wes said. "Haul from the windmill cistern, scrub the cedar logs clean, then push the cows through by sundown. No stragglers."

Eli snickered over the rim of his now-sweet coffee.

Rhett grunted. "Windmill cistern's half low. I'll haul from the spring after troughs. Won't reach the herd 'til noon."

"Cistern first, then herd," Wes confirmed, tapping once on the tabletop. "I'll check perimeter fences and the north corral— see what needs mendin'. I'll keep an eye out for brush we ought to clear before it dries and turns to tinder."

Jesse met his gaze, one brow up—steel-gray eyes and high cheekbones echoing their father's face, gone these many years but still alive in that look. *What about me?* said the lift of Jesse's brow without a word spoken.

"Check supplies," Wes said. "Then document calf drop. We've had a few births."

Jesse nodded and folded the *News* again, slipping it aside. "You remember Old Man Murphy hollerin' yesterday? South pasture by the creek—dry as old leather. I reckon you ride that way after your first loop. See if we can open the spring run."

Eli nodded around a mouthful. "Saw Murphy's stock drifting toward the timberline last evening. If they keep at it, they'll crowd our brand."

"I'll check Murphy's gate," Wes said. "If he blocked the flow again, I'll clear it. Then I'll circle back and make sure our calves have room to bed down."

Rhett shifted on his stool. "Fence Six? Saw slop there, two posts leaning, wire with a belly to it."

"I'll add Six to my list," Wes said. "I'll ride that line coming back from Murphy's—look for loose posts or broke wire. But I'm sweeping the corrals first."

Jesse's mouth edged toward a smile. "Hands full, then."

A sideways glance at the paper jogged Wes's mind. "Ran into Sam Hurlock at the store yesterday. He's selling off half his brand. Moving south."

Eli raised a biscuit slicked in grease. "Sam's spooked. Rumor is Blackwell's frontin' for some Denver syndicate. They want this valley clean for sheep."

Rhett made a face like he'd bitten pith. "Sheep." He slapped his palm on the table. "Wool-heads chew a pasture bare faster than cattle. Let 'em try."

Wes didn't bother answering. He eyed the eggs—edges crisped and going rubbery—resting beside blister-hot biscuits still steaming from the Dutch oven. The baked beans, left to cool, had stiffened into a paste that would keep a man standing through noon. He split a biscuit, found the crumb dense but honest, and washed it down with coffee that owed nothing to sweetness.

Eli and Rhett bickered their way through the last bites, the war of brothers as familiar as the stove's pop. Wes rose first. At the stable, Jeremiah whickered low as Wes laid the saddle blanket straight, cinched the latigo tight, and evened the stirrups by habit more than thought. The gelding's warm brown coat rasped his palms; no finer greeting to a day than a good horse and work waiting.

He mapped his route in his head: corrals first, then outer fence runs, eyes peeled for windfall and dead snag that needed cutting before summer set its teeth. Murphy's place would come after, though Calder work came first.

Shoulders squared like a cavalryman's, Wes tipped the brim of his weather-worn Stetson low and swung into the saddle. Jeremiah's first step rattled the gate chain. The slap of boots behind him said his brothers were finally moving. Wes drew a lungful of brisk air, gathered the reins, and rode into the pale of morning.

Minutes and then hours blurred beneath the rhythm he trusted. He liked the world best when it let him work—body busy, hands certain. No small talk. No questions that pawed at old ground. No need to keep his voice measured for anyone's comfort. The land didn't care about charm. It cared if you showed up and stayed until the job was done.

By midmorning, Jesse's horse showed at his flank as Wes angled toward the outer corrals. They let the silence carry for a while—Jesse knowing enough not to pull at threads Wes left alone.

"Need to count the new foals down there," Jesse said at last, tipping his chin toward the long corral.

Wes considered veering to the far pen and coming back later. He tossed the thought before it got air. Childish. A man did the next job in front of him so the whole didn't sag.

Jesse, bless his brother, did not try to start a conversation with Wes. Out of the three, he was the one who understood that Wes liked the peace of his work and didn't purposefully try to get him to engage in small talk or games like Eli would or silly competitions like Rhett loved to do.

They rode on. Near the corral, Wes caught a shape slumped by the fence, a hunch at the edge of vision he almost mistook for a fallen tarp or a draped saddle. He didn't stop; his mind did the arithmetic of ranch life out of habit—wondered if a foal had gone down in the night, how deep he'd have to dig if it was small enough not to drag—but as they neared, the truth settled cold and heavy.

That wasn't a foal.

The figure was motionless, curled inward against the biting wind. A puff of dust lifted and wrapped the body in eddies. As it settled, Wes caught the unmistakable slope of human shoulders.

He put a heel to Jeremiah and pushed through the gate. Jesse slid down and caught the reins without being asked, letting Wes stride ahead.

Someone was tucked against the rough-hewn planks, shadowed by the overhang. Dark-blond curls spilled over hunched shoulders, half-obscuring a bundle held to the chest with a grip that spoke of bone-deep fear. Even from a distance, he read the rigidity in her posture—the unconscious vow to protect what she held.

Wes softened his steps, slipping into the quiet he'd learned as a scout when stillness meant you kept your skin. He dropped to one knee and peeled back the edge of the blanket with steady fingers.

The morning light revealed the fragile round of a baby's cheek.

His pulse jumped hard against his throat. He held a fingertip near the child's nose, waiting—hoping—for breath. Warmth brushed his skin, a small whisper of life, and some tight knot beneath his ribs loosened without asking his permission.

His gaze slid back to the woman. Mud and dust streaked her clothes; bits of hay and grass seed stitched themselves into the weave. Wet blotches darkened the fabric in uneven spreads, like she'd crossed spring run-off or cut through a stream more by necessity than choice. Her boots were caked and soaked, leather warped from a night cold enough to stiffen joints.

Yet the bundle in her arms was dry as a parlor cushion. She'd kept the baby wrapped in a weather break of her own body. All night, maybe longer.

Wes lifted her chin with care, slow enough not to startle. Sun found her face—small, fine-boned, skin browned by weather, not softness. It struck him she looked like she ought to belong to a quiet room with light on the floorboards, not slumped against a fence where hooves could break ribs if a horse took a wrong step. What brought her into the teeth of someone else's ranch? Did she not know the danger of bedding down against a corral wall, even an empty one? Or had she known and made the calculation anyway?

He clicked his tongue and shrugged out of his duster. Warmth first. He didn't know her name, but the boots told the distance—long. The way she curled told the hours—many. The closest edge of town lay a fair piece off; on foot, in the dark, with a baby? He traced the path in his mind and set it against the country—draws and low places, creek-beds swollen with the last of snowmelt, thorn and rock, wind that knifed after midnight. Thirteen miles at least from the far side of Twin Forks if she'd started where most strangers rented rooms, maybe more depending on which roads she avoided to stay unseen. A walk like that skinned a man raw. A woman with a babe—she'd paid for every step.

He draped the coat over her shoulders and around the baby. The thick canvas swallowed her slight frame; the hem nearly brushed the dust. It made her look smaller still—small enough to stir something old and unwelcome, he didn't have a name for.

He slid an arm beneath her knees, the other around her back, careful of the child. She curled closer in reflex to the heat, not waking, only burrowing like the warmth was the first kindness she'd met in days. The protective clamp of her hands around the bundle didn't loosen even in sleep. He respected that. Admired it, if he was honest.

Jesse had stepped inside the stable, checking stalls and the near pen. When Wes carried the woman in, his brother's head snapped up, eyes going wide before his face settled into that composed line again.

"That a woman?" Jesse asked, dry as dust, like he didn't trust his own eyes.

Wes understood the disbelief. "Looks like she walked."

"Walked?" Jesse came closer, voice pitching up a notch as he took in mud, torn hem, ruined boots. "Insane woman."

"Insane," Wes agreed, but there was no bite in it. "And in need of warmth. I'm taking her to the house."

Jesse nodded once. "I'll finish this side, then open the spring run at Murphy's. You make sure she's seen to."

Wes hesitated a breath—just long enough to look down and see her shiver despite the coat—then he nodded back. Outside, he maneuvered himself into Jeremiah's saddle with the extra weight balanced careful as a full water skin. The gelding shifted, then steadied under the load, good as ever.

As Wes turned the horse toward the house, questions lined up like fence posts across his mind and kept pace with him. Was she injured? Had the cold crept too far into her fingers and feet? How long had she held the child without sleep? He felt the weight of her, not only the body, but the mystery of her; no name, no reason, no warning that the land would set a living riddle at his fence. The ranch had brought him strays before—calves bawling and motherless, a lone shepherd dog gone lame and mean from hunger—but never this. Never a woman and a baby asleep against his corral in the blue light of a Colorado morning.

He kept Jeremiah to a careful pace, one hand steady on the reins, the other braced around the bundle of woman and child, his jaw set against the thought of what kind of trouble put a mother on foot at dawn with nothing but grit to carry her. Whatever the answer, it rode with him now. And he meant to see it warm, fed, and breathing easy before the sun cleared the ridge.

Chapter Three

Time was never something Maisie could spare much of. She always had things to do, money to earn, and a house to care for. She had lived on her own for a long time before Ivy crashed back into her life. That was why Maisie would be asleep one second and awake the next. She never had time to wake up slowly.

Not this time.

Awareness crept in slow as a snail's crawl. The air smelled of aged timber and faint leather, of smoke threaded into walls by a hundred suppers. Heat pressed close. A draft slid somewhere near the floorboards, but the warmth of a woolen blanket cocooned her and tempted her to sink deeper. Her limbs ached—heavy and still, as if the blanket itself had weight. Coarse fibers rasped against the bare skin of her forearms where the coverlet had twisted.

She hadn't even realized she'd been sleeping.

She blinked. The room stayed dim and unfamiliar. Her eyes felt sluggish, as if dipped in lard, and her mind thick with the fog of too-long exhaustion. The straw-stuffed mattress whispered when she shifted, the faint rustle a stranger's sound beneath her.

A soft murmur threaded the quiet. Voices. Too low to catch words. Wood scraped—chair leg across floor?—and the tiny noise sliced the fog, sharp as a knife.

Her breath hitched. She opened her eyes fully. The ceiling above her was rough-hewn plank, not the cracked plaster of the room she'd rented these last weeks.

Memory returned in a rush—Zeke's knock, the narrow alley, the long black hours, the hissing wheat, the fence, the corral. Had he found her? Had he taken—

Her arms tightened. The bundle pressed to her chest answered with a warm, sleeping weight. Junie.

A shuddering breath leaked from Maisie's lungs. If Zeke had found them, the crib would be empty and her arms bare. She swallowed. Her tongue lay thick and dry as dust. Panic clawed up her spine. She forced another breath and then another, tasting old smoke and the ghost of coffee on the air, fighting for a steady rhythm because panic wouldn't save either of them.

Once she was sure she had her breathing, Maisie tilted her head and looked—and met the eyes of a man who would have had Ivy blushing and nudging her in the ribs, whispering names and mischief.

He was tall, broad-shouldered; dark brown hair lay in loose waves that would have curled wild if cut shorter. His eyes were a cool, unsettling gray—beautiful in a way that made her wary. *Attractive* did not cover it. Zeke had been handsome, too. There were others—men who made prettiness a kind of weapon, who liked to lord a pleasant face over a woman's choices. Pretty outside meant nothing about the inside of a man.

Men couldn't be trusted. Attractive men, least of all.

She pulled Junie closer until her fingers ached, the blanket's edge biting into her skin. Any tighter and the baby might smother, but fear had a way of dulling sense. The wool's clean, animal smell and the faint sweetness of Junie's skin filled her head, steadying her for a beat or two.

She surged upright. Pain flashed through stiff muscles. The mattress crackled; the bed frame groaned. She crabbed back until her spine hit the wall with a thud that rattled the pictureless boards.

"Where am I?" she demanded, her voice coming out stronger than the tangle in her chest felt. "Who are you, and what do you want with me?"

She twisted, turning her shoulders and the baby away, making her body a shield. Part of her almost flinched at her own tone—afraid of angering him, knowing she wasn't in any fit state to fight. If he lunged, she'd take the brunt and hope Junie didn't.

"This is my place," he said from the doorway—the only exit she could see. He didn't step closer. His voice carried easily in the still room, a deep, even timbre like far thunder: plain words, no sugar or threat. "Calder Ranch. A few miles west of Twin Forks."

He paused, letting the information land instead of crowding her with it. "We found you collapsed by one of our corrals and brought you in."

His gaze slid once toward the bundle in her arms. Maisie recoiled as if he'd reached to take it, curling tighter around Junie until the child stirred and made a sleepy, offended sound. Little fingers twitched against Maisie's blouse; drowsy blinks fluttered. *Please don't cry*, Maisie prayed silently. *Not now.*

"The baby's fine," he said, voice level. "She was cold and hungry. We did what we had to..."

Maisie's head snapped up so fast her neck twinged. Heat flared through her chest like a struck match. *"Did what they had to?"* The words scraped her like barbed wire. Who were *they?* She should have woken. She should have fed the child herself. It was her job. It had been her promise.

"You did what *you had to*?" The pitch of her voice climbed until it nearly cracked. The blankets bunched under her shaking hands.

"You were exhausted," he said, unruffled. "She was pale and cold and needed food. Are you suggesting we should have left her to starve until you woke?"

Her throat burned with all the words that didn't help—*yes,* a foolish, furious part of her wanted to say, *yes, because at least then it wouldn't be my failure.* Shame coiled low and mean. She had let them take Junie. She had slept.

She stared at the man and decided she disliked him—hated him, almost—for being calm when she was not. It wasn't logical. He wasn't speaking over her. He wasn't punishing her for her tone. He wasn't Zeke. *He wasn't Zeke,* and she hated him for it—in part because she knew how to manage men like Zeke. This kind—quiet, reasonable—left nothing to hold.

She dropped her gaze to Junie and rocked, small motions that steadied her hands. When she looked up again, the man was gone.

The quiet left room to see the place she'd landed: spare, clean, useful. Two bedside tables, a tall dresser rubbed smooth at the handles, the bed beneath her. In the corner, her bags—*all* of them, from what she could tell. No rummaging. No gaps where precious things should be.

Junie would need changing. Maisie checked and found it had been done already. Heat climbed her neck. She closed her eyes until the sting subsided, then opened them to her niece's small hand batting for her hair. "You're all right," she whispered, forehead to Junie's, breathing in milk-sweet and wool. Junie giggled and tugged, unconcerned with the size of the world's teeth. "You're all right," Maisie said again, because saying a thing twice sometimes made it truer.

A faint clack drew her head around. The man had returned, setting a glass on the bedside table.

"Water," he said, gesturing. "Drink. You'll need it."

He stepped back to the door again, keeping the distance between them like it might be a bandage on a wound. It wasn't—not really. Nothing would be, not until Zeke was a problem for someone else to fear.

She stared at the glass.

"I'm Wes Calder."

She continued staring, not giving him the answer he'd left hanging. *Wes.* Short. Simple. Nothing like *Zeke.* He wasn't Zeke. She would need to remind herself of that until she left— because she would leave. Names didn't matter. He was a man.

"Drink," he said again, not sharper, just certain.

She pushed herself up and took the cup. Better to do as asked. Better not to stir any anger. Cool water slid down her throat and soothed the scrape there.

"If you're feeling better, feel free to leave," Wes said.

Maisie's eyes flicked to his face. She searched for the telltale signs—tightness at the corners of the mouth, a flash of temper in the eyes, something that said a trap had been sprung. He looked carved from good stone. She drank again.

"What my brother means," said another voice from the doorway, "is you're free to rest for the day—two, three— however long you need."

Maisie glanced between them. The newcomer's eyes were a similar gray but muted—duller pewter to Wes's bright steel. They shared high cheekbones and clean lines to the nose and jaw: brothers, clear as anything.

"I wouldn't be surprised if you needed time to sort things," the second man added. "Please stay until you have." He cut a look at Wes. "You can't chase her out when she clearly needs rest."

Wes scowled. "I wasn't chasing her out, Jesse. She looked trapped. I was letting the lady know she can leave whenever she wants."

"Thank you," Maisie murmured, the words trained and tidy from a lifetime of using politeness as a shield.

She wanted to say no—she could feel the refusal trying to climb her tongue—but her hips and knees throbbed from miles, and her bones felt brittle as kindling. Zeke wouldn't think to look for her on a ranch. *Maybe.* That alone made this a good place to catch breath. She could stay a little, go back to Twin Forks, ask which way he'd ridden, and then take the opposite road.

"If it isn't too much trouble," she said, "I'd like to stay a day or two. Until I've got my strength. Then I'll go."

Jesse's smile was easy and quick. "I'll bring you some food. Rest while you can."

Wes left with his brother. Maisie didn't see him again until the light had stretched long and honey-colored across the floorboards. Jesse came and went through the day with quiet knocks and small mercies—bread with butter and honey, a cup of milk for Junie, broth that tasted of marrow and thyme. He asked after the baby's color, her appetite, Maisie's head and feet. Maybe it was kindness. Maybe it was a careful rancher keeping eyes on a stray. Junie needed the milk. Maisie needed the quiet. She smiled and thanked him, and swallowed the pride that wanted to lift its voice.

When late sunlight poured amber into the room, the door creaked. Maisie looked up from where she had slid down to sit on the braided rug, the blanket puddled around her hips, Junie giggling under her fingers as she tickled the round of her belly. She hadn't meant to end up on the floor, but the bed felt too big and too close, and the rug had a sturdier kind of comfort.

Wes stood in the doorway, casting a long shadow. Heat rose in Maisie's cheeks; she could *feel* the wildness of her hair and the wrinkles in her skirt. Not fit for company—even if the company had gentle eyes and a voice that didn't push.

"You must be tired of the room by now," he said, glancing around as if the walls might tell him what she thought. "Dinner's near on. You're welcome to join us—if you're up to it."

A nod came before she could think better of it. "I would like that."

It would let her see the house—count doors, find the kitchen exit, set the map in her head. If she needed to run, it was best not to learn the layout with men at her heels.

Wes tipped his head toward the hall. *Now.* Realization caught up a breath later. She scooped Junie into her arms; the baby squealed, then lunged for a fistful of hair and jammed it into her mouth with triumph. No time for smoothing skirts or pinning stray curls. Maisie's neck warmed with embarrassment. She must look like a windblown scarecrow.

Junie had eaten from what Maisie had packed and from what Jesse had left. Maybe she'd sleep. Maybe.

The kitchen was open and cool. Cornbread and woodsmoke curled together in the air. Nothing here was grand; everything was useful and well-kept. Sun slid through tall windows, painting gold across worn floors. A round table sat near the far wall, its edge polished by years of elbows and plates.

Jesse lifted a hand in greeting. Two other men sat with him, both taking her in with the frank curiosity of boys who'd spotted a bird where they hadn't expected any.

"This is Rhett—" Jesse nodded to a stocky brunette who gave her a once-over and a shrug—"and Eli—" the younger-looking man grinned with an animated wave—"our other brothers."

Maisie slowed near the table, then managed a small, polite smile. "It's nice to meet you. I'm Maisie Ward."

Only after the words were free did she realize she'd given them the truth. Maisie *Ward,* not *West.* A flinch shivered through her, invisible if one wasn't looking. She dropped her eyes to the dull pattern worn into the tabletop. A chair scraped. She looked up. Wes held a seat for her, staring in that stone-faced way that felt less like a challenge and more like a test she didn't know the rules to. She sat, stiff, cheeks warming again.

Awkward was the word for it—awkward for her, anyway. The men didn't seem to mind. They talked—well, three of them talked. Wes's contribution ran to hums and short, practical answers when asked a thing directly. Rhett and Eli turned curiosity her way: Where was she from? Where was she going? Was the baby hers? Where was the father? She gave them enough to be polite and then let silence do the rest. Passing through, she said. The baby was her niece, she said.

"Stop," Wes said at last, scowling at his brothers. "She doesn't owe us answers."

Rhett scowled back. "We just want to know who's sleeping under our roof. Can't blame us for wonderin'."

Heat crept along Maisie's throat—embarrassment, shame, habit. She hunched over her plate without meaning to.

"She didn't ask to be here," Wes said. "We offered. Enough questions."

Rhett muttered but let it go. The silence that followed felt like a blessing. Maisie ate faster than she meant to and found herself stuck, not knowing whether to take her plate to the basin or set it neat and folded-napkin tidy where it was. Wes decided for her—collected her plate with his own and disappeared to wash. She watched his back move under his shirt as if answers might be written there.

When he returned, he tipped his head toward the hall. She rose, murmured a thank-you to Jesse and the younger two, and followed Wes back to the room she'd woken in.

"You can use it as long as you're staying," he said from the threshold, one shoulder against the jamb. "It's the guest room. Won't bother anyone."

"Thank you," she said, risking a glance at his face before she looked away. She backed into the room, settled on the bed with Junie tucked close.

"Good night," Wes said.

Maisie looked up, mouth opening and closing on words that wouldn't form. He tilted his head like he might say more and then didn't. A nod. Footsteps away. The door eased shut without a click.

She rocked the baby and stared at the wood as if his shape were still stamped there. She wondered how long he would be gentle—how long before anger showed itself the way it did in most men. Deep down, in the part of her that didn't make sense and often betrayed her, she wondered if she'd feel relief when it did—or disappointment.

Chapter Four

Wes could see her no matter how far he wandered from the house or how long he stayed outside. She seeped into his thoughts like smoke curling under a door—stubborn, suffocating, impossible to banish. After showing Maisie back to her room, he turned to his evening tasks, hoping routine might settle his mind.

He walked the perimeter. The lantern's glow trembled over hard-packed earth, brushed splintered fenceposts in gold, and caught in the glassy eyes of the dogs as their shadows shifted in the flicker. Cicadas sang like they had for a thousand summers, a long, buzzing hymn that settled into bone. The wind carried the smell of dry sage and horse, sharp with sweat and dust, with a resin whisper of pine and juniper from the ridge. Somewhere, an old owl hooted—low and thoughtful—like it knew something Wes didn't.

He latched the back door and made his way inside. By the time he was done, moonlight had soaked into the floorboards, turning the knots to gleaming silver, while pale shadows stretched thin and restless along the walls. He washed up and lowered himself into bed, but sleep evaded him like a ghost slipping just out of reach.

He thought of the woman in the guest room. Skittish—not in any clownish way, but in the set of her shoulders, tight as a deer scenting smoke on the wind. She moved like a hunted thing; every footfall measured, every muscle drawn as if the shadows themselves might lunge. She hadn't answered a single question straight. Even her name had come reluctant, like it cost her something dear to give. She spoke like a woman punished for honesty who'd learned to trim her truth until it fit inside the space men allowed.

He told himself it wasn't his business. Said it the way a man might tell himself he doesn't miss a dog gone too long. He had a ranch to see to, brothers to keep in line. Whatever she was running from had no place here. She needed a safe bed; he could offer that much. Travelers, hands, friends of his brothers—folk came and went with the weather. She would, too, soon enough.

Still, she lingered in his mind like a word half-spoken, like an echo he couldn't place. It wasn't just her beauty—though she had that in spades: dusky curls, the sweet hazel eyes, sun-kissed skin. What clung was the way she looked at the world, with a quiet, unflinching strength, like she'd been through something she hadn't yet survived.

And the child. The way she held that baby, as if she had tied her very soul to the little one's breathing. Wes reckoned she'd march to hell itself before letting harm brush that child. It wasn't only protection—it felt like penance. Like a vow whispered to God or to a grave. Even near dead on her feet at supper, her back had stayed straight, arms wrapped around the bundle, picking at food while keeping the babe amused, ready to bolt at the smallest reason.

He couldn't help wondering. *What* made her like that? *Who* had left her rattled—so fierce and so afraid at once? The wondering irked him. Curiosity led to entanglements, and entanglements never did a man favors. But she looked like someone in need of help, and Wes hated walking past that kind of need.

He turned over again. The mattress creaked. The quilt bunched beneath his knees, trapping warmth in awkward folds. Lye soap and pine still edged the sheets from the wash, and none of it felt like rest. He listened to the wind prowl along the siding and felt as if it were testing seams for a way in. Outside, the stars burned in a navy sky—heavy over the prairie, winking like watchful eyes.

Somewhere in the stillness, a baby's cry split the night. The wail cut the silence like a knife through canvas, setting the fine hairs on his forearms to rise. Wes lay still, listening. It came again—softer, followed by a woman's hush, thick with fatigue. He pushed the blanket aside with a sigh and rose.

Another door creaked down the hall. Jesse's tousled head poked out, eyes bleary. Wes waved him off. "I've got it," he muttered.

He padded to the guest room, bare feet quiet on the boards. He tapped gently and waited. No answer—just the child's fretful cry and Maisie's murmur. He knocked again, then eased the door open.

Maisie stood near the bed, the baby writhing in her arms. Lamp-light showed tear tracks on her cheeks, though she seemed not to notice. Her shoulders hunched protectively; her eyes were dull with weariness yet bright with something fierce and private. Her forearms trembled with the child's weight, but she held on as if loosening her grip might unravel something more fragile than swaddling. Heat and exhaustion had blotched her cheeks. Her nightgown clung. Wes dropped his gaze to decent ground and fixed on the baby instead.

"May I?" he asked.

Maisie startled. Fabric fluttered as she spun, eyes going wide despite the rank exhaustion dragging at her. "I—I'm sorry," she whispered. "Did she wake you?" Guilt bled through the apology—fear, too—like she half-expected scolding.

Wes shook his head. He held out his hands and waited. She hesitated, arms tightening. Then, slowly, she surrendered the baby.

The child was warm and damp-faced, tiny fingers curling against his shirt. She smelled of milk and lavender, with a ghost of something medicinal—old salve, perhaps. The way she clung—pure trust with no understanding—twisted something in Wes's chest he hadn't felt since holding Eli through the storm that near took the roof.

He saw a whisper of Maisie in the little face—understandable, after all, she'd said she was the aunt. He snugged the blanket and drew a finger softly down the baby's forehead and nose. His mother's trick—simple, near wordless—had settled Jesse in '59 when fever made the boy wild. It worked now. The child's cry wobbled, fell to hiccups, then to silence as she blinked up at him. He hummed an old lullaby—Appalachian, likely. No words, just breath and memory. Lashes drooped. Sleep found her in a small puff of warmth against his chest.

He looked to Maisie. She watched the child with eyes full of sorrow and the look of failure people wore when they thought a judge stood behind every kindness. Hollow and sharp at once, braced for a verdict she believed she'd earned. She stared like she meant to memorize the rise and fall of that tiny chest—as if joy could be yanked away mid-breath and she needed to tuck each second into bone before it happened. He didn't ask. Some things a person carried too close to name.

A cradle waited by the bed—Jesse must have rooted it out of storage after supper. Wes checked its rockers and nails, set the blanket right, then laid the baby down with the care you reserve for the single thing in a room that matters. Maisie moved beside him, presence warm, uncertain.

"You're good with children," she murmured.

He breathed a hushed sound that might have been a laugh. "Oldest of four. I do what I saw Mama do. Doesn't mean I know much."

She nodded, eyes still on the sleeping bundle. "Right. Of course."

Silence rose between them, stitched with the soft rustle of a baby's breath. Then he noticed her shiver.

He had half a mind to shrug off a coat, but he wore none—just a nightshirt and old pants. The urge to shield her anyway came on foolish and strong. He settled for a nod, not trusting any other words to land right, and stepped quietly from the room.

Surely now she could rest.

Wes returned to bed, and sleep once again refused him. He wanted to blame it on the cry, but it wasn't the baby's image that lingered. It was her aunt's—standing by the cradle as if alone in a crowd, arms wrapped around herself to hold in what little warmth she had left.

He dozed in uneasy fits until dawn came quick and sharp on the rooster's cry, pale light spreading across the floorboards. He slid from bed, limbs heavy, splashed water from the basin over his face. Dust, woodsmoke, and the faint iron scent of night-air fading drifted through the window's crack.

He stepped into the hall, rubbing the tightness at the back of his neck. His eyes went to the guest room door before his thoughts had fully gathered. Closed. Quiet.

"It's strange, having someone else in the house," Jesse muttered. Wes turned. His brother leaned in his doorway, arms crossed, shirt half-buttoned. Like Wes, his gaze hung on that still door. He kept his voice pitched low. The old walls didn't hold secrets well.

Wes made a sound that was agreement and nothing more. The hands had their own bunkhouse; visitors usually took rooms in the outer cottages. The main house belonged to the three of them—built board by board by their father's hands. The ghosts in the walls were all family.

"Are you worried?" Jesse asked.

Wes lifted a brow. Plenty to worry: cattle prices, fence needing mending, the dry patch in the west pasture. What did Jesse mean, exactly?

Jesse tipped his chin at the guest room. "About her."

"She ain't danger," Wes said, and he meant it. The woman was no bigger than a sapling and skittish as a colt, but her eyes held something he trusted. Good soul; anyone could see it.

Jesse studied him, quiet a beat. "Maybe not. But whatever—or whoever—she's running from might be."

Wes's gaze returned to the closed door. Jesse wasn't wrong. The thought had gnawed at him half the night. He wanted to know where Maisie had come from, who had chased her across country and fear, who had hurt her.

Would she bring trouble to their step? Likely. Was he going to send her off for it? Not a chance.

The thought alone made his stomach twist. He saw again how she'd stood in the moonlight—nightdress slipped at one shoulder, hair in soft disarray, worn to the bone and still at post like an angel set to guard that child. The way she'd looked into the cradle, hollowed by sorrow, holding fast to hope with trembling hands.

He couldn't let that pass him by.

"If it comes to it," Wes said, voice even, "I'll handle it."

Jesse didn't answer, only watched him in the gray. Wes kept his eyes on the door.

"If trouble follows her here," he said, quieter still, "I'll carry it."

Whatever devil dogged her steps, Wes meant to face it before it crossed his threshold. She didn't have to walk that road alone anymore—not while he had blood in his veins and ground to stand on.

Not while she was on his land.

Chapter Five

Two days. That was all she'd said she would stay. But two turned into three, and three slipped quietly into five. Wes had been the one to tell her to stay on, and Maisie—worn thin and threadbare—had agreed. She hadn't any real plan yet. Still didn't.

The tension she'd carried in her shoulders, in the set of her jaw, began to ease as the mornings passed, each one stitched gently into the next with quiet routines. At night, she managed more than a few scattered hours of sleep. Junie ceased her constant fussing and took a child's delight in the smells and sights of the ranch—the creak of leather, the sun on the yard, the flutter of swallows under the eaves. Maisie no longer kept herself hidden in their room, not since Eli coaxed her out for a slow tour of the land—fields wide as sighs, barns thick with the scent of hay and horse, wind combing the sage until it rippled like water.

Food came hot and regular, simple but hearty, and she began to join them for breakfast each morning. There was comfort in the predictable clamor that rose with Eli and Rhett bickering like old washerwomen over coffee—Rhett claiming it needed to be boiled harder, Eli swearing he'd rather drink axle grease. It struck Maisie as a kind of ritual, the way they woke the house with noise and laughter like a pair of restless colts.

No one questioned her after that first night, not even Rhett, despite the looks he tossed her way—furrowed brow, pinched mouth. Eli told her Rhett was only protective of the ranch. *Don't take it to heart,* he'd said, and she tried not to. Still, guilt pricked. How could she risk Junie without a plan? She'd already swallowed her pride—downed it like vinegar. She could stomach shame and every sour emotion if it meant Junie had what she needed.

Wes never pressed. He was a man of few words, and she saw him only at breakfast or supper. He'd tip his hat, ask quietly after Junie's health, then fade back into silence as if he'd never spoken at all. His steadiness sat in a room the way a load-bearing beam did—seen or not, you felt it.

For the first time since she fled New York in the crisp light of midmorning, Maisie wasn't constantly scanning for escape routes, wasn't watching every shadow as if it were ready to grab and drag her under. Her nerves dulled—just a little.

But she knew better than to trust peace. Good things always came at a cost. They always left something behind in the ash. Life had never been kind to Maisie. Comfort and peace were not served on fine silver by a gloved hand. She had to fight for scraps of safety, dignity, hope.

It had been five days. She still had no plan. No money. Not even an idea of where to go next. Zeke could follow her anywhere, and he would. He'd done it before. He'd do it again. If she had to, Maisie would live on the run—always a shadow away from danger—but how could she raise Junie like that? She wanted more for her niece than what she and Ivy had scraped by with. And now—now Junie might have less.

At least she and Ivy had been stable. Their parents had struggled, yes, but love always sat at the table, worn but present. There was always a roof overhead, even when it leaked. Could Maisie promise the same? Could she keep Junie fed when the jobs dried up and the road stretched too long?

Sunlight slipped through the narrow, warped-glass window, thin as milk. She watched dust motes drift lazily in the beam. After breakfast, she had crept back beneath the quilt to try to think, to plan. Her mind stayed blank. *What? When? Where? How?* No answers.

With a sigh, she pushed herself upright. She couldn't keep leaning on Calder kindness. She wouldn't become a burden, no matter how soft their voices or generous their hands. She had to stand on her own two feet. She would.

Before her bare feet touched the floor, voices rose outside the door—low at first, then blistering into shouts. Boots pounded across the boards in an erratic rhythm. A harsh bark—Rhett, maybe—cut off beneath the splintering crack of something heavy slamming a wall. The whole house shuddered with it, the air tightening as if it couldn't bear witness.

Maisie froze. Breath hitched and lodged like a bone. Her heart lurched—one hard, punishing thud—and then silence roared in her ears. Her body forgot how to move.

A baby's wail cut the stillness. Junie.

Maisie jolted to her feet, scooped the child, and pressed her close, heart pounding loud enough Junie could surely feel it. *Is it Zeke?* God help her, had he come already, like a curse spoken into life? Maybe he hadn't come alone. Maybe he'd brought men. Guns. Law. Lies dressed in badges.

Last time she'd made it weeks before he caught wind of her. But she hadn't run far this time. He'd been in Twin Forks. Of course, it would be easier. Of course.

"Hush now, Junie-girl," she breathed, voice snagging. "Hush, my baby."

She drew a line down the infant's brow the way she'd seen Wes do when the baby fretted. Junie quieted at once, blinking up at her with teary eyes, tiny hand curling around Maisie's finger.

Maisie sank hard beside the wardrobe. The wood cooled her back; the floor chilled her feet. She curled over Junie like a shield and cupped a hand near the baby's mouth—just enough to hush the breath. Junie whimpered, and Maisie's stomach twisted. *Please, please,* she begged silently, *don't make a sound, baby girl.*

She rocked, willing calm into bone while panic gnawed her ribs. Hoofbeats outside pounded like a drumline through the yard.

She didn't move. Barely breathed.

Guilt crawled under her skin like fire ants. They'd taken her in without asking why, fed her, laughed with her. And now? Now they might be bleeding outside her door—hurt because she couldn't make herself leave. She should've kept moving. She knew better.

This is my fault, she thought. *Whatever's happening—this is on me.*

The Calder brothers could be in danger. Hurt. Or worse.

She should have left sooner. Should never have stayed. Zeke was coming. He would take Junie. And Maisie—

Maisie was going to fail again.

She didn't know when the shouting stopped, or if it truly had. The silence after was worse. She stayed tight beside the wardrobe like a field mouse that survived the trap but not the fear. Every creak in the house sounded like a hammer being cocked. Every second stretched thin.

The latch groaned—a low, death-rattle sound—and the door eased open, slow as a coffin lid. Her body jolted before her mind found purchase. Her lungs cinched as if a hand had slammed flat against her chest. She couldn't scream. Couldn't move.

Her eyes burned, but she blinked hard. She would not cry—not for the devil who bloodied her sister and marked her niece for ruin. No tears for him. Not ever.

But it wasn't Zeke.

Boots crossed the threshold with a muffled thud—thick-soled and familiar. Roughspun trousers brushed, the sound of them catching faintly. Wes. She let her gaze skim him for wounds. His face—always carved in stone—was drawn taut, tension sitting at the corners of his mouth, a displeased crinkle at his eyes. Lips pressed thin—not with worry now, but temper.

She'd seen him worried three days back when Eli took her to the pasture. They'd returned to find Wes pacing the porch like a penned bull, jaw locked, fury sparking at his brother for taking her out without a word. That had been worry. This wasn't.

Still, he wasn't hurt. No blood on his shirt. Collar askew, hair mussed—as if wind or his own hands had dragged through it. Her breath eased before she permitted it. Fear didn't vanish, but it settled lower, claws sheathed.

That irritated her most—how his quiet steadiness dulled the edge of panic; how her body answered calm before her mind caught up.

Wes's eyes swept the room. A frown flickered when he found her huddled by the wardrobe. He didn't seem to understand at first; then his gaze dropped to Junie, wriggling in her lap, tiny fingers tugging at Maisie's like reins.

His jaw twitched. A knowing grimace crossed his face.

"It ain't who you're runnin' from," he said low—words like a match burning out before it hit the floor.

Maisie didn't answer. *Not him,* she repeated in her mind, still half-braced for the door to open again.

"This wasn't about you."

Her head bobbed before she realized she'd moved. Wes crouched in front of her, his boots shifting on old boards. He didn't reach for her—just settled into her eye-line, steady and quiet, *there.*

His scent came faint—leather, smoke, a trace of dust. Familiar things. Ranch things. Not threat.

Her muscles tensed anyway—habits hard to shake. But when he touched her hand, it was careful, almost questioning. Junie reached for him with a bubbling giggle and eager fingers. That small, effortless trust tightened Maisie's throat.

He looked to her for permission. She gave a jerky nod, unsure if she meant it.

Junie settled into the crook of his arm as he slid down to sit beside her, his back to the wall. His boot tapped once against hers—barely there. No message. No demand. Just company.

Maisie didn't lean in. She didn't lean away.

"There's a man," Wes said quietly, "wealthy bastard out of one of the big cities. Been pressin' on this land near six months. Wants us gone so he can take it." His voice stayed even, but steel ran under it.

Her body sagged against him before she could help it. She knew she should pull away—re-stack her walls brick by brick—but didn't. Couldn't. Her spine felt like warmed wax. Her will had scattered. Her cheek found his shoulder; she let it rest there like she belonged. Guilt howled—*how dare you feel safe? how dare you need someone again?*—but Wes said nothing about it. So she pretended that meant it was all right. Just for a minute. Just for now.

"He sent another warnin' this morning," Wes murmured, voice low like he didn't want to wake the dust. "Hired men cut three lengths of fence, scattered the herd. Then one of 'em got bold—made a scene right here in the house. Told us to take the hint."

Maisie nodded faintly. Thought felt slow as leaves on a lazy creek. Junie gurgled, mouth wide for a giggle, then latched on to one of Wes's fingers to gnaw. Maisie lifted her hand and tapped the girl's rosy cheek. Junie gripped Maisie's finger in one small fist and Wes's in the other as if she'd caught two fireflies.

Maisie didn't mean to smile. But she did.

"I'm sorry it scared you," Wes said—so soft she nearly missed it.

She didn't look at him. Shrugged instead, shoulders hitching once. What sickened her wasn't the fear itself; it was how easily her mind whispered *he's found you.* How natural it felt. As if danger had become a language she'd learned by ear— weeks of whispers and half-sleep teaching her the grammar of dread.

She'd braced for impact before she understood why. Weariness rewrote instinct that way.

She didn't belong here—not with Ivy's ghost trailing her, not with worry she carried like a splinter too deep to dig out. The Calder brothers had troubles enough. They didn't need hers piling on.

Her breath came easier now. Wes said nothing about the way she leaned; didn't flinch from the contact; didn't shift or sigh. She ought to move. He likely had work waiting. But she couldn't make her body rise.

"You're safe," Wes said. "So long as you're on Calder land."

The words slipped into the quiet. Maisie barely caught them, but she held fast, tucking them away like a child hiding a keepsake in a pocket. She needed to tend to Junie. Her limbs were lead. Her mind floated somewhere near the rafters.

Junie was safe—in Wes's arms. And for the first time since everything broke, Maisie felt something close to safe, too.

She let herself sink into the dark—not because it promised peace, but because it offered rest. And for tonight, that was enough.

Chapter Six

The first morning after the attack ushered in a new rhythm at the Calder ranch. Wes rose well before dawn, the bite of chill wrapping his skin as he kicked off the quilt. His soles met plank floor cold as riverstone, a shock that ran his spine. Outside, the sky kept its charcoal cloak; heavy cloud swallowed the moon and veiled the stars.

He bent over the enamel basin and dashed his face with well water so cold it bit. It chased sleep from his eyes, not the weight from his chest. He dressed quick—thick trousers, mended shirt, coat, boots—and gave a low whistle only the dogs knew. Then he stepped into the dark to saddle Jeremiah.

Before the trouble, his patrols hugged the house. After yesterday's cuts and scattered herd, that wouldn't do. He mounted, clicked his tongue, loosed the dogs, and swung the corral gate wide.

Jeremiah's hooves settled to a muffled rhythm. Mist clung to the grass and beaded on Wes's lashes; it made the world feel smaller. Leather creaked. Once in a while, a dog barked far off where the prairie opened. He took the fence in lengths, first south, then east, then quartering north. He rode it again in reverse. He stopped to test wire, drove a staple, tightened a post that had heaved from clay and wind. He did the work the way he did all work: thorough, no fuss, until worry quieted enough for breath.

When a dog ranged too far, he whistled short, and a gray shadow slid back to his knee. His eyes kept moving—brush, draw, the little rise where the creek cut a dark seam, the low places where a man could squat and watch a house unseen. The land carried its old sounds: wind combing grass, a tick in the wire, the soft rasp of Jeremiah's breath. Under it, a sheet of silence pulled tight.

By the time dawn thinned the horizon to pearl, his spine ached from the saddle, and his thighs burned. Light feathered amber across the pasture. It brought no comfort, only another day to keep ahead of trouble. He turned toward the house, dismounted at the steps, and found Jesse on the porch with a yawn big enough to split his face.

"Perimeter check," Wes said to the question in Jesse's look, hitching Jeremiah to the post. "Not keen on being caught unawares again."

Jesse scrubbed his eyes and frowned. "I'll help. You can't cover all of it yourself."

Before Wes answered, Eli bounded in, too chipper for a man just out of bed, dragging a bleary Rhett by the collar like a pup who wouldn't heel.

"Who's doin' what on their own?" Eli asked.

Wes tipped his chin toward the ceiling—toward the guest room where Maisie and the baby still slept, or would soon. She'd taken to coming down an hour after the men, just as coffee met the cups.

"Checking the perimeter," Jesse said, chin pointing Wes's way.

"You're waking up even earlier?" Eli said, scandalized. Rhett, eyes slitted to slashes, looked ready to pick a fight with sunrise.

"We can't all be off the property at once," Wes said, meeting each brother's gaze in turn. "From now on, no straying from assigned tasks. I want to know where everybody is—hands included. We're starting a check-in."

Jesse sighed and coaxed flame into the stove. "Then we talk to Tom. Have the boys report to him and keep the tally straight. You can't watch every last man on the payroll."

Wes opened his mouth, then shut it again—agreement sticking in his throat. The floorboards creaked; all three turned as Maisie stepped in.

She framed the doorway as if the room had been built around her. Hair caught back with a bright orange scarf, apron snug at her small waist, sleeves rolled; her thick skirt was hitched a shade higher for moving. She'd dressed for work. For a heartbeat, she looked like she'd always belonged.

Wes studied her a breath longer than he meant to. Ready, not fragile. Determined. Guilt had replaced fear at the corner of her mouth. Neither was good, exactly—if he had to choose, he'd take the kind that kept a person upright.

"Could I help with breakfast?" she asked, a small smile that didn't quite reach her eyes. She looked to Jesse.

"I wouldn't mind it," Jesse said, grin warming his voice. "I'm always the one cooking around here." He tossed a theatrical glare at his brothers. "None of these bastards knows proper food."

Eli shrugged. Rhett rolled his eyes. Wes turned to the kettle; the scrape of tin on iron rang loud. Coffee lifted—earthy and honest. He ignored Eli's raised brows, tracking how often Wes's gaze, against sense, drifted back to Maisie.

It wasn't suspicion. Wasn't caution. He just couldn't stop.

"About yesterday," Maisie said, drawing every eye like a tugged rein. "Wes said someone was trying to cause trouble for y'all?"

Wes flicked Jesse a look that meant: Tell her.

"Rich bastard's buying up land 'round Twin Forks," Jesse said. "Threatens, leans on folks, undercuts supplies. He wants the whole valley. Calder ground's in his way."

Wes passed mugs while Jesse went on. "He'll cut fence, scatter stock, pay suppliers to turn their backs. What you heard yesterday was one of his 'polite' reminders."

"Sounds like a real piece of work," Maisie said, dry as dust.

"That's the polite way," Eli added.

Breakfast ran quieter than usual, different in a way that felt like someone had sanded a rough plank smooth. The biscuits were flakier; the eggs held to velvet; the gravy wore a whisper of thyme nobody named. There was gentleness in the food, and carefulness, as if she'd poured apology and thanks into every stir. Compliments circled the table—even Rhett grunted that she could "keep cookin', if she wanted."

"I'd be happy to help," she said, cheeks warming. "With the cooking. With chores. I just—well, I don't want to take advantage."

They told her she wasn't. Jesse proposed a chalk slate by the back door listing names and tasks; Eli argued for a bell code—one long, two short—if anyone saw riders cutting crosswise near the creek; Rhett wanted a strip of red cloth on the gate-latch as a sign when men were out by the east line. Wes said yes to all three and sent Jesse to speak with Tom, the foreman, about keeping the log so the many hands moved like one.

Days began to run like that. In the mornings, Maisie kept to the kitchen, though not only there. By midafternoon, she might be at the pump, sleeves wet to the elbow, or on the porch steps humming to soothe a fretful Junie, or in the yard with a laundry paddle flashing at the washtub. Once, Wes saw her stooped at the herb patch, pinching a leaf, rolling it between finger and thumb, then sniffing—head tilted like the plant might answer. She didn't say much. He didn't mind the quiet.

Wes never once mentioned her leaving.

At night, his feet took the same path whether he meant them to or not—down the hall when Junie cried. At first, it was practical—one more set of hands to wrestle a bottle or a blanket. Somewhere it shifted from help to habit, and from habit to expectation none of them named. He didn't question it. The night he sat bolt upright at the first fretful sound—shirt dragged over his head before thought—he learned something that chilled him more than the ambush had:

It had become normal.

A week had slipped by since fence and herd were cut like a warning letter. Midmorning found Wes heading into Twin Forks with Eli to restock essentials. He wouldn't send his brother alone, not with trouble stirring along the edges.

Maybe the sharpness was Army-taught from his scout days. Maybe it was simple ranch sense. Men who went alone didn't always come back.

The wagon rolled steady over ruts still slick from spring rain. Air came crisp and sunlit, with the faint green of thawed earth and sagebrush. Blackbirds argued on the fence wire; cottonwoods wore a haze of new leaf. Wes kept his eyes working—brush, draw, culvert, shadow—while Eli filled the air with talk like a man paying a debt he happily owed.

"Salt's gone up again," Eli said, squinting at the folded list.

"It hasn't," Wes said. "Jesse and I checked the invoices. Wrong line."

Eli let it pass and shifted targets. "Feels like the wagon's dragging. Back wheel's pulling harder than it should."

Wes added it to the ledger in his head. Another fix waiting its turn.

Closer to town, Eli found an old grievance. "I'm tellin' you—that damned gate hates me."

Wes grunted. Quiet roads didn't soothe him; trouble liked quiet. A hawk drew a circle; its shadow wheeled and disappeared.

"I'll try to square it tomorrow," Eli said. "Who knows how long this run'll take."

Their rhythm held: Eli offered noise enough for two; Wes guarded the edges where noise failed.

The first storefronts showed—sun-faded paint, hitching posts weathered gray. "We splittin' the list?" Eli asked.

"No," Wes said flat. "Nobody goes off on his own."

"You're a worrywart," Eli said, but softer. "We'll finish faster if we divide."

Logic didn't argue down the knot in Wes's gut. Eli saw it and changed tack. "What if somethin' happens while we're gone? Rhett's mean with his fists, Jesse's fair with a gun—but they've got Maisie and the baby to think on."

Wes muttered and nodded. "Split it."

They left the wagon at the edge of town, paid a boy a nickel and a look to mind it, and divided the list. The sky had gone the pale blue that comes after a storm scrubs it clean. Wes tugged his brim and offered a silent prayer to make business quick.

Eli took perishables, angling toward the grocer. Wes set for the hardware stalls and the blacksmith: wire, staples, two hammers that wouldn't split, gate latches, a keg of nails. After last week's sabotage, there was more break than mend to the eastern paddock; new posts would have to be set when time and men allowed. He ferried loads to the wagon twice, and each time let his gaze drift down the street—who watched, who turned away.

The forge rang clean, hammer on anvil a sure beat. The smith, arms blackened to the elbow, jotted the order and asked after the ranch as if he were asking after weather—expecting stubborn. Wes kept it short. He stepped into the square and paused as the sun caught his brim.

Across the way, a woman stood in profile, speaking to a small boy clinging to her skirts. Hair pinned high, darker than he remembered; skin pale as cream. Her dress was dove gray, the trim embroidered fine—nothing like the practical cottons she'd once worn to ride fence with him for the mischief of it.

Anabelle.

Even at a distance, he knew her laugh, the bell-bright note that had once undone sensible parts of him. The child tugged; she bent; lace at her collar fluttered like a thing that had never known dust.

She hadn't seen him yet.

A man stood beside her—a banker by the cut of his coat and the soft of his hands, Denver writ plain across his boots. The man spoke; Anabelle smiled with the polite sweetness kept always ready.

Then she turned. Their eyes met.

Her smile faltered by a hair. She dipped her head—the nod you give a stranger you're half sure you've seen. Then she turned back to the boy and straightened his little collar like love could be folded right.

Wes kept walking. His boots thudded on the boardwalk like a hammer, drowning the murmur of horses and the tin clatter of a peddler's pans.

Anabelle was nothing to him now.

She had left. Folks came and went; the ranch stayed.

He didn't look back. The blacksmith had been the last stop. He went to the wagon, sat on the tailboard with arms folded, and waited for Eli, jaw tight enough to ache.

The trip home ran quieter.

Eli—who never met a silence he didn't try to fix—started with teasing, then grumbling, then talking about small things meant to draw Wes out. Wes didn't bite. A third of the way back, Eli let quiet settle and only cut sideways looks—curious, a shade worried—that Wes pretended not to see.

Prairie softened to gold as the sun slipped west. Wind freshened, carrying new grass and horses; thaw clung in low places like winter's hand refusing to lift. The wheel complained the way Eli had said it would; Wes filed it under tomorrow.

When the ranch rose from the grass like a story you know by heart, the house sat still in the afternoon's long light. No voices, no ring of bucket—just porch boards creaking under their boots and a distant whinny from the barn.

They carried supplies inside without words.

Wes expected nothing unusual past the threshold. Jesse should be out on the east line, Rhett at the barn. He wasn't prepared to see Maisie in the parlor, settled easy on a low chair, folding laundry into neat squares while Junie slept on the settee—one small hand curled near her cheek as if she'd caught a dream.

He stopped short. Eli bumped him with a soft oof.

Maisie looked up. Met his eyes.

She smiled—gentle, soft, warm in a way that made Wes feel he'd opened the wrong door and stepped into a scene not meant for him. Light from the window made a small crown at the edge of her hair. The skirt spread around her like it knew that floor. He had the strange thought that if he left and came back three hours later, she might still be there—laughing with Jesse over spice, showing Eli how to fold a shirt that didn't look like a map, tucking the blanket to Junie's chin as if the world couldn't reach past a well-placed square of wool.

He swallowed, nodded once, and turned for the kitchen with his armful. He didn't speak. Neither did she. But he felt her eyes on his back, felt it like the heat from a stove you still carry in your skin.

He pretended not to notice.

He'd been pretending a lot today.

Still, he couldn't unsee the ease with which she fit the room, the way the light made home of her edges. She didn't look like a guest. She looked like something older than that—a thing the house had waited for and finally kept.

Something turned under his breastbone. He shoved it down.

Hard.

He set the feeling in a box in the dark and nailed the lid tight. Let it rot. He had practice.

He'd let a woman in before.

He wouldn't make that mistake again.

Not with someone he knew would leave.

Chapter Seven

It was hard to miss the change in Wes's demeanor.

He and Eli returned from their supply run, and suddenly the man would not look Maisie in the eye. He passed through the parlor with nothing more than a curt nod.

Maisie stared after him, palms paused on a stack of warm linen. Eli lingered a heartbeat longer, frowning at the same doorway.

"Did something happen?" she asked.

"He was fine on the way there," Eli said. "Quiet coming back."

"I see."

She lowered her gaze to the laundry. The cloth still held the day's sun and the sting of lye and wind. She smoothed a frayed seam on a clean undershirt, careful as if the cotton might tear under too much thought.

It stung more than it should. Wes had been cordial these days, attentive in his quiet way—asking after Junie, tilting a kettle when her hands were full, slowing his stride when she carried a basket. None of it had been flirtation. It felt like the steady habits of a decent man. But this silence felt different. It felt like a door gently closed from the other side.

She had not meant to get comfortable.

She had meant to pass through like a shadow—offer help, earn her keep, and move on before anyone looked too closely. But the rhythm of the house had a way of finding bone and breath: Junie's sleepy coos; Jesse's easy laugh; the drift of woodsmoke after dusk. Even Wes, with his quiet presence and unreadable eyes, had become a kind of compass point. She did not stare at it; she only kept true by it and hoped it would not shift.

She should have known better.

With the last shirt folded, she lifted her sleeping niece and balanced the basket on her hip. In the small hallway, she left the stack where Jesse had asked and climbed the stairs, careful of the two risers that creaked. In the bedroom, she tucked Junie into the crib and lingered, brushing a curl from the child's damp forehead.

A breeze rattled the loose pane. Outside, cottonwoods whispered. Damp earth and the ghost of dogwood curled in. The crib gave a soft complaint as Junie turned. The clock ticked. Maisie stood in the hush until her shoulders eased by a finger's width.

Downstairs, Wes and Eli were in the kitchen, unpacking the haul from town.

She hesitated at the threshold. Wes did not look up. He inspected a tin of coffee, like it held more than beans, thumb flicking the dented lid. Light from the window laid pale bars across the floor; dust motes wandered in it like seeds.

She turned to Eli. He offered a small, tired smile.

"You two must be worn out," she said.

"Wouldn't say no to food," Eli admitted. "We didn't eat much on the road."

Habit went ahead of thought. She reached for flour, the paper twist of cinnamon, a sack of dried apples tied off with string.

"That'd be fine by me," Eli added, grin nudging back.

Wes said nothing. Eli elbowed him. Wes scowled and muttered, "No need."

Maisie nodded as if he had thanked her. "Did you get everything Jesse listed?" she asked, though the table already answered: wire staples, a keg of nails, latches, a rasp, and sacks with the comfortable weight of coffee and beans.

"Yes," he said at last—clipped; final.

She could not help the quick, traitorous thought: perhaps it was not her at all. Perhaps town had scraped something raw in him—an old name, a face in a window, a word said wrong by a stranger. Men carried their hurts quieter than women, she had learned; they tucked them like letters into a breast pocket and pretended there was nothing there even when it crinkled with every breath. The guess shamed her a little. She returned her eyes to the pan and to work, which asked for nothing except attention.

She set a skillet on the stove. Butter hissed. The smell rose— sweet and rich—once apples hit and sugar began to melt. Cinnamon dusted the air. The scent tugged her back to a scuffed brick hearth in a narrow New York kitchen. There had been hunger then, constant as weather, but food had felt like love every time a pot was set down and three spoons clinked.

It was a dish their father made after her mother died, when there was enough to spare and she and Ivy were too hungry to wait for proper supper. He hummed while he stirred. Sometimes he lifted Ivy to the counter. Sometimes he pressed a spoon into Maisie's hand like she was his helper and not a child. She swallowed and kept stirring.

The kitchen spoke in small sounds—Eli sliding a crate, the stove's quiet breath, the tin lid tapping twice against Wes's thumb. Silence stretched. It pressed along the table's scarred edge. He did not owe her words, she reminded herself. He did not owe her anything.

She finished cooking without noticing how far the light had moved. She separated portions, set two plates on the table, and ladled sweet sauce over the biscuits Jesse had baked that morning.

When she set the plates down, Eli reached for a fork with a boy's eagerness. "Smells like a fair," he said, then caught himself. "A decent church supper, I mean."

Wes finally looked at her. Only for a moment. "Thank you," he said, voice even as a fence rail. It should have helped. It only marked how far away he stood inside himself. She tipped her head in acknowledgment and stepped back before the small pride that rose at his words could embarrass her.

The plates clinked. The quiet pressed. She missed noise— the scrape of boots, Eli humming, Jesse's whistle, Junie's babble while Wes crooked a finger to win a laugh. Silence like this reminded her of empty rooms and doors that had once slammed and never opened again.

She took the rest and made for the back door.

She was still on the porch when Jesse came around the corner, shirt damp with sweat, hair wind-tossed, face striped by dust.

"There's enough for you," she said, lifting the plate.

Jesse's eyes lit. "You, Maisie Ward, are a blessing I don't deserve."

She laughed, fragile but real.

The sun had slipped behind the ridge, laying long amber shadows across the yard. A robin hopped the rail and sang like a pin driven through quiet.

"Jesse," she said, "may I ask a thing?"

He raised a brow mid-bite, half a mouthful stalled.

"Do you know anyone who needs an extra hand? Seamstress, maybe. General store. Apothecary work, if there is such here. It was my trade."

Her fingers, raw from scrubbing at dawn, curled into her palms.

Jesse chewed and thought. "Can't say I do, not this minute. I'll put an ear out. If something shakes loose, you'll be the first to know."

"Thank you," she said, making the words steady.

Jesse wiped a smear of sauce from his thumb with the edge of his sleeve, then had the grace to blush at his own bad manners. "I'll ask at the post office, too," he added. "They always know who's hiring and who's pretending not to be."

"That would help," she said. "I don't need grand. Just steady. Just honest."

"You're owed that much," he said, so simply she had to look away.

His gaze lingered, reading more than she said. He turned, eyes running the yard the way a rancher reads weather. A wind rattled the barn doors. Chickens fretted dirt near the well. Storm or change, she could not tell; lately they felt the same in her bones.

"Tom!" Jesse called toward the paddock. "We could use your counsel."

An older man ambled over, grizzled hair curling from beneath a sweat-stained hat, sun-browned skin laid in lines from years of narrowing his eyes against distance. He tipped his hat. She answered with an awkward half-curtsy she could not unlearn.

"The boys haven't introduced us proper," he said, giving Jesse a glare that was both fond and scolding. "Tom Hargrove. Foreman."

"Maisie Ward," she said. "Stowaway." Humor nearly landed.

"Guest," Jesse corrected. "And welcome."

"I'm looking for work," Maisie said. "Seamstress, shop help. I've training in apothecary."

Jesse held out a leftover biscuit like a bribe. Tom took it and snorted. "Mrs. Pritchard in town keeps a dressmaker's. Contrary as a mule, but she'll hire on if the needles back up. The general store takes help toward month's end—tally and stock. I'll ask."

"That's kind," she said.

"Eat while you look," Tom added. "Hunger makes a body say yes to the wrong thing."

"I will," she lied. They let it pass.

Tom angled toward the bunkhouses. Jesse went to the pump. Maisie stood on the porch a breath longer, then slipped inside, the screen tapping like a small heartbeat.

That night, she kept mostly to the room. She tidied what did not need tidying, mended a cuff with thread pulled from a seam allowance, told herself work steadies better than wanting.

***

In the end, it was not Jesse or Tom who helped. It was Eli.

He found her the next evening after supper, lingering near the doorway to the room she shared with Junie. Maisie looked up from the yellowed pages of a tattered novel Jesse had lent— *A Lady's Promise*, sentimental and soothing. Moonlight pooled silver on the braided rug. Junie flopped on her stomach and laughed at a straw butterfly braided from hay and thread.

Eli leaned against the frame. "Jess says you're looking for work?"

"Yes," she said. "I need to save. I can't keep relying on you and your brothers."

"We don't mind," he said softly.

She shrugged. Depending on someone meant handing them the power to take it back. Ivy had taught her that lesson without meaning to: bruises and tears, apologies that did not change the night. And anyway, Wes wanted a stretch of space wide as pasture.

"You're a mean cook," Eli said. "I'll miss it. Jesse's got five meals he rotates like bad hymns."

Maisie laughed in spite of herself. The sound pried a knot loose.

Eli crossed to the bed and sat at the corner, elbows to knees. "I have a friend in town. Minnie Abbott. Runs a small herb shop out of her mama's parlor. Not grand, but honest. She could use help a few days a week. I sent word."

"Minnie keeps shelves of jars," Eli said, warming to his subject. "Dried willow bark, horehound, peppermint, comfrey. She bottles liniments that smell like wintergreen and sin. Folks swear by her cough syrup and her salve. You'd be measuring, grinding, keeping books, fetching water, that sort of thing. She pays by the day and in cash. Hours are decent unless there's a fever round. She runs straight and honest."

The picture he drew rose clear: a tidy room with light falling on brown glass, the faint perfume of herbs and alcohol, customers grateful for a small kindness in a hard week. The work touched a part of Maisie that had been asleep since New York. She set a palm on the novel to keep it from sliding off her lap. "I can do that," she said. "I can be useful there."

Maisie blinked. Relief did not rush in; something careful unfolded instead. "Thank you. That will help." She added, because he would expect it, "You truly are the best of your brothers."

"Tell 'em," Eli said, grinning. "Especially Jesse."

"He'd cry," she said.

"Flood," he said.

They laughed. Eli bent to smooth a blanket near Junie's foot with hands that did not ask permission to be gentle. At the door his voice shed its show. "Hope it lets you sleep easier."

After he left, Maisie stared at the wood a long time. It should have felt like a step forward. Instead it felt like the edge of a foggy cliff—one wrong move and down you went, no promise of soft ground.

Wind hissed against the walls. The old boards groaned. She gathered Junie and rocked. The floor was cool under her feet, uneven from years of use. Junie was heavier now, greedy for the world, growing by handfuls of days. Soon, she would not sleep for being carried. Tonight she did. The rhythm steadied both of them.

Maisie laid the baby in the crib and turned the oil lamp down until the flame thinned and vanished. Shadows pooled in the corners. A nightjar called once; a dog answered down the road; then even that sound fell away. Sleep did not.

Her thoughts walked to Ivy.

She saw her sister's face the night she turned up in New York—swollen and bruised, eyes huge above a mouth that barely formed words. Ivy clutched Junie like someone might try to steal breath. *I didn't know where else to go,* she whispered. *Junie's all that matters.*

The words had cut. *What about me?* Maisie had wanted to ask. *Wasn't I also yours?* She had not asked. She had opened the door and her stingy heart. She had kept three lives upright inside rooms that leaned.

Now she understood.

She remembered Ivy's hands shaking as she set Junie in Maisie's arms. Remembered the way Ivy pressed her face into Maisie's shoulder and wept like a wheel finally broken. Ivy had not needed saving the way stories tell it. She had needed someone to witness the breaking and stay.

Maisie understood the fear now—the protectiveness that makes a woman put everything into one small life and dare the world to try. Junie was all that mattered. Maisie agreed with Ivy in full.

She did not cry. Her eyes stayed dry as she stared at the crib and let the weight settle like a mountain she had chosen to live beneath. Two pulls lived inside her: what she owed the Calders—kindness, fairness, not bringing danger—and what she owed her own—safety enough, a roof that did not leak, and a door that would hold. Sometimes those debts ran together; sometimes they tugged a woman in two.

Junie's breaths threaded the room like a seam. Maisie pulled the quilt higher and let herself sink into the hush. Things were not perfect. They were better. Maybe the beginning of something good, if she dared name it. She did not know what came next, but tonight the unknowing did not cut as sharply.

Somewhere in the house, a floorboard spoke. The wind eased. The dog barked once and stopped. Maisie lay down, palms flat on the quilt as if smoothing cloth, and told her heart to hush. The room listened.

She let her mind run once more along the narrow track of possibility. Work at the apothecary would mean time in town. Time in town might mean being seen. The thought pricked like nettle. Yet hiding forever was only another kind of danger. A woman could vanish so thoroughly she no longer knew where to find herself.

If Zeke came within fifty miles, she would hear. Gossip traveled quicker than the post. If he did not, then every coin tucked into the tin at the bottom of her bag would thicken the wall between him and the child he thought he owned. She would write to no one. She would keep her head down. She would move if the wind changed.

She lay there until the plan was small enough to hold and not so big it frightened her. She named three things she could do tomorrow: rise early, help with breakfast, and ride in with Eli if Minnie Abbott sent word. Three things seemed possible. Sometimes, possibility was the only mercy left to take.

She turned her face toward the crib and watched the blanket rise and fall until her own breath matched it. It was not peace. It was rest enough.

For tonight, that was something she could hold.

Chapter Eight

Wes spent another night rolling in his bed, sheets tangled around his legs, sweat prickling at his hairline despite the early spring chill seeping through the windows. Sleep came in fits of brief, jarring spells where his mind dragged him back to the past, to the dirt roads of Tennessee, the scorched woods of Georgia, and the coppery scent of blood that never quite left him.

His time as a scout during the war lived deep in the locked recesses of his mind, kept there for good reason. They weren't memories fit for quiet nights or peaceful thoughts. Too many ghosts lived in those years. Too many names he hadn't spoken since Appomattox. Wes had never believed himself a hero. He'd led good men down the wrong trail—straight into an ambush. No forgiveness, least of all from himself, could ever scrub that stain clean.

He woke with a start, heart pounding, eyes snapping open in the pitch black. For a moment, he thought it was the remnants of a dream—the war creeping back in—but the sound came again.

Hooves.

Not at a walk. It was fast and uneven, and coming hard.

The wind whipped along the edges of the roof, hissing like a warning, but beneath it was the unmistakable clatter of a corral gate. Metal on wood.

Wes sat up instantly, swung his legs over the side of the bed, and shoved his feet into his boots without bothering with socks. He threw on his old cavalry coat that still smelled faintly of smoke and horse sweat and reached for the rifle leaning by the door.

The grandfather clock in the parlor ticked out a low, solemn chime as he passed it. One o'clock. Too late for any of the cattle to be stirring, especially the mothers and their calves. Moonlight spilled through the windows in fractured beams, silvering the floor and fencing outside.

He crossed the porch in three strides, boots hitting the steps with dull thuds. The cold bit at his face.

The ranch had a dozen corrals, but only a few were close enough to the main house for sound to carry. He ran toward the one used for the breeding cows, the spring mothers, and their newborn calves. Sure enough, when he rounded the tool shed, he saw the wide swing of the gate. It was open and banging lightly in the wind.

Several cows were still penned, clustered to the far side, their heads up and ears twitching. But others had scattered; he could see the blur of hides moving across the yard, hooves kicking up damp dirt as they bolted toward the lower field.

Wes didn't stop to wonder why. Later, maybe, he'd let the question rise. Was it a coyote? A person? Mischief or something worse? But now wasn't the time for speculation.

The wind tugged at his coat as he stepped into the field, boots sinking slightly in the thaw-softened earth. He kept his movements slow and practiced, his posture relaxed but firm. Panicked cattle didn't need shouting; they needed presence. Certainty. And he had plenty of that, even if it came from hollowed-out places inside him.

He cornered the nearest two, one older heifer, the other a young cow with her calf still wobbly at her side. He whistled low and steady, a practiced sound from years of rounding up panicked herds. The cows froze, their ears twitching toward him.

"That's it," he murmured. "Easy, girl."

He approached from the side, murmuring soft nonsense to calm them, then gently guided them back toward the gate. The moonlight glinted off their coats as they passed under the beam of the fence and returned to the enclosure. Wes latched the gate behind them with a metallic snap, the noise echoing across the quiet yard.

He could see more shadows moving across the lower slope. The grass there was fresh and damp with new growth, scattered with wild onions and budding clover. Wes stepped into the field, letting the night close around him. The stars were out in full above, winking through thin clouds like the quiet eyes of forgotten soldiers. The cows were farther now, skittish still, and he knew better than to rush.

As he approached, a figure darted from the far side of the shed. It looked small, lithe like a human and not a coyote as he'd assumed—hoped, really.

His chest tightened.

He moved quicker now, his boots no longer soft in the grass. The figure paused before darting away.

"Hey!" he shouted. His voice felt loud in the stillness. "Stop!"

But they were gone in the dark.

Wes didn't give chase. The cows came first.

It had taken nearly forty minutes, not counting the time to saddle Jeremiah. Still, Wes had managed to wrangle another five. The last was a belligerent calf that refused to be coaxed, finally yielding when bribed with a handful of hay from the feed shed. He rounded the far end of the fence line surrounding the main yard, breath coming steady now, the sweat along his neck cooling in the crisp night air.

Then he spotted movement.

A shadow eased along the edge of the barn, low to the ground and near another stray cow. His first thought was that the little bastard was back, the one he'd seen bolting into the dark earlier. He tensed, ready to intervene.

But then the figure raised a lantern.

The lantern flame flickered in the wind, revealing a familiar face. Maisie. Her nightgown clung to her in the breeze, one hand clutching a rope that hung limp at her side, the other holding the lantern aloft. Her cheeks were flushed from exertion or cold—it was hard to tell which—and her boots were speckled with mud and straw.

Wes slowed his approach. His eyes narrowed. How long had she been out here? The chill had only deepened with the darkness, and she wasn't dressed for it. Not by half.

As he drew closer, her voice wove through the stillness. It slipped into his chest before he could guard against it, quieting something he hadn't realized had been clawing for air. She whispered calmly to the frightened cow, the same way one might soothe a crying child. There was no fear in her expression, no tension in her limbs. She moved with the kind of steady confidence born of habit, not guesswork.

So—she had experience with livestock, then.

A corner of Wes's mind, the one he tried to ignore most days, sparked with a quiet curiosity. Maisie made it hard not to wonder. Not just about her past, but about all the pieces of her that didn't quite fit where she'd landed. He didn't need to know. But that didn't stop him from wanting to.

She spotted him just as she slipped the rope around the cow's neck, her gaze flicking up. She didn't jump or freeze, just nodded once and turned her attention back to her task. Wes stepped in silently, taking the rope from her hand and guiding the cow toward the corral.

"Are there more?" she asked, her voice slightly breathless as they walked the cow back.

"A few scattered down in the field," he replied. "I'll saddle Jeremiah and go get them."

He caught the nod from the corner of his eye before she shivered, rubbing one hand along her bare shoulder. Without a word, Wes shrugged off his coat and draped it over her shoulders. She looked up, her brows knitting.

"You don't have to," she murmured.

"I know," he said, helping her slide her arms through the sleeves anyway.

The coat swallowed her whole, the hem brushing her calves and the sleeves hiding her hands. She looked like she didn't belong to the night anymore, but to something softer. Warmer. He told himself the ache that rose had nothing to do with her and everything to do with the wind.

After returning the cow, she followed him to the stable, where Jeremiah waited, ears twitching as Wes started to wake him.

"Can I use one of the other horses?" she asked, glancing at the row of sleeping animals.

Wes frowned as he reached for Jeremiah's bridle. "I can get the cows."

"How many are still out there?" she countered. "It'll be faster if we both go. I know how to handle a skittish cow."

Wes huffed out a breath. He was too tired to argue. And truth be told, she wasn't wrong.

"Fine," he said, gesturing to a smaller mare in the corner— a soft-coated paint with white splotches down her flank.

She was beautiful and gentle, rarely ridden by the brothers. She'd belonged to Anabelle. Wes hadn't had the heart to send her to the other stables after... everything. So she stayed here, where he could look after her himself.

Maisie approached the mare with careful hands, waking her with soft strokes to her nose. Wes helped her with the saddle when she struggled, fingers brushing against hers briefly.

"Sorry," she mumbled. "I've ridden, but never saddled one before."

"You're doing fine," he said, surprising himself.

With both horses ready, he helped her mount before climbing onto Jeremiah. They grabbed extra rope and took off into the open pasture, lantern swinging from Maisie's grip like a firefly dancing through the dark.

Riding was faster. The added height gave Wes a clearer view of the strays, and within twenty minutes, they'd located the rest. One cow had nearly made it to the fence line at the edge of their property—farther than expected.

By the time they finished, Maisie's face was pink, her breath coming in short puffs, one hand rubbing at her leg where it had likely chafed from the ride. Still, she didn't complain.

They returned the horses to the stable. Maisie set down the lantern with a sigh, arms trembling slightly. She had carried it the whole ride.

Wes reached for it. "Here," he said, taking the weight from her hand.

She gave him a tired smile in return.

"Did the noise wake you?" he asked. The question felt too small for the quiet between them, but it was the only thread he had to pull. He didn't want the moment to end, not just yet.

77

The silence between them had stretched too long over the past few days, and he couldn't stomach it anymore.

Maisie shook her head as they walked toward the house. "I was feeding Junie. Got her back to sleep, then came out to see what happened."

"That was dangerous," he said gruffly. "Could've been an attack."

She glanced sideways at him. "I know how to hit a man where it hurts."

His lips twitched, but he forced it back down. "And some men know how to kill a woman."

Her face shuttered, jaw tight. He'd said the wrong thing—again. She didn't snap back, just stared ahead like she'd locked the door from the inside. He hated how easily she could do that. How quick she was to retreat.

They reached the porch. Wes took a long look at her, scanning for injury. He spotted nothing visible. His gaze lingered longer than it should have.

When she turned to look at him, her expression softened into something that was not quite a smile, but close. He didn't say thank you. He didn't have to. She nodded, like she'd heard it anyway.

She took off the coat, handed it to him, took the lantern, then disappeared inside.

Wes stood there, staring after her, the sound of the door shutting behind her muffled by the creak of the wind. He turned, eyes sweeping the dark horizon for something, anything to make sense of the mess that was his thoughts. The night wasn't over yet. There were other corrals, and he needed to be sure none had been tampered with.

Wes glanced back toward where Maisie had left. He hadn't gone looking for anything. But feelings weren't like cattle; they didn't stay where you penned them. They got loose in the night, tangled in fences, showed up with mud on their coats and her name on their breath.

She was kind.

Strong.

Capable.

Beautiful.

And none of that mattered.

Wes tightened his coat around himself, the warmth of her still lingering in the fabric, and strode into the dark.

There was more ground to cover.

Chapter Nine

Maisie brushed a hand down the front of her dress. Then again. The fabric lay smooth beneath her palm, but it didn't still the flutter in her chest. She hadn't felt this kind of nervous in weeks. Being hunted by Zeke brought a sharp, cold sort of fear. But this—this was different. Softer, almost giddy.

"You'll be fine, Maisie," Eli said from the doorway, arms crossed as he leaned against the frame.

She glanced up. He wasn't dressed for ranch work. No dust on his boots, no sweat on his collar. His shirt was neatly tucked and freshly laundered, and the sight of it made her feel guilty. He'd claimed he had business in town, but she knew better. He was only tagging along because it was her first day.

She might have told him not to bother, but Wes had spoken up at supper before she could. Said it was a good idea—safer— and that had been that.

Maisie lifted Junie from the parlor floor, where she played with a straw doll. Thirteen months old now, the little one was quick on her knees and eager with her hands. Maisie soothed her with a soft hum, bouncing her gently as they stepped outside, cool morning light slipping through budding branches overhead. Eli held the wagon reins, his usual grin in place. Damp earth and new blossom rode the air—clean as a hymn breathed straight.

As they rattled toward Twin Forks, the easy nerves faded and the other kind crept back in. What if Zeke was still in town?

Her eyes slid toward Eli. He didn't know who she was running from. None of them did. What might a man like Zeke do to the Calder brothers? Plenty, she reckoned. Men like him had reach.

Eli caught her look and raised a brow. "Don't stare at me like that, Maisie. I'll have to catch you if you fall too hard."

Her cheeks warmed, though not as fiercely as once they might've. She rolled her eyes. "My standards are too high to fall for a man as easy as you."

He clutched his chest like she'd shot him. "You wound me."

The wagon jolted through a rut; Junie fussed. Maisie hushed her and kissed her soft hair. The baby settled. A stray tendril teased Maisie's cheek; she closed her eyes a moment and let the morning touch her.

Town rose into view. Maisie scanned the fronts, wondering after the baker and his wife, though it was likely too late in the morning to find them free of the market bustle. Eli turned off the square onto a quieter side lane, toward a house behind a small iron gate. He'd mentioned it wasn't a formal shop but a parlor business.

The house was modest, lace curtains in the windows and pots of crocus bright along the porch. Warmth lived there that had nothing to do with sunlight.

"Minnie!" Eli called before Maisie could knock. "My beautiful Minnie!"

A small woman appeared in the doorway, smile fresh as rising bread. Minnie Abbott was soft of curve and gentle of eye, hair swept into a loose bun with stubborn wisps framing her cheeks.

Eli leapt from the wagon, scooped her up, and spun her laughing. Junie squealed in sympathy. She kicked to be set down, but Maisie kept her close as she climbed down.

When Eli set Minnie back on her feet, he flourished toward Maisie. "This is Maisie Ward. I told you about her. She's my new friend—so take good care of her."

Minnie huffed, fond despite herself. "Maisie, is it? Eli says you're staying out at Calder." Her gaze dropped to Junie and returned with something like gentle approval. "Poor thing, having to deal with this one all day."

Eli gasped, scandalized in play. Maisie grinned despite herself, some tautness slipping from her shoulders.

"It's been rough," Maisie said solemnly. She tilted closer; Minnie leaned in like they were old friends. "I told the boys I wanted to earn my keep, but truth is—" she slid Eli a sideways glance "—I needed a day's freedom from Eli. And Wes."

"Only those two?" Minnie cackled.

"Oh, Jesse's a sweetheart," Maisie said, laughing for real now.

Eli flung up his hands. "I can tell when I ain't wanted. You ladies enjoy your gossip—I'll leave you to it."

He tipped his hat, wounded in show. Maisie shook her head, smiling for true.

***

The parlor was cramped—that was the plain truth of it.

Wooden shelves lined the walls, every inch crowded with labeled glass: dried calendula, comfrey, pennyroyal. The room breathed soil and old petals. Even with the windows smudged open, the breeze could scarce stir those heavy aromas.

A long table near the hearth had been repurposed into a workbench. Its scarred top gleamed in the low firelight. A stone mortar and pestle sat center, flanked by linen sachets, curls of golden beeswax, a small brass scale with flat iron weights. From the ceiling beams above hung bundles of angelica, sage, rosemary. Their brittle leaves whispered whenever a draft crept beneath the door.

"Eli mentioned you have some experience?" Minnie asked.

Maisie started, pulled from reading the shelves. She flushed and nodded. "I worked in an apothecary for some years," she said, smoothing her skirt. Her hands wanted a task to steady them.

Minnie grunted approval. "I've done a bit of cleaning already, though it doesn't look it." She wrinkled her nose, and Maisie chuckled with her. "Help me stuff dried herbs into sachets and seal 'em proper. We'll see how well you know your plants, then set to work."

Maisie nodded. Junie kicked, then sneezed. Minnie's gaze softened.

"When Eli said you had a baby, I tucked away what might tempt curious fingers. You can set her down, if you like. Can she walk yet? I confess—I don't know a thing about babies."

Relief loosened Maisie's throat. She lowered Junie to the thick red-strand carpet. "Not walking yet," she said, smiling. "But she crawls quick as a mouse."

And crawl she did. The moment Maisie turned, Junie squirmed off toward something crinkly and green.

They fell into a rhythm soon enough. Maisie identified Minnie's stores, stripping plantain leaves for drying or grinding, folding parchment slips for loose teas, sealing bottles with warm beeswax, lining finished sachets neat as soldiers. The work should have soothed her.

In practice, Junie made it a trial.

The baby snatched at anything near. She toppled a jar of catnip into a fragrant scatter that set both women to their knees. She shrieked when Maisie slid the mortar out of reach, shrieked louder when told no. She squirmed to be held, then twisted free only to reach again. She cried when customers came and cried when they went.

Maisie tried. Truly. But with every fresh disruption, every polite smile Minnie offered, the parlor air thickened. Guilt weighed heavier than any bundle of herbs.

By late morning, Maisie knew. This wouldn't do.

She gathered Junie, who gurgled happily as she gummed a harmless sachet Minnie handed over, and drew a breath. "I'm sorry," she said—she'd lost count of how many times that day.

Minnie shook her head. Her smile was kind but edged with weariness. "It isn't your fault. You're working hard. Any woman can see that."

They both understood. It didn't need saying aloud. Maisie wouldn't be returning; Minnie couldn't be expected to endanger her livelihood for a stranger.

The parlor's small clock ticked toward three when Eli's voice carried in from the door. "Maisie! Minnie!" He strolled inside, hands folded behind his head, grin bright as linen on a line. Maisie managed a faint smile, turned, and offered Minnie a small curtsy.

"Thank you for the day," she said. "Truly." She gathered the baby. "Goodbye."

Eli's smile dimmed when he read Minnie's face. He lifted a hand in farewell, then fell into step beside Maisie.

She didn't meet his eyes. The dust at her feet seemed easier to look at.

How selfish am I?

"Did Junie have fun?" Eli asked as they headed for the wagon.

Maisie shrugged. Junie giggled as if to answer for herself. *Too much*, Maisie thought, and her arms ached with the truth of it.

"What do you think of Minnie? She's grand, isn't she?"

"She's kind," Maisie said.

"She is," Eli agreed, turning his gaze to the road. "Saved me once, you know."

Maisie glanced up.

"When I was younger, a city girl came through. I fancied her, but she had no time for a country fool. I made a mess—fell into the creek trying to impress her, or some such." He laughed. "Minnie saw it, hauled me out, and told me she pitied me."

Maisie hummed, not quite smiling. Something eased in her chest.

"She told me later I looked a poor, sodden fool," he went on. "I pestered her weeks after that. Wore her down into being friends." His eyes warmed. He didn't say more. He didn't have to.

By the time they turned into the Calder yard, the pasture had blued with evening, and the air carried tilled soil and alfalfa bloom. Tom tipped his hat at the well.

"Thank you," Maisie said softly as they reached the steps. "And I'm sorry to be such a burden today."

"You weren't," Eli answered, gentle but firm. "Not a lick."

She gave him a grateful smile and carried Junie upstairs. She washed the day from her hands and laid the child in the crib. Junie sighed in her sleep, a fist curled near her cheek.

Maisie brushed the soft skin with a fingertip. "I love you," she whispered.

***

Supper ran quiet.

The men glanced between her and their plates often enough to notice but not enough for rudeness. It might have made her self-conscious if she hadn't been bone-tired.

"You look a sight," Rhett said through a bite of stew, gesturing with his fork. "Must've been a hard day."

"It wasn't really," she said softly, eyes on her bowl.

Jesse traded a glance with Eli. "If Minnie's wasn't what you expected," he offered, "there's always work here. Plenty to do, this time of year. We can use another pair of hands."

The others slid quick looks toward Wes, who only chewed.

"If she's going to work with us," Eli said, stirring his spoon, "we should probably get Tom back."

Maisie looked up. "Get him back?"

"Tom usually eats with us while we set the next day," Jesse said. "When you first came, we thought it best he take his meals elsewhere till we knew more. No offense meant. Didn't want a stranger too mixed into our business."

Her stomach turned. She stared at the cooling stew.

"I'm sorry," she murmured.

"No," Wes said. His voice landed solid as oak. "That was our call."

She nodded, though the words didn't quiet the tightness in her chest.

When supper ended, appetite had long gone. She rose and gathered the dishes. Jesse had cooked alone—she'd returned too late and too rattled to help—so she took the cleanup as hers.

Chairs scraped; boots thudded. Eli and Rhett offered their goodnights. Jesse lingered a beat, then stepped onto the porch. Only Wes stayed.

She didn't look at him, though she felt him the way a room holds a small fire—there, whether you face it or not.

When the door clicked shut, he spoke.

"Tell me how it went."

It wasn't truly a question.

She opened her mouth, ready to say *fine*—to lie neat and quick. The word snagged like a thorn.

Her breath hitched. Her chest pulled taut. Her eyes stung.

A sob broke loose.

She braced on the washbasin's edge, fingertips skimming suds. Her shoulders shook with the effort to hold steady, and the tears came anyway—quiet at first, then deep and hard.

"I..." She shook her head, burying her face in her arm as she fought for breath. "Working with Junie...it isn't possible. I stopped so often to tend her. No sensible shop would hire a hand like that."

She pushed back from the basin, apron damp, and paced the kitchen. Her hands found her hair, fingers tugging what order she'd built that morning.

"It isn't like I've anyone to leave her with. And I don't have coin for help. How am I to build a life for her like this?"

Wes crossed the room without a word. His palms were warm where they settled on her shoulders. He coaxed her hands down from her hair, steadying her more than any speech might.

"I'll do what I can," he said.

Maisie kept her eyes down. She didn't want comfort. Not when it reminded her how little she could do alone.

"Junie..." The truth slipped free before she could catch it. "Junie isn't my daughter."

He shifted. She didn't need to look to know he watched her careful.

"I know," he said gently. "You told us when you came. She's your niece."

"I did," she whispered. "What I haven't said plain is this: Ivy—my sister—died a few weeks before you found me. She begged me to keep Junie safe and away from her husband."

She swallowed. Ivy's wan face lay sharp in her mind.

"That man...he didn't love anyone. Not Ivy. Not Junie. He wanted a pretty thing to show, that's all. He wanted Junie, but he'd have been a cruel father. He was a cruel husband."

Silence filled the room—not cold, only heavy.

"I can't afford to fail," Maisie whispered. "I can't lose the last piece of her I have."

Wes's hands eased from her shoulders, then returned—one light, one sure. "You won't," he said. "Not while you're under my roof."

She lifted her head. The lamplight cut across his jaw and left his eyes in shadow, but his voice held.

"If you mean to work in town," he went on, careful, "we'll set it plain. Mornings, Eli or I will see you in and bring you back before sundown. If that's too tight a tether, I can ride two horse-lengths back and pretend I ain't there. Bell code stays the same—one long, two short if there's trouble. Minnie keeps a steady parlor; we'll speak with her about hours that match Junie's naps. On days you're here, there's work near the house you can do between her sleeps—books, salves, counting stores. You won't carry it alone."

Maisie stared at the suds beading along the basin's rim. "You can't be everywhere."

"No," he said simply. "But I can be where I'm needed."

For a moment, the only sound was the soft tick of the clock. Junie stirred upstairs and fell still again.

"If I say I can ride alone?" she asked, testing where his fence ran.

The corner of his mouth bent. "Then I'll ride farther back and pretend better."

A breath left her that felt like it belonged to someone else. "All right."

He shifted, as if tipping a hat he wasn't wearing. "You'll do good work there," he said.

"I intend to."

When she turned toward the hall, he lifted the lamp higher so the light found the latch. It gilded her sleeve a heartbeat, then slid away as the door eased shut behind her. He stood a while longer with the lamp burning small in his hand, listening to the old house settle, as if the night might yet give him another answer.

Chapter Ten

Morning unraveled in a hush that felt like purpose. Thin light pooled along the eastern windows, soft and gold, carrying damp earth and the promise of new shoots nosing up through cold soil. Birds chattered as if the sky itself had thawed.

Wes checked the upstairs hall before the house fully woke.

He didn't open the guest room door. He never would. He paused at the jamb, palm braced on worn wood, listening. A faint rhythm answered from within—two sleepers breathing steady, the kind of peace that finds a body only after a hard day. He let that be enough. He set a covered tray on the floor beside the door—porridge, a heel of bread, and a small crock of stewed apples—then eased away as the staircase creaked.

Downstairs, the kitchen had already found its commotion. The room smelled of bacon and cornmeal, coffee and woodsmoke. Morning light laid buttery slants across the scrubbed floorboards. Jesse worked the stove, stirring grits with one hand and turning eggs with the other. Rhett sat near the hearth, whittling a bit of hickory; curls of pale wood rained like feathers. Eli hunched over coffee so black it smelled like penance. The back door stood open to a breeze that carried damp and the mild iron scent of thaw.

"Tom'll eat with us," Jesse said without looking up. "Eli fetched him at first light."

Eli groaned. "Did it without so much as a swallow o' coffee. Feet near froze to the step."

Wes took his place and reached for a biscuit. "Maisie and the baby are sleeping," he said. "Set a plate aside. They'll want a warm meal when they wake."

"Already did," Jesse replied.

Tom Hargrove arrived as Jesse plated up—stooped and sun-browned, sharp-eyed as crows on a fence rail. When they were settled, Wes spoke again.

"I talked with Maisie last night."

Four sets of eyes turned his way, Tom's slower but steady.

"She can't keep town work while caring for the child," Wes said. "No coin for a nurse, and no kin near. She's worn thin, and she's afraid." He hesitated, then added what mattered most. "And she told me the name of the man hunting her."

Eli's mug paused halfway to his mouth. "Name?"

"Zeke Blackwell." The room changed with the saying of it. "Her sister's husband. He's after the child. Junie is his by blood."

Silence held a beat, then two. Even the fire seemed to listen.

"That'd square the circle," Eli muttered at last. "Newspaper said Blackwell's been buying up spreads, throwing weight, making trouble." His brow pinched. "Explains why she flinches at shadows."

Rhett set his knife aside. "If he sets foot here—"

"—you'll not meet him alone," Jesse cut in. "And you'll not meet him without thinking."

Tom nodded once. "Jesse's right. Whatever else Blackwell is, he's patient and he's rich. Men like that don't care who breaks under their heel."

Wes kept his gaze on the table, appetite gone cold. "She told me Ivy—the sister—died weeks before we found them." The words came quieter than he meant. "Maisie promised to keep the girl safe."

Jesse leaned his hip against the counter and folded his arms. "Then if she stays, the staying needs a shape. Folks are already whispering. Come summer, if there's no arrangement, they'll do more than whisper."

Tom's look moved from one brother to the next. When he spoke, it was simple as fence wire. "Marry her."

The room went still.

Eli stopped mid-sip. Rhett blinked. Jesse's spoon clicked against his bowl and went quiet. Wes didn't move.

Tom lifted a brow at their surprise, as if disappointed it had taken them this long. "A wife under your roof draws no talk. A wife and child under your name draws less. It gives her shelter the law respects and gives that baby a steadiness she won't find elsewise." His gaze settled, certain, on Wes. "And it gives this house a shield against gossip gunners who'd love a clear shot."

Wes stared back. "You mean me."

"You're the head here," Tom said. "Your name carries farthest. If any Calder takes her, it ought to be the one who can swing the widest shade."

Rhett shifted. "I could," he offered, then grimaced. "But I ain't fit for quiet." He tapped the knife hilt against the table. "I got a temper and no patience with talkers. She doesn't need my kind of storm."

Eli scrubbed a hand through his hair, sheepish. "Minnie Abbott's half the reason I can't be the one. I reckon I'm fixed looking in that direction." He shrugged. "And I'm not the steady sort a woman like Maisie needs."

Jesse's mouth thinned. "I deal with suppliers and men likely tied to Blackwell. If I marry her, every negotiation turns into a

93

pry-bar aimed at our ledger. Besides,"—his tone softened— "Maisie trusts you, Wes, more than the rest of us. You're the one she lets close when the baby fusses."

Wes's jaw worked. "I've no interest in marrying anyone." He hated the way his voice roughened on the last word. "Not after Anabelle."

No one spoke. The old ache stirred under his ribs, the one he never gave voice. Anabelle's bright talk and city ways; the promise she made a game of breaking; the shame of being fooled in public while thinking himself a man of good judgment. He'd buried the notion of tenderness deep after that, under stock lists and fence lines.

Tom took a slow sip from his tin mug. "It ain't courting I'm urging. It's cover. It's decency. There are times you build a roof because the sky's black, not because you fancy the hammer."

Wes looked past Tom to the open door where branches, just budding, tapped the jamb like soft knuckles. He thought of last night—Maisie's voice wrenched small, the promise she'd made her sister, the way she'd stood in lamplight as if bracing for a blow that didn't come.

"I'll think on it," he said.

"Think quick," Tom answered. "Windows shut."

He pushed back from the table, set his mug in the basin, and went out. The breeze shifted and carried in the faint, sweet green of alfalfa.

Rhett rose with his cornbread in hand. "It's a clean fix," he said. "And it warns Blackwell he can't pick us apart with gossip." He clapped Wes's shoulder once and headed barnward.

Eli stood slower, eyeing his brother with a grin that held more care than mischief. "She'd keep us honest and fed," he said. "And Jesse's meals wouldn't taste like boiled penance."

Jesse scowled on principle; Eli gave him a mock salute and slipped out, the door hinges complaining as it swung shut.

Only Jesse and Wes remained. Jesse stacked plates into the basin and worked the pump. Water gushed and splashed hard.

"Tom's right about this much," Jesse said, voice low. "Whatever we decide, we decide for her safety, not our ease. And Wes—" He turned, drying his hands. "Of all of us, you're the one who can promise without talking it to death. She trusts that."

Wes didn't answer. He dried a plate and set it aside. Outside, a cow lowed; a chain clinked; some small thing went on being alive in the yard.

"All right," he said finally.

Jesse's eyes warmed, but he didn't smile. He just nodded and tilted his head toward the hall.

Maisie stood partway inside the kitchen, as if deciding whether she belonged there. Her hair was braided back with a bright scrap of cloth; her cheeks still held sleep's softness. When she moved fully into the room, Wes noticed the small plate already set aside—Jesse's habit—covered with a tin lid to keep warm.

"We put food by for you," Jesse said, gentling his tone. "I'm for the corrals. Would you see to the washing after you've eaten?"

"Of course," Maisie said. Her voice was wary and polite, like a guest careful not to step where she shouldn't. Jesse gave her a brief smile and slipped out.

Wes stayed. He told himself it was to speak plain, not to watch the way the room changed when she entered.

She sat and fed herself and the baby in small turns—bite for her, soften a morsel for Junie, wipe a crumb from a round cheek. Junie gripped the edge of the table with fierce little fingers and bounced her legs in triumph each time food reached her mouth.

"You missed Tom," Wes said at last.

Maisie started, then looked up with a small, rueful smile. "We must've slept hard. Thank you for the tray."

"You needed it," he said. He hesitated. "May I?" He held out his arms.

Surprise flickered across her face, then gratitude. She passed Junie to him. The child curled one hand around his finger and made a pleased sound; something in Wes's chest eased at the simple, heedless trust.

"I'm low on condensed milk," Maisie said. "And the grocer knows me now. I don't want to be in town much."

"We'll fetch what's needed," Wes answered. "I'll send Eli."

She nodded and focused on eating, but Wes saw how her jaw tightened on the word *send*—how she hated relying.

"We talked this morning," he said.

Her attention sharpened. She set down her fork.

"About what?" she asked.

"About you." He didn't leave room for doubt. "About Blackwell. About gossip. About your promise." He kept his voice even. "Tom thinks the surest shield is marriage."

The word landed like a hammer on a quiet nail—no clamor, only finality.

Color rose to her cheeks. She looked at the window, at the floorboards, anywhere but at him. "To whom?" she asked carefully.

"To me."

Silence stretched again, but it wasn't the blunt kind from the kitchen. It was measured, watchful. Wes let it be. Junie patted his jaw as if urging him to say more; he didn't.

When Maisie spoke, her voice was level. "Why you?"

He had answers ready; he chose the ones that were true. "Because the head of a house offers the widest cover. Because my name settles talk fastest. Because you trust me not to take what doesn't belong to me."

Her eyes lifted, steady on his. "Do I?"

"You've let me close when the child fussed," he said. "You've not let the others close so quick." He didn't make it a boast. "If another Calder suits you more, say it plain. There's no shame in that."

She was quiet a moment, thinking. "Eli is kind," she said slowly, "but his road bends toward someone else. Jesse's the careful one, and that would help...but he spends his days in town and in talks. I won't be the pry-bar men use to open your ledgers." Her mouth tipped, wry even in worry. "Rhett is dear in his way, but he burns hot. I don't need smoke in a room that already chokes me."

"And me?" Wes asked.

"You're the only one who's never pushed," she said simply. "Not once." She swallowed. "But I won't trade one kind of trap for another. If we agree to this, I set the terms."

"Say them," he answered.

"Separate rooms. No...expectations. I won't be forced, not by law or kindness." She steadied her shoulders. "It ends when I say it ends. If I decide to go—if it's safer to go—you'll let me. You won't stop me with your name." Her hand drifted toward Junie as if of its own accord. "And we put it on paper— guardianship provisions, who keeps the child if something happens. I won't risk her being taken by Blackwell's lawyers for want of a line of ink."

Wes nodded once, relief catching him off guard. "All fair." He paused. "And I set terms of my own."

Her chin lifted. "Go on."

"You don't leave the ranch alone," he said. "If you work at Minnie Abbott's, you ride in with one of us and back the same way until Blackwell's out of our sky. Bell code stays posted— one long, two short. If trouble comes to our porch, you take the child to the root cellar and bar the hatch. You'll carry a small knife in your pocket for your own sense if not for use. And you'll let us know if you plan to move—today, tomorrow, or three months hence. No vanishing."

Her mouth softened. "That's your fence line," she said.

"It is."

She drew a breath and let it out. "There's something else." She met his gaze head-on. "Your name will bear the worst of this. If I leave, folks will say you couldn't keep a wife. If I stay and Blackwell presses, they'll say you brought danger to good men. I won't be the reason you're shut out by churchmen or merchants or wives' talk. Are you willing to pay the cost if it comes?"

Wes considered. The answer felt simpler than it should have. "Yes."

"Because you want to?" she asked, not unkindly. "Or because you think you must?"

"Because it's right," he said. "And because when a thing is right, I can live with what it costs."

The clock in the hall ticked three slow beats. Somewhere above them, a board creaked as the house adjusted to the day.

"All right," Maisie said. "Then we'll do it. For now." She touched Junie's foot where it dangled from his forearm. "For her."

"For her," he agreed.

She wasn't smiling. Not giddy. But the strain eased around her eyes, and something steadier set in its place.

"One more thing," she added, and a spark—the old defiance—kindled in her voice. "If the day comes when *for now* isn't enough, we talk about *next*. We don't disappear on each other."

Wes's mouth tipped a fraction. "We talk," he said.

She nodded, then stood and reached for the baby. He passed Junie over; the child made her pleased sound again, and Maisie kissed the top of her dark head.

"We'll need a pastor," she said, eyes still on the child. "And witnesses."

"Pastor Crane," Wes answered. "This afternoon or tomorrow—quiet." He hesitated. "You deserve a ring."

"I deserve peace," she said gently. "And you deserve a chance to change your mind before supper."

Wes huffed—almost a laugh. "I won't."

She looked up at that. Not soft. Not hard. Only sure enough to make the next step.

"Then I'll wash up the dishes," she said, practical again. "And after, I'll mend that tear in Eli's sleeve."

He reached for his hat, which wasn't on his head, and touched the place it would have been. Habit. He stopped himself and instead reached for the water bucket to refill the basin.

"Eli will grieve the loss of his hole," Wes said.

"Eli will survive," she answered, and there was a flicker of teasing there—small, but there.

He lingered a heartbeat longer than needed, watching the way she balanced the child on one hip and reached for the crock with her free hand. Then he stepped back.

"I'll speak to Crane," he said. "And to Tom. And to Jesse."

"Speak to Eli, too," she said. "He'll pretend he isn't worried."

Wes nodded. "You see through people too quick."

"I learned the hard way," she said, and that was the only piece of sorrow she allowed into the room.

He tipped his head and turned for the door. At the threshold, he paused. "Maisie."

She glanced up.

"This isn't charity," he said. "It's covenant."

A line of surprise crossed her face, then smoothed. "Then we'll keep it," she said. "So long as it keeps us."

He went out into the yard where the air smelled like turned earth and something green pressing to be born. The wind took his hatless hair and toyed with it. He drew a breath that felt like grit and light and made for the barn, because a man with decisions to live has chores to steady his hands.

Behind him, the house settled back into ordinary sound—the clink of crockery, the baby's pleased babble, the soft slap of water in a basin—ordinary as bread and, he found, just as saving.

Chapter Eleven

The few times Maisie had allowed herself to daydream about her wedding, it had looked nothing like this.

As a girl, she'd pictured sunlight through white lace curtains, her father's steady arm tucked in hers, Ivy at her side with flowers in her hair. She'd imagined a modest gathering— neighbors in their Sunday best, lilacs scenting the aisle, a future bright as new tin. She had not imagined a borrowed dress, a borrowed name, a pastor who spoke in a voice that made the dust motes listen, and a marriage first made of paper and promise.

But she had chosen it.

Not because she loved him—she hardly knew him—but because of what they had set down together the night before: *no conjugal expectation; separate rooms; guardianship written and witnessed; a right to leave if danger demanded it; a duty for both to say so plain.* She had set those terms; Wes had agreed without flinching. The shape of that had steadied her. A covenant, he'd called it, not charity.

Minnie tightened the last pin at the nape of her neck. "Give us a turn," she said, stepping back.

Maisie obeyed. The dress, a modest blue cotton trimmed with tired lace, flared as she turned. It smelled faintly of lavender and starch, softened by many washings. It wasn't white, it wasn't new, but it fit. Minnie's hands were gentle and brisk; her mouth worked with practical little hums that kept nerves from rising too high.

"You look like yourself," Minnie decided. "That's the point."

"Is it?" Maisie managed a smile. She smoothed the bodice with a palm to still the nervous beat beneath. "I am myself, Minnie. Just... under a different roof."

Minnie tied a ribbon at Maisie's waist and pressed a small bouquet into her hand—sage and lavender for steadiness and grace. "Under a safer one," she said. "That's the point."

They rode out to a small chapel tucked among saplings and wild grass. The breeze carried turned earth and a whispering green that made a person feel the world could begin again if given half a reason. Inside, light fell in stripes across worn pews. The preacher waited at the front, his clear eyes kind. The Calder men gathered near—Jesse with his quiet steadiness, Eli already smiling, Rhett trying not to fidget, Tom stone-shouldered and sure.

Maisie's gaze found Wes.

He'd put on a clean jacket and combed his dark hair straight; a razor's fresh mark scraped his jaw. Somehow the neatness made him look younger and more solemn at once. He did not smile, but when she reached his side, his hand found hers, warm and steady, and gave the smallest answer of a squeeze—*still your terms, still our bargain.*

The preacher began without flourish. The words were old and careful, the kind hammered true by use. Maisie repeated them when bidden. Once, her voice wavered, and she lifted her chin and found Wes watching her—not to press, but to hold. The hitch eased.

When the vows were done and the ink dried on the paper, there was no kiss. Tom shook Wes's hand and, to Maisie's surprise, hers as well, with a gruff "Mrs. Calder." Rhett muttered something that might have been a blessing. Eli grinned like the sun off water. Jesse's "Congratulations" carried respect more than noise, which she preferred.

Minnie pressed Junie into Maisie's arms at the chapel door. The baby buried her face beneath Maisie's chin and sighed, as if the day were too wide for such a small body. Outside, birds trilled. Lilac buds, not yet open, promised a sweetness soon.

"Ready?" Wes asked quietly.

"I am," Maisie said, choosing the words. She had stood her ground last night and made the bargain she could live beneath; now she would step into it.

***

Midday found the house full of good smells—bread, chicken, and the sharp sweetness of preserved apples. Someone in town had sent the meal out with Jesse and Tom; Minnie took command of the table with practiced authority.

Maisie portioned soft pear and bits of bread for Junie first, as habit commanded. The baby ate with ferocious purpose and then succumbed to that warm, heavy-lidded drowse that turned the world gentle. Maisie hummed Ivy's lullaby on the way to the stairs—wind-through-grass soft, the kind of tune a body can lean on. She laid Junie down, smoothed one fine curl from her brow, and whispered a promise she could keep: "I will always tell you the truth."

Back in the kitchen, a single chair waited empty beside Wes's. The sight drew up something complicated in her chest. *A place, and a name to go with it.* She took the chair.

"Well, look who decided to join us," Eli sang, wagging his brows. "Mrs. Calder."

The name sat strange on her tongue—weighty, unfamiliar. Not heavy like a chain. Heavier like a mantle. She folded her hands. "Thank you," she said, because there was gratitude in her, even if joy took its time.

Tom lifted a tin cup that smelled of something stronger than coffee. "To the woman of the house," he said. "Welcome."

"Thank you," she answered again, and meant it.

Rhett scowled into his stew. "Smells like more chores."

"Wouldn't that be less chores?" Eli prodded, bumping his shoulder. "We just gained two extra pair of hands."

"One and a half," Rhett grunted. "The small one mostly waves."

"She'll pull her weight soon enough," Jesse said mildly, and Maisie, catching the twinkle in his eye, let a small laugh loose. It loosened other things inside her, too.

The meal was unremarkable and therefore dear: clatter of forks, small jests, the scrape of chairs. Wes did not say much. He did not need to; he was a man who made steadiness read like speech.

When it ended, everyone scattered to chores with the soft complaint men make when their bellies are too full for speed. Wes lingered by the door, hat in hand.

Maisie caught his glance. "Go on," she told him. "The ranch won't tend itself."

He tipped his hat a fraction. Not a smile, precisely. Something like it. She watched him go and turned to the dishes with Minnie.

"Does it trouble you he went so quick?" Minnie asked, not unkindly.

"No," Maisie said, setting a plate into the washbasin. "He married me to keep his word, not to sit by the stove. I'd rather a man who tends his work than one who makes pretty speeches and leaves the fence to sag."

105

Minnie leaned a hip on the table and studied her face. "And you? How's your heart?"

"It's doing what's asked of it," Maisie said. She rinsed; she dried. "I won't pretend I didn't want some different kind of day, once. But I wanted safety more. For her." She nodded toward the ceiling. "For me too, if I'm honest."

"That's honest enough for a wedding day," Minnie said. "Honester than most."

"Does honesty make a future?" Maisie asked.

"Helps you build one," Minnie said. "Hammer's no use if you swing crooked."

Maisie huffed a soft laugh. "You should write that on Jesse's ledger. He likes sayings that look like numbers."

They worked companionably until Minnie smudged her apron and went to peer into the oven. "Eat before it's cold," she scolded, shooing Maisie toward a plate the men had not devoured.

"I did," Maisie lied. Minnie let her lie. Friends learn which ones to let pass.

***

Upstairs, Junie's nap was short as a sparrow's bath. Ten minutes of peace, maybe twelve, then the thin, sharp cry that meant *the world is wrong and I can't say how.* Maisie tried all the sure ways: humming, rocking, a clean cloth, a cool sip from the bottle. The child battled sleep as if it were a thief. Crying did what it always did—turned the edges of Maisie's patience to rag and then to threads. She was not angry at Junie; she was angry at fatigue itself, at the way a day could demand more than a body had to give.

She carried the baby down and set her on a blanket in the parlor with a wooden rattle and the straw butterfly she'd twist-made last week. Junie batted at both and scolded them for existing. Maisie sat, closed her eyes, and counted five slow breaths. She made it to four before footsteps crossed the threshold.

"Looks like someone's overtired," Wes said quietly. He held at the doorway as if not wanting to intrude. "Might be worth a short walk, or we can darken the room and try again."

The words were gentle. They still snagged.

"You think I haven't tried?" Maisie heard her own tone and winced inside it. "You think I don't know my own child?"

"She's not—" Wes stopped, corrected himself. "I didn't mean to sound like a judge."

"It doesn't take much to sound like one," she said, sharper than she'd planned. The sharpness startled Junie, who keened and kicked; Maisie gathered her up at once. "I'm doing all I can," she said, quieter and truer. "Sometimes I don't know what else there is."

Wes came no farther in. "May I try?" he asked.

The question took the heat out of the room. She shifted Junie on her hip and nodded. "Take her outside. The light's softer."

He crossed and held his arms out like a man used to being refused. When she gave Junie over, he tucked the child against his shoulder and stepped back as if backing a skittish mare: slow, sure, no sudden reach. He didn't speak advice. He didn't speak at all, only hummed something shapeless and old.

"Walk east," Maisie said, rubbing a thumb across her brow. "Wind's kinder that side."

He tipped his chin and did as told.

Maisie sat on the couch and counted five breaths again. This time she reached six. She pressed her fingers to her eyes until she saw little stars. She felt foolish for snapping and more foolish for wanting to, and tired to the bone besides. Ivy would have laughed and told her mothers had been snapping and apologizing since Eve. The thought of Ivy made her throat sting, as it always did, with love and absence in equal measure.

Wes returned after a small while with a quieter child. Junie had done that heavy surrender of the limbs that meant true sleep. He laid her on the blanket and palmed the straw butterfly nearer to her cheek like it could stand guard.

"I'm sorry," Maisie said before he could speak. "I don't like the sound of my own voice when I'm tired."

"I'm sorry," he answered. "I don't like the sound of mine when I think I'm helping and I'm not."

Heat prickled her face. Not shame, not quite—something gentler, cousin to it. "You *are* helping," she said.

He glanced at the hall and then back at her. "We'll do better if we set it down," he said. "Like fence lines. Hours and hands. Who does what when the baby's fit to fight, and who rests then so there's something left."

Maisie nodded slowly. "A schedule."

"A plan," he said, and because he was Wes, the word fitted him.

She rose and went to the little desk Jesse kept for the ledger when he didn't want to take it into town. She drew a stiff scrap from the stack by the inkwell and sharpened the pencil with the knife Jess kept tucked there. "Say it and I'll write."

Wes stood near the doorway, hat in hand, more out of habit than need. "At dusk," he said, "I walk her. If I'm on fence or water, Eli walks. If Eli's in town, Jesse does." He looked toward the window, calculating. "After supper, you sleep for two hours. Bell code stays hanging by the kitchen door—one long, two short—and anyone in the house answers when you pull it. If we've a late calving, Tom will send a hand to sit on porch while you sleep so you're not alone with the door if someone comes."

"And nights?" Maisie asked.

"I take first waking," he said. "You take second. If there's a third, we'll argue then." He half-smiled and let it be brief. "Cradle should be moved away from the window. There's a draft on that wall."

"There is," she agreed. "We'll put it near the wardrobe, and I'll hang a heavy shawl as a screen. I've a mind to stitch a strip of cloth for the door—*Hush Hour*—so Eli minds his voice coming in late."

"Eli won't read a banner," Wes said, which made her laugh despite herself. "I'll tell him instead."

"Good," she said, writing the names beside the hours in a neat hand. "We'll need more condensed milk by week's end. I'd rather not take her into town."

"I'll send for it," he said. "And for a rocker. I'll build one if I must, but it'll set sooner if we fetch one from Murtry's place."

"You can build?" The question escaped on a little awe she hadn't meant to let show.

"Not pretty," he said. "Strong enough."

"That's the better kind," she answered, and the sentence made something ease in him she wouldn't have noticed if she hadn't been looking for it.

"Her gums are troubling her," Wes added, nodding at Junie's damp fist. "Tom chews a strip of clean linen and chills it in the pump for the hands' pups—says it soothes."

"I can sew five," Maisie said. "Boil and dry them on the line."

They moved through the next small hour with the simple, useful talk of a household setting itself: where to hang the shawl, where to keep a knife she could reach but Junie couldn't, which corner creaked loudest so she wouldn't step there after the baby slept. It wasn't romance. It was relief. It felt, to Maisie, like building a bridge across a narrow, cold river—two people laying planks from either side until they met in the middle.

When the pencil had more lead on her fingers than in its stem, she set it down. "I ought to apologize to you proper," she said. "I made you the face of every strain I feel. That's not fair."

"I can stand being a face for a day," he said. "Better me than a stranger on the road. But I like the plan better."

She nodded. "Me too."

A soft sound came from the blanket—Junie's little sigh that meant she'd found a good dream. They both looked at once and then, catching each other at it, looked away again like guilty children who'd peeped into a pantry.

"You said something to me once," Maisie said, watching her hands. "You said this wasn't charity; it was covenant. I can live under that word." She lifted her eyes. "I'll do my half. I expect you'll do yours."

"I will," he said. He had a way of making two words sound as binding as a signature. "If you find I'm failing it, you tell me straight."

"I will," she echoed, and felt the first clean line of trust draw itself between them, not deep yet, not wide, but true.

Wes tipped his hat—as if a hat could be tipped to a pact— and turned toward the yard. "I'll tell Jesse the hours," he said. "And Eli, the part about the banner, he won't read. I'll see Tom about a hand on the porch near midnight when there's calving."

"And I'll sew the cloths," she said, "and the shawl-screen, and that *Hush Hour* strip you say he won't read."

"He'll pretend not to," Wes allowed, "and still lower his voice."

He left her with the paper and a quieter room. The house took up its ordinary noises again: the pump handle, the light drag of a chair, a hen scolding the world from the yard. Maisie pinned the schedule to the kitchen wall with one of Jesse's ledger nails and stepped back to read it as if it were a prayer pinned to a church door.

Minnie slipped in then, cheeks pink from the air. "Well?"

"We made a plan," Maisie said, unable to keep the small pride out of her voice.

Minnie read the neat lines and clucked. "Sensible. I'll add my name to the afternoons I'm not at the parlor. You're not the only woman in this valley with hands."

Maisie swallowed around the sudden rise of feeling. "Thank you."

Minnie bumped her shoulder. "Hush Hour!" she read, grinning. "Eli will hate it and obey it."

"That's what Wes said," Maisie answered, and it felt like something to say *what Wes said* as if he were the sort of man a person quoted—not because he talked pretty, but because he talked plain.

***

Late light stretched the yard wide and gold. Work called the men out again, and Maisie set the shawl on a strip of twine to make the screen by the bed. She boiled linen, wrung it, and pegged it to the line. She moved the cradle from the draft. The small doing of these things settled her more than any speech could have. The day had given her a husband; the afternoon gave her a household.

Near dusk, Junie fretted again—the little whimper that means *I want the world quiet and the air warm and a shoulder under my cheek.* Wes lifted his coat from the peg and came to the parlor without ceremony.

"My hour," he said.

"Your hour," Maisie agreed, and handed him the child. She did not hover. She did not advise. She watched him once through the window as he paced the east side, where the wind ran softer, and then she turned to the basin and scrubbed without rushing, because there was no bell to answer for a little while and the *Hush Hour* strip—still a damp curl on the line— was coming soon.

When he returned, Junie was heavy with sleep. Wes touched the brim of his hat to nobody in particular and handed the child over with care a nurse might envy. Maisie laid Junie down in the cradle, now tucked near the wardrobe, the shawl-screen giving shade to the corner. The baby's breath settled into that small, even tide that makes a room holy if a person lets it.

"Good work," she told him.

He took that plain praise as if it were a coin worth saving. "Good plan," he told her back.

112

She wanted to say more—about how the day had begun with a vow and might have ended with her temper, if not for a man who knew how to ask *May I?*—but words, if too many, made a tangle. Better to keep the lines clean.

He started for the door. At the threshold, he paused. "One more thing," he said without turning. "If Blackwell comes, you don't look him in the eye. Not because you're afraid. Because he's the sort who feeds on it. You keep your eyes on your path. And you ring the bell."

"I will," she said. "I'll be the loudest thing in the house."

He huffed a laugh and went out.

Maisie stood beside the pinned paper and traced the names with a fingertip. She did not feel giddy. She did not feel tragic. She felt—finally—like a woman who had taken a step and then another on ground that might hold.

She took up needle and thread and stitched the letters on a narrow scrap—*Hush Hour*—in small, firm strokes. When she knotted the last, she slid the needle into the cloth as if putting away a blade and hung the strip on a peg by the kitchen door where Eli could not miss it and would pretend to.

Then she banked the lamp, drew the shawl-screen close, and sat her first hour on the new rocker Wes said he'd fetch and Tom said he'd find and Minnie said she'd bargain down two dollars—listening, not for calamity, but for the ordinary music of a house: the baby's breath, the murmur of men's voices outside, the soft tick of a clock that, for the first time in a long while, did not sound like it was counting her down.

Not a hope spoken at the ceiling. A plan pinned on the wall. And a promise—hers—to keep it.

Chapter Twelve

The echo of Maisie's quick steps earlier—the brief flare of temper both of them regretted—still rang in Wes's ears, though the worst of it had passed. They had apologized, set a few house rules on paper, and the house had quieted as if it, too, approved of sense over sharp words. Even so, the memory rode with him the way a burr rides a hem: small, stubborn, impossible to ignore.

A floorboard creaked. Eli breezed in from the side hall with hair like wind had tried to comb it and failed. His boots thudded a lazy rhythm; his grin was as familiar to Wes as the sunrise.

"I know that look," Eli said, pleased with himself. "Seen it on men who just learned their wives are better at words than they are."

Wes tipped him a stare cold enough to harden spring mud. Silence never once slowed Eli.

He leaned close, studying Wes as if he were weighing a yearling. "Tell me: did Mrs. Calder set you straight?"

Wes folded his arms and said nothing.

Eli took the non-answer for what it was and laughed. "Pricked your pride, did she? Or is it your feelings?" His eyes sharpened. "Don't tell me you've gone and fallen."

"Nonsense," Wes said. "We've fences to mend, calves to tag, water to pull. No time for fool talk."

"Mm." Eli lifted both hands in mock surrender. "Just seems to me a man doesn't stew if he doesn't care what a woman thinks."

Before Wes could answer, the front door shoved wide. Tom filled the frame, breath hard, glove braced against wood.

"What is it?" Wes was already moving.

"North fence," Tom panted. "Cut again."

A cold iron thing passed between Wes and Eli. Third time in a week. Someone wanted the Calders watching every direction at once.

Thirty minutes later, they were in the saddle, following the pale ribbon of trail through new-green. Clover nodded, balsamroot flared yellow, bees worked as if men and their mischief had never been invented. Past the rise, the line broke into open, and the hurt showed plain: wire sliced neat, posts jarred loose, a mouth of gap wide enough to swallow a small herd.

Wes swung down. His boots sank in thaw-soft earth. He walked the damage in a slow, sure loop—angle of the cut, height of the break, where a post had been shouldered instead of pried. Fresh prints lay in the moist dirt—a run by the depth of the heel—headed west before drying wind smudged them to nothing.

Eli squatted near the break. "Clean steel," he said. "No animal."

Sloppy work, though. Not the quiet kind old rivals used. This mess had a boy's boldness to it, and a boy's faith he wouldn't be caught. There were a few young men in the valley who'd try such a thing; only one had the pride to be brazen and the foolishness to leave tracks.

Jamie Grayson.

The Graysons had been Sunday-table friends once. Wes remembered setting a squirming Jamie on his knee so their fathers could finish a talk uninterrupted. Last spring, the elder Grayson died, and Jamie started living past his means. First, he borrowed and bought wrong. Then he looked east at Calder pasture and saw a solution that wasn't his to take.

Wes had tried talking. Then firmness. Offered the sheriff, offered to sit the two brands down with witnesses. None of it took. The boy wanted land and thought theft clever.

"Back to the break," Wes said. "Tom?"

"On it," Tom answered. "I'll fetch the hands and tools."

"Eli, you stay and keep watch while they mend," Wes added. "No sense letting the day's work get cut twice."

"What about strays?" Eli asked.

"I'll sweep the south flats and bring in what's wandered."

Jeremiah carried Wes an hour along rolling green. The sky spread wide and patient, as if it could outwait men's meanness. No strays turned up, which sat uneasily on him; no cattle could slip through that mouth and not stop to crop sweet spring grass. He patted the gelding's damp neck and turned toward home.

***

Dusk laid a warm hand on the house. Windows caught light like coins; the kitchen smelled faintly of coffee dregs and clean wood. The place was quiet—the particular quiet that means men are still out and work is not done.

Soft steps in the hall. Too light for any of his brothers.

Maisie came in with the child dozing on her shoulder, thumb tucked, lashes heavy. The baby's curls clung to her brow; sleep had pinked her eyelids. Maisie's own face carried the day's work—tired at the edges—but the sharpness from noon had worn away. She met Wes's gaze for a breath, then looked down, worrying her lower lip.

He had the foolish thought to free that lip with his thumb. He folded it away. Married or no, a man didn't touch without leave.

"I'm sorry," Maisie said, voice barely above a breeze through orchard branches. "For earlier. I was tired. I shouldn't have snapped."

Wes should have answered at once. The words stuck, as if some tight band round his chest had finally loosened and startled him. He nodded, once. "I said it poorly. I'm sorry, too."

Her shoulders eased. A few curls had wriggled loose from her scarf. She set Junie on a braided rug, where the baby rolled onto her belly and blinked at the room. Maisie went to the shelves and began to gather the makings of a simple supper.

"Where's Jesse?" she asked, frowning at the window. "He's usually rattling pans by now."

"With Rhett. Counting heads," Wes said. "Eli's at the north line. Tom's likely gone back with tools."

"This late?" Her hands stilled. "Again?"

"Cut fence," he said. "Not the same breed of trouble we've had before. This is local foolishness."

She looked over, questioning.

"Jamie Grayson," Wes said, accepting the bowl of potatoes she passed and the paring knife beside it. He fell into the easy rhythm of peel and turn. "Our families were close once. He took the brand too soon and thinks swagger can stand for sense."

"What will you do?" she asked. Not fearful; simply direct.

Wes considered the clean curl of peel in his hand. "I've offered the sheriff, offered witnesses, and talk. He laughed at both."

"And fists?" she asked, one brow lifting, not as a dare but as a measure.

"I know how," he said. "And how it ends. I'd rather it didn't end that way."

The war had taught him that. He had gone east a young man who thought a rifle was weight and iron; he came home a man who knew it was decision. He had scouted the cuts through timber no one else could see, found ford and rise and safe gulch with a fox's habit. He had put men on those paths. Once on a night ridge above a black river, his hand sign sent a squad down a trail that turned under them and became a trap. He'd fired and reloaded blind. At dawn, he carried a boy whose name he'd known for two years and couldn't recall for an hour. He had also killed a man in a hedgerow south of Dalton—close enough to see the man's surprise. Those two memories had taught him most of what he knew about lines a man chooses and the weight that never lifts.

Maisie stirred the pot, the steam lifting between them. "You'll find a way that's firm and not cruel," she said. She did not say it to flatter him. She said it like naming a road she knew he'd take, whether she approved or not.

The words landed where he kept things he didn't show. *Kind,* she'd called him yesterday. If she'd seen the hedgerow, would she still say it? Maybe the measure wasn't spotless hands; maybe it was what a man did with what he knew they could do.

A hiccup—half burp, half surprise—popped from the rug. Both of them looked down at once. Junie sat blinking at the sound of her own small thunder, hair standing like thistle down.

Maisie bit back a laugh and failed. It came out soft and warm as a hand on a cheek. Wes felt his own mouth tip. The day, which had sat like a stone in his chest, shifted lighter.

He peeled in quiet while she knelt and smoothed a hand over the baby's hair. The shovel-scrape of Jesse's boots did not sound. Neither did Rhett's door-slam walk. The kitchen had the suspended feel of a room between breaths.

"Teach me the way you knot wire," Maisie said suddenly, looking up. "If I'm to be useful outside the house as well as in it, I ought to learn it proper."

Wes blinked, then nodded. He wiped his hands, drew a length of kitchen string from the drawer, and laid it on the table. "You twist to take up slack," he said, looping and pinching until the string held. "Then this half-turn bites it. Keeps the wind from singing it loose."

She watched, then took the string and copied him, tongue caught between her teeth, frown pure concentration. Her second try held firm.

"Good," he said. Praise moved through him awkwardly but honest. "You've a steady hand."

"I had to learn one," she said, and didn't have to add *for tinctures and measures and saving pennies.*

They moved easily around one another—knife, peel, stir, pinch of salt—like they'd been taught the same kitchen. When the pot thickened to a comfortable burble, Maisie wiped her wrist with her apron and, without looking at him, asked, "What did you do—during the war?"

"Scouted," he said. Truth, but not the whole. He added it. "And fought when there was no choice. I've put men in harm's way. I've killed, too. Some things sit on a man's hands even when he washes."

She did not step back. She ladled a little broth into a saucer, blew once, and held it out. "Taste this for salt."

He tasted and nodded. "Right."

She set the ladle down. "Thank you for telling me plain."

Junie made another comic little sound that put laughter back in Maisie's mouth. The sight tugged at Wes more than he liked to admit. His hand started for her cheek of its own accord, stupid as a yearling's first bolt. He stopped it and turned the movement into reaching for the towel.

Maisie looked up, puzzled at the aborted reach. He cleared his throat. "Your hair," he said, faltering and then setting it right. "You'll get flour in it. Do you—may I?"

He opened his palm, showing the narrow length of faded blue ribbon Minnie had left on the sill after mending. He felt ridiculous and, at the same time, more himself than any clever sentence would have made him.

Maisie's fingers hovered at her nape. A smile flickered, small and true. "You may," she said.

He stepped close as a man steps into a pen with a colt— slow, even, so no one startles. He gathered the loosened curls, careful of her scalp, and smoothed them back. The ribbon turned obedient in his hands; he tied a square knot without tugging. Her breath touched his wrist and made him think of quiet things.

"Better," he said, and the word meant more than hair. He stepped back.

"Thank you," she answered, and the words meant more than ribbon.

He could have stayed there longer than sense allowed. Instead, he set the knife by the board and reached for his hat. "South line needs looking before we lose the light."

"I'll have a hot plate when you come in," she said, promise without fuss.

He paused at the door and, this time, didn't manage to keep his hand to himself. He traced a loose curl that had escaped the ribbon and then, remembering himself, let it fall. "If the wind comes up, pull the shawl across the cradle," he said, practical to cover the softness of the moment.

"I will," she said. "And ring the bell if I need you."

He tipped the brim and took the steps in two strides. Jeremiah shook out a snort and carried him toward the south fence at a ground-saving trot. The work steadied him. So did the memory of a blue ribbon and laughter that warmed a kitchen the way a stove can't.

***

He rode the south line as the light thinned. Wire sang a little where wind touched it; he checked the ties, thumb-tested posts, stamped a footing that had frost-heaved crooked. The ranch spread quiet around him, honest as a ledger kept square. When he turned back, the first evening star blinked up. He let Jeremiah choose a slower gait home and, over the steady creak of leather, found himself thinking less of Jamie Grayson and more of the way Maisie had watched his hands and then made the knot herself.

Inside, the house held the best smell a man can come to—supper that someone cooked for him because he belongs where it's served. Jesse and Rhett had come in muddy to the knees but grinning; the count was good, the hands cussing in a cheerful way about wire and boys who thought mischief was clever. Eli arrived late with a coil of fresh line on one shoulder and a complaint about splinters; he read the *HUSH HOUR* strip Maisie had sewn and hung and pretended not to, lowering his voice on instinct anyway.

They ate. The talk was easy—fence mending, a mare ready to foal, Rhett's insistence that a rooster was looking at him sideways. Maisie laughed, small and surprised by herself, and topped off plates without fuss. Junie passed from arm to arm until Wes cleared his throat and Eli, smirking, relinquished her.

After, the men ghosted back to their chores with that slow drag men make when there's less light than work. Wes lingered in the doorway. Maisie stood with her back to him, dish towel in hand. He had the thought—foolish and sudden—that he could stand in that doorway every evening and be content with the sight.

"South line's sound," he said to the room in general and to her in particular.

"Good," she said without turning. "Eat before it cools."

He did, and it felt like a blessing.

Later, near dusk's full surrender, he took Junie for the hour they'd agreed was his. He walked the east side so the wind would be kind and hummed nothing in particular. The baby's head grew heavy on his shoulder. When he came in, Maisie had drawn the shawl-screen and laid out tomorrow's list beneath the pinned schedule: condensed milk, rocker if Tom's bargain held, linen for teething cloths. *A household speaking to itself,* he thought, and beyond the list, something quieter threaded under everything like a low hymn—choice.

Not Tom's idea. Not a town's gossip. Theirs.

He handed Junie over. Maisie settled the child in the cradle, then set her hand on the schedule and, for the briefest moment, set her other hand over his.

"Thank you," she said.

"For what?" The question came out rougher than he meant.

"For choosing this with me."

He didn't trust his voice. He covered her hand with his for a heartbeat and then drew back before he forgot himself entirely.

Out past the porch, the night air smelled of damp soil and a promise of rain that might or might not come. Wes stood with it a while and thought about hedgerows and blue ribbons and boys who hadn't learned yet what choices cost. He'd never be rid of all the weight he carried. But some weights a man sets down not by forgetting, but by picking up what's his and holding it steady.

He squared his shoulders, tipped his hat to the dark, and went to set the second lamp on the porch rail—a little circle of light that said *home* to anyone who had the sense to look for it.

Chapter Thirteen

Time slipped by faster when a day had shape. Marriage to Wes hadn't changed Maisie's life in any grand, sweeping way, but it had shifted its edges. She took on more of the housework, was included—quietly—in talk about the ranch, and saw Tom more often at the table. With Junie's care on top of it all, Maisie found herself with little time to sit and think. It was a blessing and a quiet sorrow. Little thinking meant less fretting over Zeke; little thinking also meant the ache of what she'd lost had fewer places to go.

A week after the wedding, Minnie arrived without warning, all sunshine, bustle, and determination.

"You need a proper breath of air," she announced, clapping once. "We're going to town. No arguments."

Before Maisie could work up any, Junie was in Tom's arms, and she was bundled into the wagon beside Minnie, rolling down the road while the morning fog still clung to the trees.

At first, the freedom felt strange—like a dress cut too loose. She wasn't used to being anywhere without a purpose now, without a baby on her hip or dinner to consider. But as Twin Forks rose ahead—its boardwalks busy, dogs yapping, a blacksmith's hammer ringing—the tightness in her chest eased. The air smelled of sun-warmed timber and horse sweat, and the noise of the street wrapped around her like a quilt.

"Look at that," Minnie teased, bumping shoulders with her as they walked. "You're breathing again."

"Thank you," Maisie murmured, unsure what else to offer.

"Come on," Minnie said, looping an arm through hers. "You'll want to know who's who. It saves time later."

They strolled past the seamstress's shop where gingham and muslin hung in the window.

"That's Miss Abby. Kind, fair prices, gentle pins. Avoid Tina Hekkle if you can. Charges too much and talks twice it."

"I'll remember," Maisie said.

They passed the grocer. "Mr. Lyle and his boy. Good apples if you go early. He'll try to sell you 'special molasses.' Don't be fooled by the ribbon."

The bakery door was propped open, and sweet heat drifted out. "Mr. Dobbins," Minnie said. "Cinnamon rolls that could turn a sinner. Eli once ate six and claimed he saw the Lord halfway through the fifth. Cissy was near beside herself with delight."

Maisie laughed before she could help it. "You and Eli were close?"

"We were children together," Minnie said, her smile softening. "He got into mischief, and I tried to drag him back out." She glanced aside. "There's still a glint in him. Like he's always thinking something he knows he shouldn't say."

Maisie looked down, the feeling that followed hard to name. Minnie gave her arm a little squeeze.

"You're not alone here," Minnie said. "Folks will learn you. You're Wes's wife now, sure—but you're also Maisie. That counts."

"Thank you," Maisie said, swallowing a sudden lump.

The bell over the general store door jingled. Inside, the air held sawdust, tobacco, and dried lavender. Glass jars lined one wall—nails, marbles, penny candy, buttons. A long-bodied cat dozed on the counter.

"Jesse said thread and sugar," Minnie reminded. "Come see where they keep the useful things."

They moved down the aisles. Lamp oil was, for no good reason, tucked in a dim corner; thread was in a basket near the front.

"Coats brand," Minnie said, frowning at a tangly skein. "The local stuff knots like sin."

As Minnie measured ribbon, Maisie's attention slid to a man standing near the window. He wore a long duster and a hat pulled low. A folded newspaper rested in his hands, but he wasn't reading it. Every so often, his gaze lifted—and found her.

Unease ran along Maisie's arms like a draft.

Perhaps he was only curious. Word traveled fast. Wes Calder had married, and people liked to put faces to names. Still, the way the man watched her—quiet, measuring—made the air feel thin.

"You all right?" Minnie asked, glancing back.

"It's warm in here," Maisie said lightly, turning toward the counter.

The man stepped closer as they set down thread and sugar. He tipped his hat with a slow flick. "Afternoon, Minnie."

"Afternoon, Mr. Danner," she returned, pleasant but brisk. "We're just fetching a few things."

He looked to Maisie. "Ma'am," he said. "Roy Danner. Knew Wes's folks."

Minnie gestured with a little flourish. "This is Maisie Calder."

Roy's eyes stayed on Maisie. "Welcome to Twin Forks," he said. "You marry into the Calder name, or are you kin to the old lot before you wed?"

The way he set the words down sounded plain enough, but the interest beneath them felt too sharp by half. Maisie kept her smile steady.

"I married Mr. Calder," she said. "We're settling near the south pasture."

"Mm," Roy said, still watching. "You mean to stay on?"

"I'm married," she repeated.

Minnie's hand landed at last on the sugar sack. "We'll be letting you get back to that paper, Mr. Danner."

"Sure," he drawled. "No harm in passing the time."

Maisie counted coins with careful fingers and stepped outside without looking back. Minnie joined her a breath later.

"You all right?" Minnie asked.

"I left Junie with Tom," Maisie said too quickly. "I shouldn't stay away long."

Minnie studied her and then nodded. "Of course."

"Thank you for today," Maisie added, softer. "It meant a great deal."

"Anytime," Minnie said.

The wagon rolled home through light that had sharpened to gold. Fence posts slid by in a steady rhythm. The air tasted of warming earth and sweet hay. Maisie held the reins and kept her eyes forward. She was grateful for the errand; she was also grateful for the lane that led back to Calder land.

By the time she turned into the yard, the horses were warm and blowing. She climbed down and headed for the house, skirts brushing dust from the grass.

Wes stood near the barn with his sleeves rolled, sweat darkening his collar, dirt streaked along one forearm. He looked up and smiled as he came toward her, brushing his hands on his trousers.

"How was town?" he asked.

"Fine," she said, not quite slowing.

"Minnie show you around?"

"She did."

"You don't sound fine," he said, falling in beside her.

"I'm tired," she answered, sharper than she meant to. "I ought to check on Junie."

He stopped but kept his eyes on her. "I was going to speak with you, if you've a minute."

She paused at the porch step and tightened her grip on the paper parcel. Her shoulders felt like they were bearing down under a fresh weight. "Can it wait?"

"Did something happen?" he asked more gently.

"I said I don't want to talk about it," she said, her gaze fixed somewhere over his shoulder.

Silence stretched. The porch boards creaked. A wind moved through the bare branches by the lane.

"You won't look at me," he said quietly.

"I'm looking at you."

"Then talk to me."

She drew a breath that scraped going in. "I shouldn't have gone," she said. "I shouldn't have left her."

"She was with Tom," Wes said. "He's steady with her."

"That isn't the point," she snapped. "I walked into a place where I don't belong and was looked at like something laid out on a shelf."

Wes's jaw set. "Who?"

"It doesn't matter."

"It does to me," he said, voice low. "If we're to share a roof—if you want the safety that comes with my name—you have to let me in."

She flinched, like the word had struck. "Safety," she said, softer, with an edge. "I am inside walls that aren't mine, among people I didn't choose. I cannot step into a store without eyes taking the measure of me. And now I am to stand on a porch and offer a full account?"

"I'm not asking for an account," he said, holding the step between them. "I'm asking not to be shut out. You're pulling away. I can feel it."

"I married you for Junie," she said, trembling. "I hardly know you."

"I know," he said, quiet but firm. "Neither of us asked for this. But I'm trying."

She stared at him and swallowed. The paper parcel had softened where her fingers gripped it. She thought of Roy Danner's slow smile and the way his gaze had felt like a thumb pressed too hard into bruised fruit. She thought of how her own feet had moved toward the door without waiting for her mind.

"You can't fix it," she said. "Not the thing that happened, not the look on a man's face."

"Then let me be angry on your behalf," he said. "Let me stand there with you. That much I can do."

Her shoulders sagged as if some hidden rope had slackened. She was tired of being watchful. Tired of packing down fear until the lid bulged. Tired of making her voice gentle when she wanted to bark like a dog at a stranger's shadow.

"I'll tell you later," she said at last. "Not now."

His gaze softened. "All right."

She turned and went inside. The screen door banged louder than it should have. In the hallway, she paused, hand on the latch of the spare room that had lately become hers and Junie's. She could still feel Wes watching her from the yard— present, steady, not pushing her past what she'd offered. That steadied her, too, though she wouldn't have said so aloud.

She checked on Junie first. The baby lifted from Tom's arms with a happy squirm, then settled her face against Maisie's collarbone like that was where she'd meant to live all along. Maisie breathed her in and carried her up the stairs.

She couldn't bring herself to tell him about Roy Danner. Didn't mention how his eyes had followed her like they'd left a stain. Didn't say how his voice still echoed in her ears, or how she felt scraped raw beneath her skin.

That night, for the first time since arriving at the Calder ranch, Maisie turned the key in her bedroom door and locked it.

Chapter Fourteen

There were more things in life that soured Zeke's temper than ever managed to please it. He was a man with more ambition in the crook of his finger than most men gathered across a lifetime. He knew what he wanted. He knew how to get it, and Heaven help the fool who stood in his way.

Maisie Ward was standing in his way.

She was the very embodiment of what rankled him most: naïve, meddlesome, and worst of all, a woman who fancied herself bold—bold enough to speak, to work, to believe she had a place in a man's world. She ought to have married some witless workhorse and stayed tucked away in the quiet corner of the world where he'd left her. Instead, she'd run off with something that belonged to him, and Zeke was wasting precious time hunting down a girl who didn't know her place, and the child she'd stolen with her.

He'd scoured the city's underbelly, from the soot-choked fringes of Manhattan to the boarding houses that sagged along the Hudson. He'd paid barkeeps and laundresses, hack drivers and newsboys, men with crooked fingers and women with sharpened tongues. Most hadn't seen her, but a few had: a fair-haired woman traveling with a baby, never in the same place long, eyes always searching a room's edges. That trail had carried him west once already, to smoke-filled depots and stage roads where telegraph wires sang in the wind and information moved faster than wagons.

News of a body found in the Ward sisters' rooms had reached him weeks later by a short, clipped wire. He hadn't lost a wink over it. Ivy Ward had been a tool, nothing more. Her death meant little beyond the fact he'd been robbed of the satisfaction of teaching her what came of betrayal.

But Maisie—Maisie still lived. And for Ivy's crimes as well as her own, Maisie would serve.

She would serve long and slow. Zeke didn't believe in quick punishments. Pain lingered best when it came in pieces. Regret did its finest work in silence, and Zeke had perfected the art of silence. He could wait—coil like a spring beneath polite words, draw it out like a butcher with a blunt knife.

A knock interrupted his thoughts. Zeke looked up from the accounts spread across his desk, statements from his many dealings, some proper, most not.

"What?" he barked.

"Telegram, sir," came a reedy voice through the door. "Routed from Colorado Territory by the Denver office. Marked urgent."

Zeke scowled and leaned back, then flicked his fingers. "Bring it."

A small, narrow-shouldered clerk stepped in, eyes fixed on the carpet. With trembling hands, he set the folded form on the blotter. Zeke snatched it up, already waving the man away.

"Get out."

The door clicked shut.

Zeke unfolded the flimsy and read. His mouth curved, slow as a cat's stretch.

FOUND WOMAN ANSWERING DESCRIPTION IN TWIN FORKS STOP IDENTIFIED BY LOCAL TIPSTER R DANNER STOP TRAVELS WITH INFANT FEMALE STOP LIVES AT CALDER PLACE SOUTH OF TOWN STOP MARRIAGE TO W CALDER RECENT STOP WILL SEND DETAILS IF PAID STOP

He didn't care if the tipster was honest or a liar, so long as the bait held. The important parts were plain: a location, a husband's name, and proof she'd put down roots. He tapped the wire against the desk, savoring the feel of the thin paper under his thumb.

He didn't keep a man on salary in a place like Twin Forks. He didn't need to. Coin did better work when scattered. For months, he'd been seeding the routes—quiet notices with express agents, station clerks, and county papers from Albany clear to the Front Range: INFORMATION WANTED, PRIVATE MATTER, REWARD OFFERED. A woman matching certain particulars. Traveling with a girl child. No names typed, only marks to make the right people wonder. Someone always fancied himself clever enough to sell a rumor. This time, the rumor had a spine.

He rose, pushed back from the desk, and rang for his valet.

"Pack for a week," he said. "Cold nights, dust roads. Send word to the broker to hold all appointments. Wire the Denver office: I'm en route. I want a room secured at whatever passes for respectable in the county seat, and a driver waiting to take me on to Twin Forks when I arrive."

"Yes, sir."

Zeke crossed to the tall wardrobe and opened a narrow compartment only he used. He took out a small velvet pouch and checked the two glass vials inside—laudanum, properly labeled in a physician's tidy hand—and a slim set of restraints wrapped in oiled cloth. Not because he expected trouble, but because he respected it. Maisie had proven herself more stubborn than most women, and now she had people— neighbors, a husband—the kind of circle that mistook defiance for courage.

Courage cracked just the same.

He paused, letting memory work. He had seen the child twice back in New York when she was small enough to fit along the bend of one arm—at Ivy's bedside, then again dozing in a cradle near the parlor stove. Stout lungs, a fierce cry. Not a newborn by then, but young enough that the world hadn't yet marked her. He hadn't taken proper notice. A mistake. The child would help mend what folk whispered about him: the philanthropist widower doing his duty, reclaiming his blood. A man must tend his name like pasture; leave it unmended and the weeds would own it by fall.

He left that afternoon on the first train west. The journey took days, not hours. Rails rattled under him from the Hudson to Chicago, then again toward the mountains. Telegraph poles unspooled beside the cars like counting sticks. In the parlors between stops, he let the other men murmur of cattle prices and mining claims while he studied maps. From Denver, he hired a seat on a coach bound north and west, where the land opened, sage-sweet and washed with spring light. He did not sleep well. The road shook the marrow, and with each jolt, he rolled the wire's words again through his mind until they were memorized.

By the time the stage set him down in the county seat, the sky had gone pearly with late afternoon. He cold-combed travel from his cuffs and took a room above a mercantile that boasted "quiet" and meant it. After a bath and a shave, he stepped out again, walked the one block to the telegraph office, and sent three messages: one to the Denver broker to draw funds on his account, one to a certain attorney in the county seat—a man pliable when paid—and one to the tipster, via the banker who'd relayed the wire. PAYMENT ON PROOF, the last line read. DETAILED STATEMENT BY RETURN OF POST. SILENCE PAID LESS.

He did not go straight to Twin Forks that evening. He preferred to place stones before he crossed the river.

In the morning, he called on the attorney—Amos Kearney, narrow-shouldered, with teeth like fence slats and a handshake that tried too hard. Zeke had used men like him before in other counties. They didn't require loyalty. They required coin and a story they could repeat without blushing.

"I want formal papers prepared," Zeke said, taking the chair by the window as if the office were already his. "Petition the brand inspector to review the Calder stock books. File notices with the sheriff asking him to examine irregularities at the south water gate. Nothing loud. Nothing that sticks yet. Just enough paper to put a question in folk's mouths."

Kearney's pen scratched like a beetle in a wall. "And you, sir?"

"I am a concerned party," Zeke said smoothly, "who believes a certain infant may be held under false guardianship. I'll need custody papers drawn in advance, to be lodged when I say. Allegations of neglect will do. They don't have to sing; they only have to hum. Leave room for a doctor's affidavit, should I bring one. The phrasing must read like worry. Can you manage worry, Mr. Kearney?"

The lawyer's smile was damp. "Worry is my stock in trade."

Zeke left him to it and hired a driver toward Twin Forks by the back road, not the main. He wanted the shape of the land in his eye before he met the town head-on. The hills wore a pale fuzz of spring. Willows greened along creekbeds. The air had that wet, iron scent of thaw. It was good country. He found himself disliking it for that alone.

He reached Twin Forks near dusk. The sign on the saloon's porch creaked, and lamplight smeared golden of an evening over dusty panes. He stepped inside to the usual reek of smoke and pine cleaner. Men at the tables paused mid-hand. The barkeep—Burke, barrel-bellied with a jaw like a shovel—looked up from polishing the counter.

"Zeke Blackwell," Burke said without warmth. "Didn't expect you."

"I don't warn people," Zeke replied. "A room."

Burke reached beneath the bar and set a key on the counter. "Second floor. End of the hall. You're paying up front."

Zeke laid coin with two fingers, took the key, and climbed. He wasn't here for company. He was here to look down on the street, to watch who crossed which threshold and who lifted a hand to which neighbor. Trouble in a town like this was a web; you learned more by listening to the flies.

The room smelled of tobacco and old soap. He cracked the window and let the night air creep in. Somewhere beyond the dark swells of pasture, tucked among cottonwoods just leafing out, Maisie Ward slept under another man's roof. He imagined the set of her jaw. He imagined her checking a latch twice. He did not imagine her prayers. A woman like that had learned the use of silence.

Originally, he had planned to take the child without noise: hands hired by proxy, a quiet trade after supper, a letter to the right official to make everything look tidy after the fact. But the Calders' name complicated such plans. He didn't fear them; he simply disliked needless mess. Their reputation ran deep as a well. Everyone bought from them, borrowed from them, nodded when they spoke. That kind of standing was worth more than cattle. It was the very thing he wanted most: presence.

Perhaps he ought to thank the little thief for leading him to it.

He sat at the small desk and wrote by lamplight. The first letter he drafted was to Kearney, polishing the points they'd discussed: requests for review, neighborly concern, a tone clean enough to pass through any open door. A second note, he worked in cipher—nothing fancy, just a pattern he and three men knew. If any other eyes read it, it would appear to be a gentleman's inquiry about freight schedules. Beneath that, the message was simple: APPLY PRESSURE AT WATER, BRAND, AND BANK. TEST THEIR FRIENDS. PAY FOR SILENCE.

He sealed both and left them on the table to go with the first post. Then he took out the telegram and read it again. The name CALDER sat there plain as print can be. He rolled the flimsy tight and slid it back into his pocket.

Control a story and you control a town for a season, sometimes for good. With the right complaint lodged in the proper office, a sheriff might look the other way. With the right rumor planted at the bank, a loan might come due a touch early. With the right show of concern, decent folk could be made to wonder at neighbors they'd trusted for years. He had learned that lesson in New York. He meant to use it here.

He blew out the lamp and lay back in the narrow bed. He did not sleep much. Dawn inched up anyway. A rooster yelped somewhere beyond the river. A cart clattered over the ruts. He washed, dressed, and stood at the window as the street brightened by degrees.

Maisie Ward thought she'd outrun a man like him.

Zeke Blackwell didn't chase.

He hunted.

Chapter Fifteen

Three days.

Maisie sat with the weight of that number heavy in her chest, as if each hour had turned to stone and settled beneath her ribs. She kept seeing the man from the general store—hat brim low, a folded paper he never read, eyes that measured. The memory didn't unravel her; it sharpened her. In those three days, she'd moved Junie's cot farther from the window, checked the back latch twice each night, and set a small bag under the bed with a spare blanket, bottle, and the few coins she had. She asked Tom, lightly, if he'd noticed any strange riders near the lane. He had: a sorrel gelding tied a bit too long by the cottonwoods, boot marks at the pump house that weren't any Calder man's.

That was enough to keep sleep thin and thinking close.

She still startled at sounds—boards easing, wind fingering the shutters—but she made herself breathe through it. Fear, when it had work to do, was steadier.

By the third night, sleep abandoned her altogether. The parlor clock below ticked its slow sermon; Junie's small breaths rose and fell like a creek in quiet weather. Maisie lay awake and counted the steps from bed to door, door to stairs, stairs to kitchen, kitchen to yard. Twice she rose and tested the latch with her thumb. The moon put a pale square on the floor. She watched it slide.

What if a man somewhere held her name in his mouth like a coin?

She could not be the reason trouble crossed the Calder threshold.

With a breath thin as paper, she swung her legs from the bed. The plank was cold beneath her feet, waking truth. She dressed by touch: plain skirt, dull bodice, shawl. Her cloak still held a faint whisper of lavender Minnie had tucked in with surplus cloth—kindness caught in wool. She hadn't worn it since arriving wet and worn with only Junie and guilt to show.

The room told on her. Her things weren't packed like a soldier's kit anymore. They had wandered—comb in the washstand, extra linen folded in the drawer, Ivy's silver thimble on the dresser where the light could catch it. A life that had tried, without permission, to take root.

Her throat burned. She packed what mattered: the coins, the thimble, a strip of clean cloth, Junie's bottle, a tin of salve, and two small jars tied with colored string—yellow for comfrey, orange for marigold—Minnie's leftovers Jesse had told her to keep on the high shelf, out of reach of small hands. Wes had seen her label them. He'd only asked that the cupboard latch catch true.

She wrapped Junie snug and lifted her. The child sighed once, then softened against Maisie's shoulder.

At Jesse's little writing table, she left a note. No sad poetry—just what men of plain sense would need: I thank you. I do not bring danger to your door. Forgive me. If God is kind, I will send word.

She stood a heartbeat longer and let the room settle in her bones—the rocker with its patchwork throw, the smell of beeswax, the soft breath of warm ash in the grate. "Thank you," she whispered, not sure to whom.

She went.

Down the stairs on the sides of her feet, past the door where the key turned smooth from years of use, and into air that held damp earth and the last sweet edge of thaw. The yard lay in soft shadow. Far off, a coyote threw a question to the hills and got no answer.

Where to?

East was a thought, if only because it seemed the one place Zeke wouldn't expect. Or north to the freight road, where she could fold into a caravan and be no one at all. She didn't know. She only knew she wouldn't draw fire onto this house.

The barn loomed a few paces ahead, a dark shoulder against paler sky. She aimed for the narrow service gate by the tack room—the one Tom kept for quick ins-and-outs—then checked herself. In the blue wash of the moon, grass flashed with something dull. Wire, half-buried near the post. The hands had mended the fence after the last cutting, and scraps sometimes strayed when men worked tired.

She adjusted her step; her boot met nothing but air. The old coil lay a hand-width farther than she'd reckoned. It whipped her ankle and cinched.

She folded around Junie as she went down. The ground rose hard. Breath fled. Junie woke and cried, shocked more than hurt.

"Hush now," Maisie managed, tapping a rhythm at the small back. "I've got you."

Boots came fast across wet grass.

"Maisie?"

The moon slid from a cloud and put Wes's face in silver. He dropped to one knee without a word and reached for the wire. His nearness hit her—warm breath, woodsmoke on his shirt, the clean bite of lye from his cuffs. Her free hand, braced on the ground, found the hard line of his forearm. He was all steadiness.

"Hold still," he said.

"I'm all right," she lied. Pain ran hot from ankle to shin.

He found the end of the coil and worried it loose, patient as if untangling reins rather than flesh. The brush of his knuckles skimmed her calf; heat arrowed up her leg, startling and not unpleasant. When the wire fell away, he slid one arm behind her back and the other under her knees.

"I'm going to lift you," he said. "Ready?"

She nodded—more habit than sense—and he rose, careful of Junie tucked between them. For one breathless second, she was entirely in his keeping—weight gathered, chest close to his, the solid breadth of him steady as timber. She felt the strength in him, yes, but also a carefulness that undid her. Her hand, seeking balance, caught his shoulder; the muscles there moved under her palm. He didn't flinch. He only held on.

He caught up the small bag with one hand, hooked it on his shoulder, and carried it in.

The kitchen held only the low red of banked fire. He settled her in the chair by the stove and, when Junie's cry peaked, he leaned close so the baby could see his face. "There now," he murmured, voice low as a lullaby. The sound rolled through Maisie like warmth.

Wes moved the way he always did when something needed doing: no waste. He set a kettle to heat and reached for the cupboard latch he had himself mended last week.

"Top shelf," Maisie said, voice tight. "Yellow string. Then the orange. Comfrey and marigold."

He took both down.

"The ones Minnie sent?" he asked, only to be sure.

"Yes." She swallowed. "Jesse said to keep them here. I keep the lids tight."

Wes nodded. "You do." He set the jars by the basin, then looked to her for what came next.

"A pinch of each," she said. "Steep it. Cloth in the water, then on the ankle. It'll take the swelling down."

He worked quiet. His hands were ranch hands—scored and strong—but they pinched herbs like they might break. Steam rose, carrying the clean, bitter-sweet of leaf and flower. He wrung the cloth once, then knelt and eased off her boot.

The first touch of heat made her hiss. He paused, waiting for the breath she'd lost to return.

"Easy," he said. "Breathe. I've got you."

Her gaze, dragged to him, found the angle of his jaw and the faint pale scar near his ear. She wanted—absurdly—to trace it. The cloth moved again, slow, sure. His thumb anchored just above the swell of bone. Every second beat, he looked up to check her face. When their eyes met, something quiet passed between them, simple as a nod and somehow more binding.

"You ever done this before?" she asked, because talk steadied a shaking thing.

"No." His thumb kept that light circle. "But you said how."

The pain eased back to a manageable throb. Her skirt lay bunched to the knee, her calf in his hand. It was nothing and everything all at once. The air felt close—bread-warm from the stove, tinged with herb and him. She became absurdly aware of his breath, the slow in and out of it; the way his lashes shadowed when he glanced down; the shape of his mouth when he concentrated.

"You'll be off it for a few days," he said after a time. "We'll rig a chair near the stove. Bring work to you rather than the other way."

She nodded. "All right."

He lifted his gaze to hers. He didn't look at the bag by the door. He didn't look at the cloak. He just looked at her.

"Were you leaving?" he asked, quiet.

There was no room left for lying. "Yes."

"For where?"

"I don't know." She tightened her hold on Junie.

"If you decide to go," he said at last, "I'll take you. Not in the dark with wire underfoot. We'll plan the road and who you ride with and where you sleep. But don't walk out alone."

Something in her loosened at that—a knot she hadn't known she'd tied. "I didn't want to ask you for more."

He stood, fetched a strip of linen, and made a soft wrap. When his knuckles grazed her skin, heat flared again—quiet, sinking, not at all like fear. The room had taken on the steady hush of a sickroom—water whispering in the kettle, the stove ticking as it took heat. Outside, the wind came thin from the north.

"You trust me," she said, the words smaller than she meant them to be.

"I do." He tied the linen off with a neat knot and let his palm rest a heartbeat at her knee—steadying, not claiming. Still, her pulse leapt. His gaze tracked the jump of it at her throat, then returned to her eyes, and the look there made her feel seen in some new, unnerving way.

Maisie shook her head. The ache in her shin throbbed; the rest of her felt oddly light, as if she'd set down a load and only now discovered how heavy it had been.

He took the cloak from the peg and laid it over her knees, his knuckles grazing her calf—one more small spark. He felt it, too; she saw the breath he caught, the way his mouth softened before he steadied it. He drew the rocker near. "I'll sit the first hours," he said. "You sleep. If you wake and want to talk, you'll find me right here."

"Wes—"

He paused, one hand on the chair back.

"Thank you," she said. Simple as that.

Chapter Sixteen

The morning after he'd found Maisie in the yard with her bags—like a ghost fixing to vanish—Wes couldn't shake what the sight had put in him. Unease clung to his ribs like damp linen. He'd dozed toward dawn, if at all, and rose early, restless. He set to work before the sun had properly shaken off the mist, starting with the short stretch of wire by the barn—the very coil that had cinched her ankle.

It wasn't a true break in the fence, nothing like the outer line that kept getting cut. More the sort of loose end men left when they'd mended in the near dark. Accident or not, it was a hazard too close to the house. He pulled the old strand free, set a new staple, and drew it tight while swallows scissored the pale sky and dew clung to his cuffs. The creak of wire and tap of hammer wore the edge off him. When the job sat right, he saddled Jeremiah and rode a short circuit, frost-laced breath silvering the air in front of them where the pasture dipped toward the creek.

By the time the kitchen smoke lifted straight and steady, he came back to the house, boots leaving damp prints across the porch. He climbed to the guest room and rapped his knuckles lightly against the jamb.

"It's me," he called.

Fabric rustled inside. He frowned. He'd told her to keep off that foot.

"Come in," she answered, voice soft.

He pushed the door and stepped into the low morning light. Maisie sat propped against pillows, Junie sprawled heavy across her lap. Her braid had loosened in the night; wisps framed her face in little curls. The color hadn't quite returned to her cheeks. She'd changed into a plain day dress—faded blue cotton with neat mending at one cuff—and an apron, though her movements were careful, like each shift was a thing to weigh. She had that look he'd come to recognize: braced without meaning to be, ready to set her jaw against pain before it spoke.

Wes crossed to the bed and lifted her injured ankle with both hands, gentle as he could manage. Heat still lay under the bone, swelling at the outside. "How's it feel?"

"Not as bad as last night," she said. A smile tried at her mouth and almost made it. "I can manage."

He hummed. Maisie had a way of admitting less hurt than she held.

"I can take you down and set you in the front room," he said. "Unless you'd rather stay up here."

"Downstairs," she answered, already reaching to steady Junie. "Please."

He bent and gathered her. Junie tucked in the crook of her arm, her breath warm through the blanket. For one beat, all three of them were one bundle in his hold—woman, child, and the ache that had taken up residence under his breastbone without asking. Pine soap clung to her skin; smoke and coffee drifted up from below.

Jesse stood at the foot of the stairs, a frown tugging his brow. "What happened?"

Wes glanced down. Maisie had gone still, like a skittish mare told to stand. He met Jesse's eye. "Trouble sleeping. She stepped out to breathe and caught wire by the barn. Sprained her ankle."

Maisie's gaze flicked up to him, startled, then eased. She let herself settle heavier into his arms.

Rhett's head poked round the kitchen door. "Wire?" Eli came behind, brows high.

"There was a loose length in the grass," Wes said. "Close to the tack-room gate."

Guilt swept over Rhett's face. "Hell. That's on me. I planned to pick it up yesterday after chores and clean forgot."

Eli cuffed him lightly. "You leave a trap like that where a baby crawls and a woman walks?"

"I had a lot on my plate," Rhett snapped, then looked down, chastened. "I'll see to it proper."

Wes kept his voice even. "It's fixed. After breakfast, meet me at the barn."

Rhett nodded once. Jesse stepped aside, opening the way. "I'll handle the cooking," he said, offering Maisie a quick, steady smile.

Wes carried her into the front room and lowered her onto the settee, then propped her leg with a folded quilt. His hand rested a breath at her knee.

"Rest today," he said.

Color touched her cheekbones. She looked aside and nodded.

"I'll bring your plate," he added, and left her to the quiet.

Tom came through the back while Wes was crossing the hall, a coil of chill air riding in with him. He shook off his hat and squinted. "Where's the missus?"

"Sprained ankle," Jesse said from the stove. "Set up in the front room."

"How'd she—"

"Wire by the barn," Eli answered. "We'll mind it closer."

Tom's jaw ticked once. "Good. She's a sturdy one, but that don't mean we make her prove it."

He went to look in on her. The back door clicked soft behind him.

Rhett huffed and threw a look at Wes. "What were you doing out so late anyhow? Moon would've been high."

"Work," Wes said.

Eli slid onto the bench with that slow grin of his. "Not following her out? Not playing knight-errant, cloak flapping?"

Jesse snorted into the skillet and tried to school his face. Wes scowled for the sake of keeping order.

"Mind the grits," he told Jesse. "Don't scorch 'em."

Breakfast gathered itself: coffee bitter and black, cornbread cut into squares, eggs turned soft. Wes fixed two plates and carried them to the parlor. Maisie had Junie settled in her lap, tapping a quiet rhythm against the small back. The baby's eyes were heavy but curious, hands opening and closing as if catching air.

Wes set one plate on the small table and kept the other on his knees, eating beside her. Sunlight slipped through the warped glass and warmed the rug. The window stood cracked for air; a thin line of breeze moved the curtain. He registered how her gaze slid there now and again—small, measuring looks that told him her worry hadn't gone anywhere, only gone quiet.

"Tom," he said when the older man stepped in, "check on her through the day. She's not to put weight on that ankle."

Tom tipped two fingers. "Aye."

Maisie's lashes lowered. Guilt came off her like a draft through a gap in the door. He hadn't meant it to feel like censure; he meant to keep her safe. Still, he felt the prickle of it and wished the words had landed softer.

When the table cleared and chairs scraped back, Wes took his empty plate to the kitchen and didn't linger. Work held him to itself for the morning: a slipped latch to fix, seed to shift to the near shed, a gelding's left hind to pick and clean. The kind of tasks that kept hands busy and left a man alone with his thinking. Trouble didn't shout, he knew; it seeped. By late afternoon, the light had gone golden and heavy, and the smell of warmed soil rose up. He'd had enough of being away.

In the hall, he paused. A voice like thread in a loom drifted from the front room. Maisie was singing—soft, low, the melody the same one he'd caught now and again when she walked the baby in the night. It wasn't the sound of a woman carefree. It was a steadying sound—like a hand laid firm over a shaken heart. He stood a moment and let it wash over the day's hard edges.

He fixed a light tray in the kitchen—coffee, a heel of bread, stewed apples Jesse had put by—and carried it in.

She didn't see him at first. She had a small basket of linen at her side and was creasing a blanket with slow care. Someone—Tom, most likely—had carried the crib down. Junie slept inside it, thumb half in her mouth, lashes like soot on her cheek. The hush about the room felt like a church when folks had left, but the candles hadn't been snuffed yet.

"Good day?" Wes asked.

Maisie started and put a hand to her chest. "Mercy," she breathed, and gave a little sheepish laugh. "You gave me a fright."

Embarrassment brought color to her face; it faded fast. "Yes. Better than it might have been." Her eyes slid to the window and back.

Wes set the tray on the table and crouched to check her bandage. The linen had loosened some. "Needs changing," he murmured, careful to keep his tone easy, no press in it.

He didn't ask about the bags she'd packed or the road she'd weighed. Not yet. Whatever had put the notion in her hadn't passed; he could feel it in her silences, in how her shoulders stayed just shy of relaxed. If she wanted him to know, she'd tell him when her own words were ready.

He fetched warm water and the same jars she'd named—yellow string, orange—then set to work. He unwound last night's wrap, dabbing slow over bruising that had come up in dull purples, shallow scrapes red at the edges. The ankle had puffed up some, but not like it might've. He laid a steeped cloth over the swell and felt the heat of her skin through it. She drew a breath, caught, let it go.

"Easy," he said. "Breathe."

Her hands had steadied on her skirt; the tremor he'd seen last night was smaller now. He eased fresh linen around the joint and tied it off, thumb anchoring just above the bone. Every few beats, he glanced up, reading her face like the weather. When their eyes met, something passed that didn't need a name.

"This ranch," she said after a time, watching his hands, "it's the bones of you."

Wes's mouth tipped. He kept working, but the words came as they wanted. "My great-granddad raised the first house with cottonwood he cut himself. My grandpa set the south fence and said the river shape would hold even in dust

years—and it has. We've got good grass, water that keeps to its course, neighbors who'll ride when you holler, and town close enough to trade but not to stare."

It wasn't boasting, only plain speech of a man who knew what he stood on.

"Sounds like a place that asks a body to be steady," she said. "To belong."

"That's the idea." He smoothed the last of the wrap and sat back on his heels.

She held his look. "Then why marry me?" No more sting in it than curiosity. "A man with land thinks ahead—wife to run a house, children to pass it on. You didn't need me for any of that. You've got brothers."

"I do," he said. "And one day they'll set their own tables. It doesn't all fall to me."

She waited. He took up the towel and dried his hands, the room quiet but for the soft tick of the stove and the low, even breath of the sleeping child.

"I didn't marry you for the ranch," he said at last. "And I didn't marry you to make a show."

Her eyes didn't leave his.

"There was a girl," he went on, as simply as he knew how. "Annabelle. We were fools together, and then I went to war. By the time I came back, Ma and Pa were in the ground, my brothers were near wild, and the ranch needed two men to be one. I tried to hold everything in both hands. I squeezed so

151

tight there was no room left for her. She left. I wasn't kind about it in my head. I am now."

He scrubbed a hand over his jaw and let it fall. "I built a life that didn't let anyone close. It kept things running. It kept me quiet inside. It weren't much good for anything else."

"And now?" she asked, voice low.

Now, he thought, you were halfway down the lane with a baby in your arms and I wanted, more than I've wanted breath, to be the reason you turned around.

"Now I'm trying to do better," he said.

She didn't smile, but he saw something ease in her, a softening that felt like trust trying its legs.

He opened his mouth to say more.

A crack ripped the air outside—sharp as bone splitting. Gunfire.

Another shot, nearer. The sound tore the quiet in half. Junie startled and whimpered, then went still again, thumb working faster.

Wes was on his feet before the echo died, crossing the room in two strides. He took the rifle down from its hooks and checked the chamber by habit. Loaded. Always.

"Down low," he said, voice clipped. "Keep Junie close. Don't open for anyone but me."

Maisie's breath hitched, but she didn't freeze. She reached into the crib and drew the baby against her, then slid herself lower on the settee, leg protected beneath the quilt. The look she sent him wasn't the wild panic of three nights back; it was the sure, tight look of a woman taking stock of what she could hold and doing it.

He spared one last glance—her hands firm at the child's back, chin set—and then he was moving, boots loud on the boards, the front door flung wide to meet whatever had come looking for them.

Chapter Seventeen

It was a small mercy the baby didn't cry at the first crack. Perhaps the Lord pressed a finger to her lips for one breath, just long enough for Maisie to move.

She didn't leap for the door—her ankle wouldn't have allowed it if she'd tried. Instead, she did the arithmetic of the room the way frightened mothers have always done: windows, doors, angles. She slid from the settee with Junie clutched tight, kept low, and crabbed along the wall to the inside corner—no glass, no line from the yard. One-handed, she dragged the horsehair chair a half-foot to give them a bit of cover and eased the crib so it broke the room in two, a small barricade between the door and their hollow. It wasn't much, but a body works with what it has.

Another report split the air—closer, wood splintering. Not a shot aimed to kill; a post or plank hit hard to make noise. The baby started then, a thin, scared sound. Maisie set her jaw, tucked Junie's face against her shoulder, and counted four steady pats before laying her in the crib. The bonnet had skewed; she fixed it because busy hands steady a mind. Then she tucked a folded napkin along the rail so the child wouldn't bruise her head if she thrashed. Tender, without halfway in it—like she'd been doing for months, like Ivy would have done if she could.

Another bang—this one a boot against a porch step. Men's voices carried, rough with whiskey and bravado, chopped apart by the wind. Underneath, she knew the Calders: Eli's even call, Jesse's low reply, Tom's barked word. And Wes— short, clipped commands that put men where they needed to be. It steadied her more than any prayer.

Fear wanted fog; she would not give it fog. She put water on in the little iron kettle—hot cloths help shock and swelling—

and by the stove took out the small tin of salve Minnie had given her and set it within reach. She tested the back latch with her palm to be sure it had caught and slid a length of kindling to wedge the kitchen door. The front latch had a habit of sticking; she pressed her shoulder to it until the catch found the strike. Work. Do the next thing.

She limped back, breath measured, and pulled the parlor curtain barely a finger's width. Outside, six riders fanned the yard. Two sat their mounts broadside to the porch; two more flanked the barn. One hung back to the lane where the road bent; a sixth, tall in a long coat, took the center like a man admiring his own work. She knew him: the watcher from the general store whose paper had never turned a page. No crest, no fine mark—nothing but that easy, knowing smile that looked like he'd already bought the land beneath his horse.

A chip stung the window frame and dust peppered her cheek—someone had put a ball into the porch post. Testing. Proving they could reach. From the side yard, Rhett's voice cut like a whip—"Back off!"—followed by the double-thunder of the shotgun he favored for snakes. The nearest rider's hat jumped; he swore and wrenched his horse away. Not a hit, but a lesson.

"Look, Calder," the man in the coat called, casual as a shopkeeper haggling over nails. "You're a decent fella by all accounts. Don't want fuss. Hand me the woman who don't belong here and we'll ride on."

Gravel scraped under a boot. She didn't have to see to know Wes had stepped into view. His voice came back cold as creek iron in winter. "You don't call the belonging on this land. Turn your horse. Last word I'll waste."

A quiet laugh drifted from the man in the coat. "Think on it," he said. "I'll be back. You keep her, you keep her trouble." He turned his mount with no more hurry than a church elder leaving a pew, and the rest peeled off after him, hoofbeats beating a fast, receding drum.

Something hard settled in Maisie at the sound—not a crack, a set. She let the curtain fall and sat back on her heels, breathing slow. The room hummed with the kettle, ticking faintly as the stove took heat. Junie hiccupped, then went quiet, one thumb finding her mouth like a compass point. The wind found the sash and worked it; she could smell dust and powder and the faint, clean bite of lye from the scrubbed floor.

The door opened; Wes was a hand and a shadow first. His palm landed on her shoulder, warm and steady, as if he knew exactly how far away she'd drifted and meant to call her back without a word. She looked up. He wasn't full of talk. He never was. But his silence made space instead of walls, and she stepped into it. She rose as far as her ankle allowed and leaned, cheek to the hollow of his throat. Smoke and sweat and sun-warmed cotton—safety, plain as bread. He gathered her—and, with care, the crib—into the lee of the room where the walls met, then eased her to the settee. Junie let out a small, sleeping protest; Wes touched the child's back with two fingers and she settled again.

"Everyone whole?" Maisie asked.

"Whole," he said. "One post ruined. That's all." Then, voice pitched to reach the hall, "Jesse, close the shutters. Eli, ride to Tom's line and make sure no one's lying in that grass. Rhett, leave the shotgun. Take the carbine and circle the cottonwoods. Slow. Tall man's not stupid; he'll keep eyes on the lane."

"Aye," came Jesse. The slap of shutters followed, one and then another. Eli's boots thudded past, quick. Rhett muttered something like an apology as he swapped guns and went out the back way. The house answered each order with a sound. The sounds made a net.

Maisie drew a breath she hadn't managed since the first shot. "Wes," she said. His name felt like an anchor cast into deep water.

He sank to a knee beside her and checked the bandage with a careful thumb above the swelling. "Hurt worse?"

"It will," she said, wry because she needed to be. "Later."

The window's edge held the line of the lane. She glimpsed a last shimmer of dust and then only the cottonwoods, still as witnesses. She had two choices: keep her mouth closed and let the men who'd fed her stand in the dark—or speak.

"Zeke Blackwell," she said.

It took the stiffness out of her throat to say it plain. She saw the name land in Wes's eyes; he didn't flinch. He simply waited the way he always did—like a man who understands a skittish horse and holds still until she sniffs his sleeve.

"At the window," Rhett said from the doorway, low and tight. "That was Roy Danner riding center. The one from town. Looked pleased with himself."

Maisie nodded. "He watched me at the store. If he rides with them, he rides for Zeke." She swallowed and kept her voice even. "My sister married him. Zeke. He used her like a thing he owned. She was allowed nothing that wasn't his say-so. If she pushed back, he called it 'teaching' and left the kind of marks that don't show in daylight." She would not dress those memories up to spare anyone. Not now.

Eli came back through, hair wind-tossed. "North line's clear. Tracks in the soft patch by the pump house, headed west. No one laying doggo in the grass. They were probing." He looked at Wes. "Sheriff'll take half a day to stir; he won't cross Blackwell's coin to do more than frown. We'll have to handle this."

"We will," Wes said.

Maisie set both hands flat on her skirt to keep them from shaking. "When Ivy was with me back East," she went on, "she jumped at doors. She slept with a lamp burning. She—" The next words clogged. She felt Wes's fingers wrap around one of her hands, not squeezing, only present. It cleared the way. "She got sick. Fever. It took her quick. She made me promise I'd keep Junie from him. So I left and kept leaving until I couldn't—and I thought I'd done wrong by bringing my wrong to your door."

"You brought yourself," Jesse said, shutting the last shutter and setting the bar. "That's different."

Maisie managed a small smile she didn't trust. "The man in the coat said he'll come back. He'll mean it." She met Wes's gaze straight on. "He doesn't give up."

"Neither do we," Wes said, simple as the sky. Then, to the room at large, "He wanted a look. That's all. He learned we shoot. He learned we're not quick to panic. He'll try a different lever next."

"Fence," Rhett said, already thinking three steps. "Water. Stock."

"Town talk," Eli added. "He'll pay for mouths to wag. Put our name in the wrong people's ledger."

"Then we get ahead of it," Jesse said. "Tom's talking to neighbors even when he's not trying. We make sure the right stories walk first."

Wes turned back to Maisie. "You stay where the wall's at your back and the stove at your side. We'll move the crib in here until this goes quiet. Tom will sit mornings. Jesse afternoons when he can. Evenings, I'll be here."

"I can work from a chair," she said, bristling because dependence chafed. "I won't be useless."

His mouth tipped a hair at the corner, fond without teasing. "I know. We'll keep you busy. And safe." He eased another folded quilt under her ankle and re-tied the bandage he had just checked, this time adding a steadier brace. His knuckles grazed her skin—small, incidental—and heat moved up her calf that had nothing to do with pain. He felt it, too; his breath hitched once and smoothed.

Eli set a rifle within reach of the hearth, butt to the baseboard and barrel safe of small hands. "Loaded," he said. "Half-cock. If you have to lift it, thumb it back before you think about the trigger."

Maisie met his eyes. "I know how," she said, not proud, not embarrassed—just true.

"Good." Eli gave her that quick grin that always tried to sew a tear with humor. "We'll hope you don't need to prove it."

Rhett handed Wes a folded scrap—splintered wood from the porch post, a dark crescent in the grain where the ball had bit. "Closest they got," he said.

Wes turned it in his palm, weighed without speaking, then set it on the mantel like a note to himself. He looked back at Maisie. "When he comes again," he said, "he'll expect fear to make us foolish. We'll not oblige him." He tipped his chin toward the kettle. "Drink. Then rest.

She poured, and the simple act felt like choosing to live ordinary in the teeth of a threat. Steam fogged the air between them. Junie sighed in her sleep and rolled, thumb never leaving her mouth. The room—shutters drawn, stove ticking, men moving with a new purpose that was not fuss but plan—felt like a fort made of small, exact things: bars set, rifles placed, chores assigned, faith named without saying it.

Maisie found Wes's hand again before she had time to decide if she meant to. He didn't startle; he simply turned his palm up and let her fingers fit. The world beyond the walls had turned meaner by one measured degree. Inside them, steadiness answered.

"Zeke Blackwell won't get near either of you," Wes said at last.

It was only a line of words. On his tongue, they had weight. She believed him, and the belief itself put a little strength back in her bones.

Chapter Eighteen

If the man weren't useful, Roy Danner would have worn Zeke's coffee instead of hearing him breathe over the rim of the cup. Zeke had given simple orders: get the woman and the brat—and do it quietly.

Not like this.

He leaned back, one finger marking a steady tap against the scarred tabletop. The oak chair creaked along with the floorboards of the saloon's back room. Lamp hiss, scorched coffee, sweat—nothing human in the room but the two of them and a plan that had frayed.

Danner sat with his hat on his knee and that easy look Zeke disliked—a man too sure of his own value.

"You weren't told to make a show," Zeke said.

"It wasn't a show," Danner answered, shrugging. "A probe. Your girl's tucked under the Calders. They move fast. I wanted to see who steps up and how quick."

Zeke let that hang. He hadn't "happened" to be in Twin Forks. Three days by rail to Cheyenne, another day by coach south, after Burke's wire: *Woman matches description—living on Calder land. Danner can verify.* Zeke had wired his attorney the same afternoon. Nothing about this was accident.

"You were told to keep my name and my men out of it," Zeke said. "That mark on your tie was for rooms like this—never daylight. You invite gossip when you advertise."

Danner's mouth quirked. "Folks in town saw a horseman and a handful of riders. That's all."

"Enough," Zeke said, setting the cup down. "What did you learn?"

"Rhett had the scattergun. Wes stood center, rifle leveled. Jesse barred the windows. Eli flanked north. They're practiced. Sheriff Lane? Dead asleep by all accounts unless pushed."

Zeke nodded once. "Then we'll push him."

He drew a folded paper from his inner pocket and smoothed it with two fingers. It was brought at noon, court seal hard and clean: a petition for temporary guardianship and a writ commanding Sheriff Lane to produce the child Juniper Blackwell at the Benton courthouse the first Monday next month. His lawyer's work. The thread he'd set running the hour Burke's wire reached him.

"We use this first," Zeke said. "Serve it at the noon hour when the boardwalk's crowded. Let half the county hear the name 'Calder' and 'to appear' in one breath. While tongues wag, we tighten elsewhere."

Danner leaned in, elbows on the table. "Fences, freight, and friends."

"Freight first," Zeke answered. "Wire and seed go missing two nights, then turn up 'misrouted.' Telegraph holds their messages for a spell—line to Laramie can be 'down.' A neighbor or two who owes them remembers a sudden bill. No big noise. Just drag."

Danner nodded. "And fences?"

"A post or two after dark at the north line. Enough to make their herd drift and their men split. If you fire, fire once and fade. This isn't a powder war—it's patience."

"And the woman?"

"Watched," Zeke said. "If she rides, you mark who, where, and how. No daylight snatching. The court paper gives us a handle; the quiet work turns the screw. Then we lift."

"From where?" Danner asked.

"The churchyard if they're fools," Zeke said. "If not, the creek above the east pasture—brush for cover, water for noise. You'll be in place when the time's right."

Danner's grin thinned. "You mean to own the ranch and the child with the same stroke."

"I mean to take what's owed," Zeke said.

He kept the rest of his thoughts close. He'd rehearsed Ivy's part in this until the telling wore thin. He did not need the old story to steady his hand. He had gone back to Maisie's rooms in Albany after the neighbors' hush had hardened into truth—*fever took her* was all they'd say, and the boards still smelled of boiled cabbage and old sickness. He'd not seen a body; there had been no body to see. That did not matter. Whisper became print, and print required coin to bury. Weeks had been wasted clearing his name while the trail went cold. That part he remembered clearly.

Juniper remained useful—a public proof Ivy had lied, a small weight for the respectable scales when he chose to tip them. And Maisie Ward had made herself an obstacle. Obstacles were to be removed.

A boy in a cap tapped once and ducked in with a second paper. "From the lawyer," he said, breathless. "Judge Markell signed a temporary order—child not to be removed from the county until hearing. Sheriff to enforce it." He thrust the paper, then fled.

Zeke read fast. No possession yet, but a trap all the same.

"If the Calders keep her home," he said, folding it neat, "they do it under paper, and every neighbor knows it. If they try to ride her over the ridge, they break a judge's ink. Either way, we're waiting."

Danner rubbed a thumb along his jaw. "They won't scare easy."

"They don't have to scare," Zeke said. "They only have to tire."

He pulled Burke's old invoice book close and wrote three short notes in a hand that had charmed Albany boards and chilled debtors: one to the freight yard boss authorizing a bonus for "mistakes," one to the telegraph agent reminding him of the favor already owed, one to Sheriff Lane—*serve at noon, not before.* He sanded the ink and sealed each with a neat press.

"Anything else?" Danner asked.

"Burke keeps a ledger of tabs," Zeke said. "Find every name that eats at a Calder table—hands, neighbors, strays. Pay half their accounts ahead and let it be known the Calders were asking credit at Hart's this week. Let talk do its work."

Danner's smile returned. "Long game suits you, Mr. Blackwell."

"I don't play games," Zeke said, standing. "I settle accounts."

He did not enjoy errands. Enjoyment belonged to men with time to waste. He preferred results—the kind that left competitors staring at ledgers, wondering when the numbers turned.

At the window, he watched late light wash the street old-copper. A woman crossed with a loaf wrapped in paper; a boy clattered a stick along a fence; a team stamped and jingled. If

Sheriff Lane posted the notice on schedule, Hart's stoop would carry the news farther than any wire.

Zeke put the petition and the order back into his pocket and slipped a penciled map from the desk drawer—trails sketched from saloon talk, creekbeds shaded. He marked the bend above the east pasture with a small cross.

"You asked for action," he said to the empty room—Danner, the judge, Burke, the town that loved a Calder's handshake. "You'll have it."

He blew the lamp out and let the dark come up like clean water.

Chapter Nineteen

There was a calendar—hand-painted by Minnie—that hung above the hearth. Smoke and sun had gentled its colors, but the thing still brightened the kitchen. Eli had insisted it go up.

Most mornings, Wes ignored it for his ledger. He trusted figures more than flowers. Near late-morning, when light struck the page just so, a square a few days off snagged his eye. Jesse's tidy hand had marked it: Eli's birthday.

Wes blinked. With fences cut, freight late, and strangers testing their gates, he hadn't marked the season's turn. Yet there it was in the window: bees among clover, cottonwoods leafed, the air warming toward summer.

The back door creaked. Tom stepped in, dusting his sleeves, hat already in his hand.

"Jesse around?" he asked.

"Office," Wes said. "Sorting bills that don't mean to sort."

Tom turned to go. Wes stopped him. "You notice how it's got quite warm all of a sudden?"

Tom peered toward the yard, then gave a rueful huff. "Snuck up while we were busy not looking."

"Eli's day's near," Wes said. "I was thinking a small gathering. Neighbors we trust. Let folks breathe. Let them see we're still standing."

Tom's mouth tipped. "You mean it?"

Wes nodded once. "We'll keep a watch posted. No foolishness."

"Then it's a fine idea," Tom said. "I can have a quiet word up and down the lane, if you like. The right mouths carry news better than a bell."

"Hold a spell," Wes answered. "I'll tell the boys first."

***

He didn't sleep much that night. Not from worry so much as the steady thrum of plans. They hadn't marked an occasion since Ma and Pa died. There'd always been too much frost in their days back then—and in Wes's chest besides. But there was sense in a little light now: a crowd as witness, hands to help, laughter to loosen tongues grown too fond of whispering. And for Maisie, maybe a way to settle—on her terms—before the next wind swung against them.

He'd ask her plain.

***

Morning came clear and gold. The kitchen held coffee steam and bacon salt. Jesse worked the stove; Maisie kept to a low stool near the table, ankle wrapped and propped on a second chair, a board set across her lap. She hummed a quiet measure while she chopped onions, slid them toward Jesse with a little nod, then measured lard by feel, passing what he asked without the need for words. On the floor, Junie made it her aim to crawl under every boot in the county.

When they were seated, Wes cleared his throat. "I've something to put to you."

Eli winced theatrically. "Mercy. He's about to say 'prudence' and 'fences' again."

"Eli's birthday's upon us," Wes said, ignoring him. "I'd like to hold a small gathering—neighbors we trust, sundown to moonrise. Food. A fire. We post a watch while folks are here."

Eli clapped his own shoulder. "A party? For my tireless service and general handsomeness? I accept."

Jesse's mouth tugged into a smile. "We can send a few notes this afternoon."

Wes turned to Maisie. Her fork had stilled above her plate; her wrapped foot rested where he'd set it. He didn't miss the wariness that lived behind her eyes, the way her gaze kept flicking to the door and window before coming back to him.

"If we do this," he said, softer, "I'd like to introduce you proper. Folks who count will see you and Junie under this roof. It won't stop talk, but it puts faces to names—and eyes on you that mean well. Only if you want it."

She looked at Junie, who had discovered the wonder of a wooden spoon and was beating the table with it, solemn as a drummer boy. "I think it's wise," she said. "And...kind." Fear lingered in the small pause before the second word, but it was a fear she'd turned toward usefulness. Wes recognized the shape of it.

"Invite the Graysons?" Rhett asked, already scowling.

"I'll ride out and hand the note myself," Wes said. "Better to give the boy a chance to be civil in front of witnesses. He's bolder in shadow than in lamplight."

Tom snorted. "Wolf from a distance, coyote up close."

"We'll post men," Wes added. "No one comes or goes without a look."

Eli, as ever, dragged the talk back toward the bright side. "Minnie will handle flowers," he said, already up. "If I ask sweet." He sent Maisie a wink. "We'll pretend it's for me, but it's to make you welcome."

Tom tipped his hat. "I'll see to tables, chairs, and lamps. Rhett, you're on wood."

Rhett grunted, but his eyes warmed a fraction. "I'll cut enough to burn to morning."

"Jesse?" Wes asked.

Jesse tilted his head toward Maisie. "If she's willing, she and I can plan the food. I'll keep to the hot pans. She can show me what to do while she rests that foot."

Maisie's mouth lifted. "I'd like that."

***

Toward afternoon on the day itself, Wes came in from the north pasture and near stopped in the hall. Minnie stood on the porch stoop with a pin in her mouth, fussing with a pale scarf at Maisie's throat. Maisie sat in the shade, foot bound neat, skirts smoothed over her knee. Her hair—usually tamed—had been let half-down, curls catching light like warm wheat. Minnie turned her face this way and that, set the knot just so, then laughed at some quiet remark Maisie made. The sound skated along Wes's ribs.

He hadn't meant to stare. He hadn't meant to feel anything at all. But something in him tightened, low and clean, at the sight of her—arranged without ornament, and somehow more beautiful for the mercy of it. He had seen women dressed to be looked at; this was different. This made him wish to look and keep looking, and that unsettled him more than any man at his fence.

He stepped back before they noticed and stood a breath in the dim, palms open till the pulse in them let go.

***

The yard wore its best. Tom and Rhett had raked the ruts flat and strung lanterns along the fence line. Tables were laid with blue-washed cloths and borrowed crockery, jars of lemonade beading with sweat. Wildflowers—Minnie's choosing—sat in stoneware pitchers, all larkspur and white yarrow and a few early roses from her mother's yard. Strips of bunting ran from porch post to elm, bright against the deepening sky.

There were people, too—plenty. Hart the blacksmith and his wife came with three red-cheeked boys. Mr. Lyle from the store, his lad minding the crate of apples like a general over provisions. The Dobbinses, bearing a pan of cinnamon rolls that perfumed the whole stretch between porch and barn. Widow Clark, hat pinned firm, with her sister from over the ridge. Two hands from downriver with their families and the quiet men from the line-camp, all scrubbed and buttoned. Minnie, tidy as ever, with a sprig of green at her throat and flour on one knuckle from last-minute fussing. Even Sheriff Lane walked through, tipping his hat, taking coffee, saying little but seeing much.

Rhett and Tom kept to the edges, rifles racked but close, eyes skimming the lane. Eli moved like bright wind through the crowd, laughter chasing him. Jesse stationed himself at the sideboard. Wes kept the long look—counting, weighing, measuring how many of their people stood near.

Maisie stayed near the porch, foot still wrapped. Wes had set a slat-back chair for her with a second to prop her ankle. She wore a summer dress of white muslin, the hem brushing her ankles; a soft scarf at her throat; her hair half-loosed, a few curls freed by the light breeze. Her stays were laced easy— sensible for work and the heat. She spooned mashed carrots toward Junie's solemn mouth and laughed when half of it missed.

Wes slowed. He didn't mean to stare, but the look on her face tugged at him—guarded, yes, yet quieter in its guard. Watchful without being hunted. The line of her throat above the scarf, the way a loose curl brushed her cheek when she bent to the child—he felt the awareness of her the way a man feels weather turning. He was not a boy. He knew better than to be obvious. Still, when two of the line-camp hands let their eyes linger a blink too long in passing, Wes's jaw set. It was not anger so much as claiming—no, not claiming; he would not lie to himself—protective heat laid against bone. He answered it by doing the only decent thing a man could do in a yard full of neighbors: he put himself at her shoulder and kept pace.

She felt his shadow and looked up. "Wes," she said, and his name in her mouth was warmer than the day. He had to clear his throat.

"You look..." The plain word would not do. He tried again. "You look real fine."

Color touched her cheek. "Thank you."

"You ought to hear it from me," he added, forcing his voice even. "Not just from every soul with eyes."

At that, something startled through her, quick as a bird under brush. She set the spoon down and smoothed Junie's sash, more to have her hands occupied than for need of straightening. His own fingers wanted—foolishly—to catch that loose curl and tuck it back, and he had to shift his weight and fix his gaze on the far woodpile to keep from it.

Junie spotted him and reached, small palms opening and closing in petition. Maisie looked to Wes. "She wants you."

He hesitated, not for doubt but for permission; Maisie nodded. He lifted the child and settled her against his shoulder. As he took her, his fingers brushed Maisie's wrist—bare, warm from the afternoon—and a quiet spark went through him that had nothing to do with firewood. She felt it too; he saw her breath catch, the quick flicker of her lashes before she looked away. He should have stepped back. Instead, for two counts of his own careful heart, he did not.

"You're good with her," she said softly.

"I do as I'm told," he said. "By women of sense." He tipped his head toward her wrapped foot. "And I mind orders myself. You needn't be up and down."

"I am seated," she said, a near-smile tugging. "You've given me a throne."

A guitar found a tune near the woodpile. Someone started "Red River Valley," and a handful took the second part with the ease of folks who had known it since they had teeth. Minnie's laugh rang once, clearer than the notes. Eli, predictably, bowled a Grady girl into a peal by tossing her just higher than her father would have dared. He returned her to the ground with theatrical solemnity and surrendered the serving spoon to Minnie with a bow that made three old ladies tut and smile.

"They suit," Maisie murmured, following Wes's look. No envy—more like wishing for a familiar seat at a table that hadn't been hers before.

"They've been tripping each other since they were knee-high," Wes said. "He rattles what she keeps too neat. She makes him kinder than he knows how to be."

"Some folk lean each other straight," she said, eyes on the crowd. "Some go crooked together."

"That a warning?" he asked.

"A thought," she said.

People came by in ones and twos to greet her. Widow Clark pressed Maisie's fingers in both of hers and declared Junie "a blessing with lungs." Mr. Lyle's boy offered the child the first apple from the crate; Junie examined it with grave attention, then drooled her approval. Hart's eldest asked after the fence mending and promised to send over a coil of wire he'd meant to bring two days ago and forgot. Sheriff Lane tipped his hat again, and if his glance took in the posted rifles and Rhett's quiet patrol, he said nothing to shame such prudence.

Wes kept introductions simple. "Mrs. Maisie Calder," he said, so that anyone who needed to hear the name could hear it in his voice, with the mild iron there that made men think twice about careless talk. He watched the way some men's eyes corrected when they heard *Mrs.* He did not crowd her; he did not stray far. When a fellow from downriver let his smile hang too easy, Wes put the child on his hip and set his other palm to the back of Maisie's chair—casual to any watching, steadying to the woman seated there. Her shoulder eased.

Near sunset, he brought her lemonade. As he passed the tin cup, their fingers touched the rim at once. She did not snatch back. Her lashes lifted slow. "Thank you," she said, and he heard more than manners in it.

"Always," he answered before sense could sit on his tongue.

The word stayed between them like a warm coin.

The Graysons did not come.

After sundown, Rhett touched a match to the stacked wood. The fire climbed slow at first, then took with a soft whoomph, and the ring of chairs inched back in a practiced shuffle. Stories rose with the smoke—calf-roping misadventures told on themselves, the way winter had left a thaw in the root cellar, the one time Eli tried to shoe a mule that bit hats for sport. Laughter hung like lantern light.

Maisie's fingers found the edge of her chair whenever someone raised a voice too quick or a bottle clinked too hard.

That lived reflex did not shame her; she let it be, then let it pass. The fear hadn't left her. She'd set reins to it.

When she rose to carry Junie in—careful on her bound ankle—Wes was already there with his hand beneath her elbow, not presuming, just offering. She took it. For three steps across his own porch, he was foolish enough to think he could feel every bone of her trust through his palm.

Inside, she settled the baby. He came back to the yard with the ache of that brief nearness pulling at him like a burr.

When the last cup was drained and the last goodbye called, Jesse and Wes stacked plates in a quiet made easy by work and weariness. Outside, Eli and Rhett folded tables while Tom doused the last lanterns.

"It was a good day," Jesse said at last, laying utensils to dry.

"It was," Wes said. "Shame the Graysons didn't take the chance."

"Or maybe not a shame," Jesse answered. "Some snakes rattle more when they're cornered."

Wes grunted. He dried a plate. He could feel Jesse thinking beside him.

"What?" Wes asked without looking up.

"You looked right with her," Jesse said, mild as spring. "Not easy, not done, just...right."

Wes scrubbed a little too hard, then set the plate down before he broke it. He didn't know what to do with the picture Jesse had drawn—the three of them under a roof, the small middle-of-the-night moments when Junie fussed and his feet took him toward that door without asking his head. Those hours left an ache behind his ribs he couldn't name and didn't trust.

"You've smiled more," Jesse added.

"Don't tell Eli," Wes said.

Jesse chuckled. "Wouldn't dream."

Wes rinsed the last pan and set it on the board. He braced his hands on the sink and listened to the low sounds of his house—the ticking stove, the murmur of men outside, the soft footfall above that had become as known to him as wind.

"We'll keep a watch these next nights," he said.

"We already are," Jesse answered.

Wes nodded. It was all he could offer a woman who had chosen, for now, to sit instead of run: a yard full of neighbors who had seen her under his roof, a family that would meet trouble at the fence, and the slow, careful work of learning one another without borrowing tomorrow's vows.

Chapter Twenty

By the morning of the gathering, Maisie's nerves kicked like a startled mule. Wes had asked, not presumed—that helped—but the thought of being looked over by near every decent soul within riding distance put a twist in her stomach. She agreed because it was wise, and because he'd asked plain. After that, the day ran on rails: Jesse at the stove, Eli in and out with errands and grins, Tom and Rhett working the yard until it looked near respectable, Minnie fluttering in with a basket and opinions.

Maisie kept to a stool in the kitchen with her ankle wrapped and propped on a second chair, a board laid across her lap for chopping. She measured lard by eye, passed Jesse what he asked for, and hummed when Junie grew restless at her skirts. Fear was still there, kept on a short rope; work shortened it further.

By late afternoon, the yard had put on its best. Lamps hung from the fence line and porch posts; wildflowers—Minnie's choosing—stood in pitchers along the tables. Folks began to come. Hart from the smithy with his boys; Mr. Lyle from the store; the Dobbinses bearing cinnamon rolls; Widow Clark and her sister; hands from the line-camp scrubbed and solemn; Sheriff Lane for a turn through with coffee and quiet eyes. There were no Graysons. Rhett and Tom posted themselves where a man could see both lane and barn. Eli moved like bright wind. Wes kept near the edge of things, counting, minding, and when he came to Maisie's shoulder with a cup of lemonade, she found she could smile without it breaking.

As evening slid to dusk, she slipped inside to settle Junie. Minnie followed, delighted for the errand and already speaking of where she meant to sleep. The cottage by the cottonwoods had been aired that morning; Minnie had made much of it, carrying in clean sheets and declaring herself satisfied as a queen.

"It's been a good day," Maisie said, once Junie's lashes lay on her cheeks. The truth of it surprised her. No tremor in her hands. No iron band around her ribs. She had simply been— looked at, yes, asked a hundred small questions, yes—but held by it rather than chased. It felt like a mercy.

"The menfolk are cleaning up. Ought we help?" Minnie flopped onto the bed and swung her feet like a girl.

Maisie lifted a brow, mouth twitching. "Are you going soft on me, Miss Abbott? I am the mistress of this house now. Duty requires I drag you along to yours."

Minnie sat up, pressed a hand to her heart, and made a sorry curtsy. "Forgive me, Lady Calder. I should be flogged for my laziness."

"No," Maisie said gravely. "Hanged. We'll send for the sheriff."

They choked on their own giggles and stifled them with their wrists, then tiptoed out, shutting the door to the baby's quiet.

Downstairs, Wes and Jesse stood shoulder to shoulder at the basin, sleeves rolled, forearms wet, moving in the steady rhythm of men who preferred work to talk.

"Well now," Jesse said over his shoulder, "if it isn't two hens come to peck."

Maisie cleared her throat and aimed for prim. "We came to lend our hands."

Wes shook his head. "We've got it. Help Minnie settle the cottage."

Minnie brightened at once. "Excellent idea. We require a bottle of wine."

Jesse barked a laugh. "You'll be disappointed. There's cider in the icebox and coffee on the stove. That's the lot."

"Tragic," Minnie sighed. "Men do know how to ruin a party. Come along, Maisie, before they make us drink water."

Maisie lifted her left hand so the lamp caught the ring. "Too late for running. I'm already within their folds."

Wes's glance found hers and held just long enough to warm. Her breath hitched; she looked away and took Minnie by the arm as if linens couldn't possibly fetch themselves. In the back hall, a voice came out of the dim.

"Food?"

They jumped. Eli stepped from the shadow with bunting and ribbons in the crook of his arm, a sprig of something green stuck behind his ear.

"For the cottage," Maisie said.

"I'll carry it over," he offered. "Might even remember the sweets."

Minnie shot him a look that was half dare, half fondness. "That would be a first."

They crossed the yard slow. The lanterns along the fence threw small circles onto damp grass. Farther off, men's voices rose and fell with the untying of knots and the stacking of chairs. A nighthawk cried once, then again.

"You and Eli seem closer of late," Maisie said.

Minnie's mouth tipped. "He's been finding a reason to come by my shop most days. Somehow always forgets what he came for."

"For a man who flirts like it's his trade," Maisie said, "he's remarkably slow."

"That's how you know it matters," Minnie said. "He talks to me like a person, not a picture."

The little cottage glowed behind clean windows. Inside, the bed was turned down, and the kettle sat on the hob with a shine. Minnie sank into the rocker, still smiling to herself, then turned sly.

"And how is married life, Mrs. Calder?"

Maisie eased into the chair opposite, the hum of the day still warm in her bones. "He's kind," she said, surprised by how simple the answer was.

"Folks forget that about him," Minnie said. "All they see is that jaw and those quiet eyes. But there's a good fire under that stone. Not the burning kind. The kind you come to when frost sets in."

Maisie folded and refolded the corner of a towel, then let it go. "If I'm honest, it's hard not to catch feelings." Her voice went small. "But I don't know where we stand. We married for safety. I don't want to presume."

"You hope," Minnie said, not as a question.

"I do."

She wasn't fool enough to misread a man entirely. She had seen the way Wes's mouth softened sometimes when he looked at her, seen the unpracticed half-smile that came and went like a shy bird, seen how he placed himself between her and the door without seeming to. He did not look at her like an obligation. He looked the way a man looks when he has already decided you belong in his keeping and is trying to learn the right way to hold you.

They said good night not long after; being away from Junie too long set Maisie's skin on edge. Eli met them halfway with a basket on his hip, bowed exaggeratedly to set Minnie laughing, and veered toward the cottage.

The yard had quieted to the slow business of putting the day to bed. Lamps glowed in a few windows; their light fell in bright slats across the dirt. It smelled of trampled grass and cooling coffee. Wes stood on the porch rail, hat tipped back, gaze stitched to the high scatter of stars. Maisie climbed the steps careful of her ankle. The boards gave a soft groan and told on her. He didn't start; he knew her tread already. She came to stand beside him, shoulder to shoulder, and looked where he looked.

"It went well," she said at last. "I'd forgot how to have fun."

"It was a good day," he said, and when he turned his eyes to her, there was thought in them, and something she did not dare name. "You fit. Folks saw that."

"I hope they did." She smoothed a wrinkle from her cuff that didn't need smoothing. The question rose, and she let it, rather than swallow it down and let it turn to ache. "For how long?"

Wes was quiet for a spell, then turned to her so the brim of his hat shadowed his eyes. "When Tom first put the notion of marriage in my ear," he said slowly, "I didn't think past the doing. I reckoned we'd do what had to be done and keep our feet under us." He drew a breath. "Things change."

Her heart stumbled once.

"I don't aim to find another woman for this place," he said. "Don't want one."

180

Her fingers went to her middle for no reason but to anchor herself to bone and breath. She bit her lip, and the smile she tried to tame rose anyway. "I don't want to leave it."

She didn't want to be the woman who ran. She wanted to be the woman who knew which board creaked, which drawer stuck, where the morning light fell across the table. Maisie Calder, not Maisie Ward. It felt as simple as setting a name down and lifting another.

"Then stay," he said, voice rough with something that widened the space in her chest.

She looked at him, truly looked—at the care around his eyes and the steadiness of his mouth—and nodded. "Okay," she said, soft and whole.

He lifted his hand toward her face. It hovered a heartbeat from her cheek, asking. Her breath fanned across his fingers. The air between them tightened sweetly, like a rope drawn snug. He bent, just enough that she forgot the porch and the sky.

Junie cried.

The sound cut the quiet. Maisie startled and laughed once, breathless from the jolt and what had been about to be. "I should—" She swallowed. "She'll settle for me."

Wes's hand dropped. He stepped back as if giving way was the only decent move left to him. "Go on," he said. "I'll douse the lamps."

She went inside and climbed careful. Junie quieted the moment she was lifted, as if the baby had only wanted to prove she could be heard. Maisie pressed her mouth to that warm brow and let the heat there steady her. He'd been about to kiss her—she was sure of it. Lord help her, she'd wanted him to. Wanted him for weeks. And still she'd turned at the first crack in the moment. Maybe there was more of the old Maisie left than she liked to admit. Or maybe this was what going slow looked like: not flight, just prudence. The wanting hadn't gone anywhere. It would keep.

When the baby slept again, Maisie stood in the doorway and watched the dark room take back what the day had laid down. She could hear Wes moving below—one step, the sound of a lamp being trimmed, the click of the bolt. Her body loosened at those small proofs. Fear still lived with her; it had simply learned where to lie down.

She crossed to the little desk Jesse had set beneath the window and sat a moment with the window cracked to the night. The air smelled of lilac and ash. On the scrap of paper that held her few figures, she wrote nothing new, only smoothed a crease and smiled at herself for smoothing it twice.

Downstairs, a chair scraped soft. The house settled with Wes in it, the way houses do when they know the weight that keeps them standing. Maisie banked the lamp and lay down beside the baby. It took longer than usual for sleep to find her; when it came, it was the deep kind that waits until a woman's set her burdens in the proper places. She dreamed, not of running, but of a porch where the boards knew her step and a hand that hovered and did not have to hurry.

Chapter Twenty-One

The porch boards still held a memory of their nearness. Wes could feel it under his boots—the same way a rail keeps the day's sun long after dark. The lamps were trimmed, the yard gone quiet but for a nighthawk's cry, and the house breathed its slow, end-of-day breath. Inside that quiet lived the thing they hadn't quite done, warm as banked coals.

He hadn't misread her. He knew that now as sure as he knew the shape of his own hand. She'd leaned as he had; the air between them had tightened sweet and good; then the baby had cried, and the right thing had been to let the moment go. Prudence wasn't the same as fear. They would come to it proper.

He rested his palms on the rail and let the last of the night's talk settle. No brooding, not tonight—only a steadiness he hadn't felt in years and the small, astonished pleasure of knowing she meant to stay.

A thin sound threaded the quiet—soft at first, then sharper. Not a full-throated wail, but that fretful fuss babies get when sleep has slipped its hold. Junie. Wes tipped his hat back and listened. Another little cry came, higher, quick as a hiccup. He didn't wait for a second.

He crossed the threshold, eased the bolt, and went by feel through the dim parlor and up the stairs. The crack of light beneath the spare room's door made a pale stripe on the hall floor. He pushed the door with two fingers so it didn't creak.

Maisie sat propped against the headboard, hair loose, a shawl drawn around her shoulders, ankle still wrapped and set on a folded quilt. She looked like what she was—tired from company and the long tenderness of seeing to everyone. Not a ruin; not a mess. Simply spent. She rocked Junie in the crook of her arm, low and careful. The baby had that late-evening, over-full day about her—too much light, too many hands, too many voices to sort—but the cry wasn't fear. It was plain fuss, the kind that answered best to patience.

Maisie lifted her gaze as he stepped in. Even worn, her eyes held a little light. "She slept," she whispered, as if embarrassed to be caught in the falter after such a good day. "Dreamed herself awake ten minutes back. I think the commotion stirred her too much."

"Likely," he said. He kept his voice near the floor. "You want me to walk her?"

She did not hesitate; she never had to with this. She had let him take the child often of late—short watches after supper, the hour between first sleep and true rest, the bit of dawn before chores. But it always touched him, the small grace of it. She shifted, and he slid his hands in where hers had been. The pass was practiced now—Maisie's palm steady at the back of the small head, his hand sure under the weight—and then Junie was on his shoulder, her breath bunching against his collar, her warm cheek set along his jaw.

"Too much biscuit," Wes murmured into the baby's hair. "Too much being admired." He took to the slow figure-eight he'd found worked best in this room, between the foot of the bed and the rocker by the window. "Your aunt fed you pride today, little one. No wonder you can't settle."

Junie hiccupped, offended and soothed at once.

"You're wicked," Maisie said, a smile skimming her mouth. It put a spark back in her face and softened the day's edges. "And right. I should have watered down her mash when Minnie slipped her those sweet bites."

"She'll forgive you by morning." He patted the small back, gentle and even. "So will Minnie."

A tiny sound caught in Maisie's throat that might have been a laugh. She eased down another inch against the pillows and drew the shawl higher. "I feel foolish," she said after a beat, quiet. "After such a day. As if I've no sense at all."

"You're not foolish," he said, and meant it. "You did the work of three women and half a gale. Parties take it out of the strongest."

"Still," she whispered. "It was good. Better than I'd hoped." A flicker passed through her eyes, shy and pleased both. "Even the porch."

He felt the truth of that in his hands. "Even the porch."

They let that sit between them—named and simple. He could have reached for the rest of it, but there was nothing more to ask of the hour. Junie settled by degrees: first the fists unclenched, then the hitch in the breath smoothed, then the little head grew heavy where it rested near his jaw. He kept walking through the last of it, the way a man rides a horse down after a hard run so the animal doesn't cramp.

When he judged it safe, he set his palm under the small weight and tipped the baby back enough to see her face. The lashes lay dark against her cheeks; the mouth was slack and damp with sleep. "All right," he breathed to her and the room. "Let's do this clean."

He slid the clean diaper from the washstand drawer with two fingers, worked by feel so the lamplight stayed soft, checked what needed checking, and set her down only long enough to switch wet for dry. She barely startled. He eased her into the crib—Tom had carried it down the day before, and Jesse had made a joke about spare beds for honored guests—and tugged the thin quilt to her middle. The house still held a whisper of the day's heat. Anything more would have been too much.

"Comfrey and marigold still in the cupboard?" he asked over his shoulder, voice even. "Your ankle looks puffed."

"Top shelf," she said, embarrassed to be caught out. "I thought I'd keep off it. I forgot once things got lively."

"I saw you standing more than you should." No reproach in it; just fact. He went to the little table where she'd set their small stores, fetched the jars by the colored strings she'd tied—yellow and orange—and brought water from the kettle on the landing. Steam rose; the room took on that bitter-green, clean smell. He dipped a cloth, wrung it hard, then settled on the edge of the bed and reached toward her ankle.

"May I?"

Her answer was a quiet "yes" that warmed him more than the steam. He rested her heel in his palm and lifted, careful as a man carrying a thing that matters. The wrap had kept its place through the day, but the skin beneath showed the mottled map of healing—blue and yellow fading to the brown of old flowers. He worked in slow circles, pressing heat in, drawing ache out, saying nothing while the herbs did their small good work.

Maisie let out a long, unguarded breath. "That feels like mercy," she murmured. "I didn't know what that word meant for a long time."

He looked at her then, proper. She wasn't the ghost he'd found at their fence weeks back. Tired, yes. The day had put a polish of weariness on her. But the fear that had lived under her skin like a burr had lain down. She met his gaze and did not look to the door.

"Mercy's simple," he said. "It's just a hand where you need one."

Her mouth bent at the corner. "And if I need two?"

"You'll have two."

Silence took the room for a span. It wasn't hollow. The baby's breath from the crib made a kind of tide; the lamp's little hiss kept time. He shifted the cloth, found the tender place over the bone, and kept on.

"I meant what I said," she whispered after that span. "On the porch."

"I did too."

Her eyes moved to his mouth—no more than a flicker, but he felt it. Heat slipped under his ribs, the clean kind, not the old kind that burned a man from the inside. He drew the cloth away and wound a fresh strip of linen, snug and neat, tied with a square knot that would come easy when it should. His knuckles brushed the skin above her stocking; he felt her breath catch and steadied his own.

"If I'm slow," he said, choosing care over flourish, "it isn't for lack of wanting. I'd rather set a good beam straight than hurry and have the roof fall when it storms."

Something like relief crossed her face. "I know," she said. "I wanted you to know I'd not run from it."

He nodded. He would not count that as a promise; he would not need to. A man can tell when a door has been opened to him. He set her heel back to the quilt, eased her foot down, and only then let go.

"Sleep," he said. "I'll sit a little."

"You've been on your feet since dawn."

"So have you."

She smiled at the foolishness of arguing kindness with him and slid lower on the pillows. He tugged the shawl so it covered her shoulder, then took the rocker by the window where the night came in a thin line at the sash. The moon had set; the yard was all dark shapes and the hint of the cottonwoods beyond the barn. He could hear Tom outside, his step making a short patrol between pump and gate. Good. That watch should hold until the first gray split the east.

Maisie lay quiet, not yet shifting into sleep. She turned her face toward him in the lamplight. "You were different today," she said, almost as if confessing. "At the party. Nearer to me without crowding me."

"I was just where I should be," he said.

"That makes two of us."

He let out a breath that might have been a laugh if he'd given it more voice. He watched as her lashes sank, rose once, sank again. She worked her fingers against the shawl edge as if smoothing it could smooth the whole of her life. Then her hand went slack, and that was that for the day.

He stayed. The rocker made a soft sound, wood on wood, familiar as the click of a bit. He thought of the way she'd looked on the porch—light from the house on her mouth, stars in her hair, the kind of yes that lives in a woman's stillness. He thought of the way he'd have to ask when the hour was right: not with words only, but with the whole of himself. There was a kind of vow in that quiet. He said it the way a man prays who's learned to keep prayers short and plain.

Lord, keep them. I'll do my part.

Junie gave a small sleep-sneeze and startled her own hand. He rose, checked the blanket, and set the little palm where it wanted to be—curled near the mouth like a cat's paw. He set a fingertip on the tiny wrist and felt the drum of life there, quick and sure. The thought that came next wasn't new; it only had more weight tonight. Somewhere between the first week and this one, he had quit thinking of the child as something that belonged only to Maisie and Ivy's memory. The word that fit wouldn't be pried loose by sense or caution.

Daughter.

He swallowed against it—against the want in it and the oath that came chained to the want. "All right, little one," he whispered. "Sleep while you can. There's work enough in a good life."

He checked the lamp, turned it down a trifle, and came back to the bed. Maisie had drifted fully. Even her mouth had softened; the hard brace she sometimes kept in the hinge of her jaw was gone. It made her look younger by years. He sat on the edge and, after a breath, reached to take the ribbon of hair that had fallen across her throat and lay it back behind her shoulder. His fingers did not tremble; he did not let them.

The bootlaces had come loose sometime after supper. He slid the boots off and set them neat, toes out, the way she had begun to do with his when she fetched them dry from the kitchen hearth. He wasn't sure when that small exchange had started. He was sure he never wanted it to stop. He lifted her wrapped foot onto a second quilt so the joint would lie easy, drew the shawl to meet the quilt, and tucked it just enough.

At the door, he paused, listening. The house answered like a body at rest: a beam settling, a draft in the chimney, Tom's tread outside falling steady, and beneath it all the paired tide of two sleepers' breath. His home had learned new sounds. It wore them well.

He stepped into the hall and pulled the door almost to. The strip of lamplight fell across his knuckles, then vanished. He didn't go down at once.

His home was no longer his alone.

And he wouldn't have it any other way.

Chapter Twenty-Two

Maisie jolted upright, a sharp breath caught behind her teeth, as though the remnants of sleep had tried to keep her tethered. Her nightgown clung damp at the collarbone, cotton chilled by the early morning air. Moonlight laid silver bars across the wall. The dream clung warm and stubborn.

It hadn't been one of the tormenting ones. No boots in an alley. No sly echo of Zeke's voice. No cold in Ivy's eyes. This dream had been of Wes.

Arms like a hearth-warmed quilt—firm but never confining. His chin light atop her head, the slow thud of his heart under her ear. No words in it. Only the sense of home she had been too long denied. Wanted, held.

She pressed her hand to her chest and felt the ache it left behind. Not just the almost-kiss on the porch, but everything unspoken inside it.

She swung her feet to the floor. The cradle beside the bed held Junie curled small, fist tucked under her cheek. Moonlight turned the baby's down to silver. Maisie smoothed a curl from the child's brow. Junie murmured and kept on sleeping.

It hadn't always been like this. When she first came, Wes had looked like a fortress—tall, quiet, set. She'd braced for the quiet to turn cold. It never had. He'd fetched water without asking, kept watch when the house was shaken, tended her ankle with a care she hadn't known how to accept at first. When she told him about Zeke, he'd simply nodded and said, You're safe now. No flourish. Just certainty. And she had believed him.

She rewrapped the healing ankle by touch, tied off the linen, and eased from the room. The boards creaked; the air had that hour-before-dawn chill. Downstairs, a low light showed in the kitchen. Coffee and pine met her on the threshold.

Jesse sat with a mug and a neat stack of papers, ink by his thumb. He looked up, that river-smooth smile of his finding her. "Mornin', Maisie. Restless night?"

She drew her shawl close. "Couldn't sleep." Her gaze dipped to his papers. "You're early."

"Work waits for no man," he said, mouth quirking. "Wes set me a list—livestock numbers, tack repairs, who we trust for freight this month." He flipped a page. "We're low on thread, molasses, liniment. I'd ask Eli to ride in, but he wanders. Tom's already carrying half the ranch on his shoulders."

She took flour and eggs without looking, the small labor steadying her. "Want me to go to town with Tom?"

"If you feel up to it," Jesse answered, gentle. "You've been penned in a spell. Might be good."

Her hand stilled at the bowl. Town. She breathed once, even. "I'll go. Junie stays here."

"Understood." No argument. "We'll watch her close."

She poured batter into the skillet; the hiss was a comfort. Jesse watched her for a time.

"I don't say this lightly," he said at last. "You've become family here. You and that little one. We've got your backs."

Family. The word found some hollow in her and filled it. "Thank you," she murmured. "Truly."

Breakfast passed under low sun, chores divided easy. She and Jesse added to the list—waxed thread for canvas, a tin of lye, liniment, a sack of oats, soapstone for the slate. Ordinary things wore a shine on a morning like this. Here, she wasn't a burden to be solved. She belonged.

By mid-afternoon, saddle leather creaked in the yard. Tom swung down, the air of a man whose day had already been long. "You ready?" he asked, reins over the wagon rail.

She set her basket on the seat, took a steadying breath, and climbed up. The road ran dusty and rutted, cicadas humming in the tall grass. They didn't talk much. Tom's hands held the lines as if they were holding more than horses. Maybe they were.

Twin Forks stirred ahead—women dickering over cloth, boys racing with sticks, a team backing to the freight platform. Tom drew up near the market. "I'll see to the heavy things," he said, a soldier's scan in his eyes. "Meet me back here."

She nodded and stepped down. No Roy Danner at a glance. No face that tugged an old fear. Relief came thin and real. The mercantile's bell chimed like any other day.

Minnie's apothecary smelled of lavender, rosemary, and old wood. Minnie glanced up from her mortar, her eyes lighting like colored glass in sun. "Maisie Calder! A sight for sore eyes."

"Errand run," Maisie said, smiling back. "Jesse sent me in. Truth is, I wasn't keen to come alone."

"You never need excuse for company." Minnie untied her apron in one tug. "Let me fetch my bonnet. I've a mind to close early."

They took the boardwalk arm in arm, basket swinging between them. Minnie's skirts whisked the planks; her laugh chimed. "You hear about Eli and the mayor's prize pig?" she asked with a wicked grin. "Swore blind it was a bear. More likely, he wanted to tackle something."

Maisie laughed before she could help it. "He cleaned up quick after that one."

"Always noisy, always up a tree," Minnie said fondly. "Jesse's a thinker. And Wes..." Her voice eased softer. "Wes is still water. Deep and steady."

At the general store, they slipped through familiar smells— sawdust, burlap, beeswax. No Danner. Minnie plucked waxed linen from the shelf. "Canvas repair. This won't fail you." They moved aisle to aisle—sugar, oats, lye, ink. Minnie shared an elderberry trick; Maisie recounted Eli's latest misadventure with a calf and a too-clever pig. Minnie dabbed laughter-tears with her cuff. "Mercy. He's a walking storybook."

"Wes just watches and sighs," Maisie said, warmth rising with the words. "Like Eli can't help himself."

"That's family," Minnie answered. "One steadies, one stirs. Both needed."

Sun pooled in the street. The air smelled of peaches. Maisie talked more than usual—small stories, scraps of days. Minnie let them go by without tugging.

They paused at Mrs. Gable's pies, crusts burnished and fragrant. "Only thing that cures Eli's foul moods," Minnie said.

"Then we'd best buy two," Maisie replied, real laughter bubbling up. She thought of a mother's flour-dusted hands long ago and a cold New York parlor where warmth had been borrowed. She wrapped a pie warm in paper.

They turned back toward the counter with their goods. The bell over the door jangled again. A man in a tan vest stepped in—hat in his hand, badge on his breast, dust on his boots.

"Afternoon, Miss Abbott. Mrs. Calder." He tipped the hat with plain respect. "Deputy Pike."

Minnie's posture straightened a hair. "Deputy."

He held a folded packet sealed with blue ribbon and a county stamp. "I'm to serve this on Mr. Wesley Calder or an adult in his household." His gaze moved to Maisie, not unkindly. "You'll see it to him?"

Her mouth went dry. "What is it?"

"Petition and summons," Pike said, voice neutral as water. "Filed this morning. Guardian matter. Order to bring the infant Juniper before Justice Markell in ten days' time for inquiry. There's a writ attached—temporary—says she ain't to be taken out of the county." He shifted, uncomfortable. "I don't write 'em. I only carry 'em."

"Who filed?" Minnie asked, already bristling on Maisie's behalf.

"Signed by Silas Hartley, attorney," Pike said. "On behalf of a... Zeke Blackwell, Albany, New York." He said the name like he'd found a burr under his collar. "I'm sorry for the errand."

Minnie reached for Maisie's wrist, quiet and firm. "We'll take it."

Pike set the packet on the counter rather than hand it to her, as if lowering a weight. "Hearing's set two Fridays hence. Paper says Mr. Calder can answer in writing, but the judge'll want to set eyes on the child. Sheriff Lane says if you need the timeline moved, come ask. We're not looking for trouble—only to do it by the book."

Maisie's world narrowed to the blue ribbon and county stamp. Her ears rang; Minnie's fingers kept her anchored. She found her voice that wouldn't wobble. "I'll see Mr. Calder gets it."

Pike nodded, relieved. "Obliged. Mrs. Gable—put it on my tab," he called as he backed toward the door, already fleeing the discomfort of it.

He was gone. The bell stilled. For a beat, the store hummed like nothing had happened. Someone laughed near the flour barrels. A broom scratched across boards.

Minnie broke the seal with her thumbnail and skimmed the top sheet, eyes flicking. "He went to Hartley," she said, disgust curling the word. "I knew it." She looked up at Maisie. "We'll do nothing from behind this counter. We take this to Wes. Not a word to a soul that doesn't need to know."

"I can't let them put hands on her," Maisie said, the words scraped raw, breath tight at the edges—but she did not shake.

"They won't," Minnie said. "Not without stepping over Wes Calder and half the county." She slid the packet into the basket between oats and pie, hiding the blue ribbon. "We walk like any other errand. Then you ride like a woman with sense, not panic."

At the door, Minnie paused, then turned back to the proprietor in a voice meant for everyone's ears. "Mr. Lyle, you tell Mrs. Gable her pies were the saving of us last winter. We'll take two."

As they turned from Mrs. Gable's stall, Minnie steered them toward Hart's. "Thread first, then I'll get you home before Tom thinks I've kidnapped you," she said, eyes bright.

The bell over the mercantile door gave a thin jingle. Mr. Hart looked up from his ledger, mouth already forming his shopkeeper's smile. It faltered a hair when his gaze slid to Maisie.

"Afternoon, Mrs. Calder. Miss Abbott," he said, smoothing his vest. "What can I do for you?"

196

"Waxed linen and canvas needles," Minnie said, easy as anything. "And I'll settle Jesse's account while we're here."

Hart cleared his throat. "About that account. I've had... inquiries. Fellow was in yesterday, asking whether the Calders were taking on more credit than sense. Left a sum on the counter—said to apply it toward your bill as a kindness." His smile didn't reach his eyes. "No name he'd give me."

Heat climbed Maisie's neck. Minnie's chin tilted a degree. "We'll pay our own way, Mr. Hart. Kindly put that 'kindness' on a separate page and send it wherever stray money goes when it's got no business here."

Hart's ears went pink. "No offense meant. It just... looked tidy in the book."

"Tidy ain't the same as right," Minnie said. "Ring us up proper."

He fetched the cord and needles, still fussing. "Telegraph's down, too, if you were of a mind to send word. Line went dead some time in the night. Freight clerk's in a state. Says two of Calder's crates that should've come on Tuesday are 'misrouted.'"

"Misrouted how?" Maisie asked before she could stop herself.

"Paper says Denver. Man says Cheyenne. I say it's a mess." Hart pushed the small pile across the counter. "Sorry for the trouble."

Outside, the street looked the same as it always did—sun on dust, a dog asleep under a wagon, a woman haggling over onions—but something meaner moved under it for Maisie now. She tucked the packet into her basket.

"Heard that?" Minnie murmured as they walked. "Money left on counters. Wires cut. Freight 'mislaid.' That ain't luck."

"No," Maisie said. "It's a hand we can't see, pressing."

"We'll press back." Minnie's smile was all teeth this time. "You get home. I'll put it about—quiet-like—that anyone taking mystery coin in this town will find themselves short of my cough tincture come winter."

Maisie huffed a laugh despite herself. "That's near cruel."

"So's a man who thinks he can buy a family's name out from under 'em," Minnie said. "Go on. Tom'll be waiting."

Minnie tucked her arm close to Maisie's and did not let go until they reached the wagon.

Tom stood with a sack on his shoulder. He took one look at Maisie's face, then at Minnie's, then at the basket. He didn't ask. He loaded the last barrel and helped Maisie up with a palm firm at her elbow.

They rolled out under a sky gone violet at the edges. Wind took the sweat off their temples. No one spoke for a while. Two miles out, they passed a neighbor turning hay; he lifted a hand; Tom returned it. The world looked as it always did. It felt different.

"Deputy served papers," Minnie said at last, low. "Hartley filed for Blackwell."

Tom's jaw flexed once. "Judge?"

"Markell. Ten days. Order not to take the baby out of the county."

Tom nodded, as if adding a fence post to a map only he could see. "We'll be home before full dark."

They were. The yard wore the evening—blue at the edges, gold still on the high boards. Jesse came from the pump, sleeves wet to the elbow. Eli and Rhett were arguing about a bent gate hinge. Wes stepped from the barn, rubbing a bit of oil from his palm.

He saw them, then saw Maisie. The steadiness in his face shifted a fraction. He came straight and took the basket without a word. Minnie passed it to him, heavy with more than groceries.

"In the kitchen," she said.

They gathered there—the long pine table, lamp turned up, the ordinary clutter of a day set aside. Tom took the back door and folded into the shadows by habit. Minnie stood with her hands on the basket rim. Jesse wiped his palms clean and leaned on the counter. Eli and Rhett came in fast, noise dropping when they read the room.

Wes broke the blue ribbon and read. He did not rush. His eyes moved once, then again, a muscle ticking in his jaw. He set the top sheet down, took the next. When he finished, he stacked the papers neat, squared the edges with his thumb, and looked at Maisie.

"Deputy Pike served you proper?"

"He did," she said.

He nodded once. "All right." He set his palm lightly on the stack, as if to pin trouble in place. "We go to town in the morning. Jesse, ride ahead at dawn to Pastor Howell—ask him to sit in, eyes on the judge. Stop by Sheriff Lane's. Tell him we're not looking for a ruckus, but we'll not hand over a child without a hearing on the square. Minnie—can you send word to Mr. Jonas Park? He's the only lawyer I trust to keep his hands clean."

Minnie's chin lifted. "I'll have him waiting at his desk."

"Tom," Wes said, without looking, "double the night watch around the house. No gaps. Rhett, you and Eli bring the small pen closer to the kitchen door. If there's any question about who's got the right to hold this child, we'll make sure every eye that matters has seen how she's kept."

Jesse's mouth tugged. "Letters?"

Wes nodded. "Neighbors who'll speak. Mrs. Gable, if she'll come. Mr. Lyle. Schoolmistress. Any soul who's seen Maisie with the baby these weeks. We'll have statements by sunup the day after tomorrow."

"Judge Markell's fair as judges go," Tom added from the dark. "Don't like men who come in from outside with paper and coin."

Eli, who had been quiet longer than suited him, let out a soft oath. "He's a snake, that Blackwell."

"He is," Wes said, voice even. "But he's a snake who's chosen to crawl into daylight. That's better than brush, for our purposes. We'll meet him proper." He looked to Maisie again. "We're not letting them take her. Hear me?"

"I hear," she said. The tight band around her chest loosened, not by much, but enough to breathe.

"Good. Eat." He slid the pie across the table like it mattered as much as the rest—which, in a house like theirs, it did. "We'll need sense more than speed."

They ate warm slices at the edge of the table—apple and cinnamon, the taste of ordinary. Plans knitted themselves between bites. Minnie wrote a neat list for Jonas Park. Jesse drafted names for letters. Eli, sent for once on a simple task, ran to the smokehouse and came back with meat for morning provisions, no flourish in him now. Rhett fetched twine and set to mending the gate hinge that had started the earlier argument, his hands easy now that there was something he could fix.

After, Wes walked Maisie down the hall, where it was quieter. He handed back the empty basket, then caught himself and set it on the bench instead.

"You did well," he said simply.

"I didn't feel like it," she admitted.

"That's not the same thing." He hesitated, then, careful as always, said, "We'll be side by side in that room. If the judge's questions cut, you look to me and not to Hartley."

A laugh—small and frayed—escaped her. "Minnie says Hartley slants the truth like a roof in a hailstorm."

"She's kind." His mouth tipped. It wasn't quite a smile, but it was the shape of one. "Get some sleep."

"I'll try," she said. "Thank you for... for not making me feel foolish about being afraid."

"Fear's a tool," he said. "We'll use it to make our plan tight."

She nodded and turned toward the stairs. Halfway up, she paused, looked back. "Wes?"

He lifted his chin.

"Whatever happens," she said, voice steady now, "I don't regret coming here."

He looked at her like a man takes light after a long dusk. "I don't either."

She went on up. In the spare room, the cradle was where she'd left it, Junie's breathing soft and sure. She bent and laid her palm lightly over the small ribs, counting—quick and steady. She tucked the quilt and straightened. Out the window, night spread over their fields like a dark shawl. Somewhere, Tom's boot tapped a slow line on the packed earth. In the hall, a floorboard spoke and fell quiet. The house had learned new sounds. It wore them well.

Maisie set the summons under the lamp and read it through once, lips moving. The words were stiff with law and distance. They did not name who had kept the child warm through cold mornings, who had boiled bottles in a house where the kettle never got a rest, who had sung a fretful babe into sleep. Papers could not tell those things; people would.

She turned down the wick and lay down beside the crib. She didn't dream when sleep took her. She didn't need to. Morning would bring more than chores.

At first light, the yard would wake to motion—Jesse already saddled for the pastor and the sheriff, Minnie's message flying to Mr. Park, Rhett shifting the small pen in closer, Eli, for once, minding the list put in his hand. Wes would be at the door with his hat and the packet under his arm.

Plot could not be outrun. It could be met. And she was done running.

She laid her hand against the rail of the crib, wood warm from the room, and closed her eyes. The house breathed. She breathed with it. Whatever came, she would walk into it with her head up and her people to either side. That was the difference now. That was everything.

Chapter Twenty-Three

The air in the Calder kitchen had turned thick, not with steam and coffee as mornings usually brought, but with the weight of what had been done in the night. Light slid thin through the windows and made long bars on the floor. Jesse stood at the stove with a cold tin mug he hadn't drunk, jaw tight as a cinch. Rhett paced a rut into the boards.

"Five head, Wes," Rhett said, voice raw. "Not trampled. Cut. Clean through." He slashed a hand in the air. "Same place as last month, only worse."

Wes kept his hat on. He'd never been a man to let anger run the room—anger wasted feed—but it was there, steady as heat in a banked stove. He'd ridden the north fence at dawn and read the story plain: two lengths of new wire sheared like thread; boot prints in pairs; a narrow-shod bay that toed in; drag marks where cattle had been pushed quick in the dark.

Jesse set his cup down harder than he meant to. "We can't patch as fast as they cut. That's coin bled and winter feed gone."

Eli leaned in the doorway, older-looking than the day would warrant. "Maybe we go straight to Jamie and be done with guessing."

"We will," Wes said. He didn't add he'd already warned Grayson once. Saying it now would only kindle more words. "Tom, hold the yard. Jesse, sit Maisie with the list—what we need for the week. Eli, you and Rhett ride with me."

He meant to keep the storm out of the house. He failed by one step. A sweep of blue cotton passed the window—Maisie, Junie on her hip, a basket of linen in her other arm. She came in on the last of Jesse's words and let her smile falter when she read their faces.

"Everything all right?" she asked, quiet.

Wes poured fresh coffee he didn't taste and put it in her hand. "We'll see to it," he said. His knuckles brushed hers—only a whisper of touch—and it put a steadiness in him he could use.

Junie studied him solemn, round eyes tracking his face. "Don't work too hard," he told Maisie, with a roughness that wasn't reproach. Then he went out where the heat could be used.

***

The ride to Grayson's place ran along the ridge where the grass showed pale in the morning and cattle dotted the lower draws like dark buttons. Rhett took the lead and worked his jaw as if there were a nail in it. Eli hummed under his breath until Wes sent him a look that cut it off. No one mentioned Zeke's name; none needed to. Trouble wore its shape without letters.

Jamie Grayson's yard had never been neat, even on good days. Today, the gate hung crooked on one hinge, and a shirt flapped from the porch rail like a surrendered flag. A boy dragged a slat-backed chair across the yard, hands black with oil. Grayson himself stepped out at the sound of three riders and put his hand to his eyes.

"Calder," he said, and tried a grin that didn't reach anything. "You come to buy a bull? I got one mean as a deacon."

"Fence on my north line was cut last night," Wes said, keeping his horse a length back so the talk stayed clean. "Five head drove through. Your side shows sign."

Grayson's gaze flicked past them, scanning for a temper he didn't want to meet. "We had sign too," he said. "Hell, Wes, I ain't taking your cattle. I'm trying to keep my own."

"Who cut it?" Rhett snapped.

"I don't know." Grayson's mouth thinned. "Men working nights, I don't hire. Two of 'em, maybe three. Come through the dry creek where the willow hides the line. One rides a pigeon-toed bay, short tail, left fore shod narrow. The other chews cigars till they look like sticks and spits like he's angry at the earth." He hooked a thumb toward his barn. "Found this in the grass at sunup."

He ducked inside and returned with a pair of new nippers, the cutting jaws bright. "Didn't belong to me. Too fine," he added, disgust in the word. "Ain't no ranch stamp. Bought with cash and quiet."

Wes took the tool. The bite on the cutting edge was small but sharp. A square-nail scar marked the handle where someone had used it for what it wasn't built for. Tom would read it like scripture. Wes could read enough: not a boy's mischief, not a storm-lifted post—work done quick by hands that knew how to hurt.

"I don't want your trouble, Wes," Grayson said, voice going soft. "But it's nippin' at me whether I want it or not. Two nights back, a rider set his horse in my lower pasture by the cottonwoods like he owned it. Told me a man from the East had business in these parts and good pay for anyone with a loose fence. I told him to get and take his coin with him. He laughed. Said fences got loose all on their own."

"Name?" Eli asked.

"You think men like that give names?" Grayson looked at his boy and back again. "But I seen him in town come last week, playing cards at Burke's. Hard eyes. Hat pulled low. Scar near his ear. Talked soft, like he liked hearing himself. I kept my head down."

Rhett shifted in the saddle, the motion short and ugly. "Danner," he said, teeth on the word.

Wes slid the nippers into his saddlebag and set his palm on the horn. "Jamie, if I ask you to sign a statement—what you just told me, in your own words—will you?"

Grayson swallowed. The movement worked hard down his throat. He looked past Wes to the ridge where his own cows stood thin as always. "If it means keeping that kind of man off all our fences, I will," he said. "But I got a wife inside and two boys you can see. Don't put my name where it gets someone killed."

"It'll go to the judge," Wes said. "Not the saloon."

"Then I'll sign."

Wes tipped his hat. "Appreciate you." It wasn't gratitude for talk of making peace with a rattler; it was for this—putting a line of ink where fear had told him hush.

They turned for home at a pace that saved the horses and their tempers both. At the dry creek crossing west of their land, Eli pulled up and pointed at the sand: two sets of fresh tracks, iron shoes with square nail heads—the pigeon-toed bay and a heavier mount. The line of the cut fence glinted through the willow like a clean wound.

"Tom'll want these before the wind takes 'em," Wes said.

They followed the sign long enough to know where it went—east to the road and toward town. No need to chase smoke. Better to set a trap for fire.

***

Back at the ranch, they circled into the yard hot and dry-throated. Tom met them before they'd swung a leg over. He took the nippers in his hands and turned them under the light like a man reading weather in a glass.

"Bought in town," he said, "not the smithy. New. See here? That nick's from prying a staple. Whoever carried these used 'em wrong and in a hurry." He sniffed at the handles and made a face. "Whiskey and cheap cigar."

"Grayson puts riders at the cottonwoods nights not his," Wes said. "One with a pigeon-toed bay. Scar by the ear, soft talker. Burke's man."

Tom's mouth went thin. "Danner."

Eli let out a soft curse, more prayer than cussing.

"Jesse!" Wes called, and his brother came from the office with ink on his fingers. "We need paper drawn for Judge Markell. Your cleanest hand. Statement for Jamie Grayson to sign. Keep it spare and true."

Jesse nodded and was already moving. "Minnie can witness," he said over his shoulder. "She'll have the right pen."

"Rhett," Wes said, "you and Tom set bells on the north run— old mule bells, low enough the wind won't chime them. Tie white cloth at the breaks so we can see new cuts easy by lantern. String fresh barb in the willow swale. And I want two on watch from dusk. Rotate every two hours. No hero work. If they come, you mark them and hang back."

Rhett's grin came mean and honest for the first time that morning. "Been waiting to do something that bites back."

"Keep it lawful," Wes said. "We've got a judge in ten days. I won't put us on the wrong side of his bench for the satisfaction of a bruised knuckle."

Rhett's grin stayed, tempered by sense. "Lawful," he said.

"Eli, ride to Sheriff Lane. Tell him we've got outside men cutting our line; ask for a deputy to pass by the north ridge at odd hours. Let Burke know I'll hold him to account for who plays cards at his tables." He felt the old heat rise and kept his voice even. "No dust-ups. We're gathering witness, not making more trouble."

Eli shoved his hat on and was already gone.

Wes turned and found Maisie at the edge of the yard, Junie on her hip, watching the circle of men like she could see the shape of the plan forming. She lifted her chin the smallest bit when his eyes met hers. Not a question. A trust.

"We'll keep it tight," he said, mostly to himself, and set to the rest.

***

By late afternoon, the yard had a purpose to it that fit like a well-made glove. Bells tied low on wire, white flags patched at old breaks, fresh staples hammered home. Tom's night chair sat where the willow opened to the creek, a blanket thrown over one arm and a rifle leaned unobtrusive against the post. Jesse returned with a stack of papers and ink dried neat. He had already sent a hand to fetch Minnie to witness Grayson's statement.

Maisie moved through the work without getting underfoot. She kept the men in biscuits and coffee and saw to a sore-kneed gelding with a poultice of comfrey and marigold while Junie clapped the spoon in approval. When Jesse asked for her eyes on the list again—what would feed the men on watch—she put down pork and beans, coffee, hoecakes, and the last of Mrs. Gable's apple. It was the kind of help that held men together without drawing notice, and Wes felt it like a hand steady at the small of his back.

Near sundown, a whistle lifted from the north line—two short, one long—the call they'd agreed on if a watcher wanted eyes without bringing the whole yard. Tom was already walking. Wes fell in beside him. Rhett came from the other side with a coil of wire draped over his shoulder.

They slipped into the willow where the creek ran low. The light there stayed green and close. The bell nearest the cut lay still. The white rag on the far post hadn't moved. Then Tom pointed, two fingers low. A fresh nick in the top wire, no more than a kiss from the nippers, and a scuff in the dust where someone had put a boot to test the post.

"Didn't like the bell," Tom murmured. "Didn't like the flags. They're reading us back."

A flicker moved beyond the trees—just a horse's shoulder easing away, then gone. Not a challenge. A measure.

Rhett took a breath like he meant to go through the brush and tear the measure to pieces. Wes caught his sleeve. "No," he said, low. "We give them a clear note to carry to whoever sent them."

He took the small tin whistle from his pocket—one Jesse had traded off a peddler for fun years back—and set two sharp notes through it. Up the creek, Eli returned the same. Then the yard bell sounded once, solid as an oath.

"We see you," Wes said to the trees, not loud. "And the judge will too."

They stood until the last of the hoof-scuff marks settled and the willow leaves stopped whispering. Then they mended the nick, re-tied the bell lower, and walked back without looking over their shoulders.

***

Night laid itself over the ranch in good order. The bunkhouse carried talk in low lines. The kitchen threw gold on the porch. Tom took the first watch in the willow, a chessboard in his lap he'd never learned to love, and a churchman's patience. Rhett sat the second, chewing on a stem like it could keep him still. Eli, coming back from town with Sheriff Lane's word of a deputy to pass by twice before dawn, pressed two cigars into Rhett's hand—"For bait," he said, and Rhett grinned like a boy.

Wes walked the yard's edge until his feet told him what his head already knew: the ranch held. He climbed the porch steps and found Maisie at the table with paper, Jesse's pen sitting beside her hand. She was writing slow and careful, Junie already asleep in the cradle pushed in close to the warm of the stove.

"What's that?" he asked.

"Names," she said. "Folks who've seen me with Junie. Mrs. Lyle. Mrs. Gable. Schoolmistress. Minnie, of course. How they'd say it plain." She glanced up. "If it helps."

"It will," he said. "We're taking a statement to Jamie in the morning. Minnie'll witness. Sheriff's sending a man by, odd hours. We set bells and flags. They tested and left. Saw us seeing them."

Her shoulders let down a measure. "Good."

He reached for the pen, drew the ink down the point with his thumb. "We'll do the hearing on our feet. We'll do the fence on our feet. I won't split a path between the two."

"I didn't think you would," she said, and the quiet held something like a pledge in it.

From the yard, a single bell chimed and went still. Wes listened, counted heartbeats, heard Tom's low whistle answer. The house breathed.

Eli came in, dust at his cuffs, and dropped onto the bench. "Lane'll swing by twice before daylight," he said, then added to Maisie, "Burke says he don't pick his patrons' souls, but he'll make sure no man sits at his tables with new nippers in his pocket." He lifted one of the cigars and wrinkled his nose. "Reckon this smells right. Cheap and mean."

Maisie made a face that almost tugged a laugh out of Wes. "Don't smoke it near the baby," she said, and Eli held his hands up in surrender.

Wes sat, elbows on his knees, and looked at the map Jesse had sketched on scrap paper—fence lines, willows, bells marked with Xs. It wasn't beautiful work. It was the work that kept people fed and kept them from being taken.

Rhett stuck his head in and tipped his hat. "I'll swap with Tom," he said. "If those rats try for the nick again, they'll ring our bell this time."

"Stay hid. Stay lawful," Wes said, and Rhett rolled his eyes like a boy who'd been told to mind and still meant to do it.

When the door shut, the quiet filled back in. Maisie folded her list and slid it on top of Jesse's stack so it wouldn't get lost.

"I heard what you told Rhett," she said. "About the judge. About keeping it lawful."

"Gives us firmer ground," he said. "And keeps my brothers alive."

She nodded, then surprised him with a small grin. "Also keeps me from having to mend bullet holes in your shirts."

He looked up at that and felt the curve of something near a smile answer. "That too."

She rose, slow and careful with her healing ankle, and set a small plate near his hand—two biscuits, cold now, and a piece of apple pie that had somehow lasted all day. "For strength," she said lightly.

He took it, and the bite tasted like the kind of ordinary men fight to keep.

"Wes," she said, pausing at the doorway with her hand on the jamb, "thank you for going to Jamie yourself. For not letting this get turned into men bragging on porches."

"That's not how fences hold," he said.

"I know." She looked like she meant more and let it lie, the way wise people do when the hour's not right for bigger words. "Good night."

"Good night."

He listened to her steps fade up the stairs, the small hitch where the board near the landing always lifted, the hush when she reached the room where Junie slept. The bells on the north run stayed quiet. Somewhere by the willow, Tom turned a chess piece and sighed.

Wes set his hand flat on the table over the map. He thought of his father's old saying Tom had quoted back at him that morning—about fear making men choose wrong. He thought of Grayson's hand shaking when he'd agreed to sign. He thought of Danner's soft talk and the clean bite of the nippers. He thought of ten days and a judge who would want to set eyes on a child who had learned to clap on the downbeat and sleep to the sound of a ranch breathing.

He lifted his hand and smoothed the edge of Jesse's paper like it would keep the rest of his life from fraying.

"Let him come," he said, low enough the table could keep it and no one else.

Chapter Twenty-Four

The ranch had learned a new kind of quiet—one with its ears pricked.

Maisie felt it in the pauses between chores, in the way the house held its breath when a rider's shadow crossed a window, in the long looks the brothers traded without words. Bells now hung low on the north run—old mule bells tied just above the wire where wind wouldn't find them—and white rags marked the weak spots like stitches in a wound. A watch rota lived beside Jesse's ledger, names penciled neat, two men posted from dusk to dawn, two hours on, two off. Sheriff Lane knew. Burke had been warned about the men who chewed cheap cigars and smiled too soft. Judge Markell would hear them in ten days' time if the Lord willed it and papers held.

It should have made her easy. It did not.

She kept moving. The ankle that had near done for her was better by the day, though the wrap still hugged it snug, and she minded steps. She cooked for the watchers—pone and beans that sat warm on the back of the stove, coffee always thick and ready—mended a shirt while the kettle grumbled, set Junie on a quilt with a tin cup for drumming. It was the quiet moments that scraped. Between one task and the next, guilt pressed up under her ribs like a mismatched board. None of this had been the Calders' to carry. Zeke's shadow had lengthened and found a roof to settle on. Her roof.

She folded a stack of dishcloths and made herself look out the window. The yard moved with purpose, not panic. Tom crossed from pump to gate, a coil of wire over one shoulder, whittled to the bone by work and years. Rhett fixed a broken hinge with a temper he kept tamped like a stove banked for night. Eli limbered a saddle and whistled a tune he didn't finish. The sound that was not there was the one that threaded

Maisie's nerves tight—the clean, startled call of a bell from the north run.

Junie flung her cup and crowed at the crime. Maisie went to fetch it, easing down on the wrap, and caught her breath when the joint complained. "All right," she told it under her breath, half to the ankle and half to herself. "We're mending, not marching."

By noon, the men came in on a tide: Jesse with ink on his fingers and a list in his pocket; Eli with dust in his hair and magnolia leaves hooked in his spur from cutting across the creek; Rhett with a nick on his knuckle and a grin he didn't quite mean. "Bell chimed once," he reported as he wolfed bread. "False. Just a mule wandering his curiosity." He tilted his head toward Maisie's wrap and scowled on her behalf. "You keeping off that ankle like Wes says?"

"As much as a woman can in a house that feeds six," she answered, easy, and set beans on his plate before he could make more noise about it. It won a real grin.

Jesse tapped the ledger with his knuckle. "Minnie'll come up this afternoon and ride out with Tom to Jamie Grayson's. We'll get that statement witnessed proper. Lane's sent word his man will pass the north line odd hours to keep it unpredictable."

Maisie let the news sink. It was more than bells and biscuits. It was law on paper. "Good," she said, and meant it. "Tell Minnie I'll have coffee waiting when she comes back."

"Tell her yourself," Eli said, already backing toward the door with his hat dangling off one finger. "You know she likes you better than any of us. I'm just the man she lets sweep her porch."

"She lets you talk too much on it," Jesse muttered, but his mouth had softened.

The hour after dinner stretched. Junie seized sleep like a prize and surrendered to it with her face mashed against the quilt. Maisie set the cradle near the open window to catch the faint breath of wind and, with the house briefly tamed, let herself stand still. The lull stitched her to old thought. When Ivy had run, Maisie had been the one with a plan folded crooked in her pocket: south, then west, then farther west, past the reach of money and men who thought money could buy the world. She'd made promises at a graveside and then made more at a kitchen table in a house not her own. Now the promises had grown legs and walked around the yard in the shape of men she had not meant to love.

She needed to do something that was more than dishes.

Behind the barn, the shade held a mercy the yard did not. Eli had a feed sack slung over one shoulder and a latch spread out on the upturned crate like a broken jaw—hinge pin bent, wood chewed from a winter's worry. He had a nail between his teeth and one eyebrow up when she came limping down the path.

"You come to steal my job, Mrs. Calder?" he asked around the nail. "Because I'll warn you now: it don't pay in pie."

"I came to ask if there's something useful I can do." She squared her shoulders. "Not housework. Something that bites back."

The eyebrow climbed higher. He spat the nail into his palm and set it on the crate. "You already do more than you think. Men like to pretend they're made of iron. They ain't. Coming home and finding a house lit and a baby laughing—" He shrugged, sudden and honest. "It makes us remember what we're standing in front of."

"That's kind," she said, and then, because kindness could feel like a pat on the head when a woman wanted a tool in her hand, "but what can I carry that frees your hands?"

He studied her the way a man studies the sky before a ride. "Hold that latch mouth for me," he said finally, "and don't tell Wes I let you."

She braced the two ragged boards, heel set, and wrap steady. Eli worked the hinge pin with a cold chisel he shouldn't have used for the job and did anyway. The metal complained and then relented. Sweat pearled and ran. He blew it off his upper lip and grinned sideways at her.

"You see Minnie today?" she asked, just to see him squirm.

"Maybe," he said, and the word shaped itself like a boy caught in the cream jug. "She's coming later to ride with Tom. To—uh—witness."

"Minnie could witness a cyclone and make it behave," Maisie said, and earned his laugh.

The hinge pin slid at last, clean and seated. Eli sat back and flexed his hands. "You're a good foreman, Mrs. Calder. I might have to hire you on."

"Don't pay in pie," she reminded him.

"Pays in good company," he shot back, then pushed his hat higher on his brow and let the grin slip into something truer. "I liked her a long time," he admitted, as if the latch's straight line had made him line up too. "Trouble is, she's known it longer. I got to earn what she already knows."

"Minnie Abbott does not spend her afternoons with fools," Maisie said. "You be steady and honest. She has an eye for that."

His grin went crooked and boyish. "You think?"

"I know."

He stood, the feed sack over his shoulder again, lighter for being no lighter. "Thanks," he said, plain as bread.

"You're welcome," she answered, and meant that plain as well.

They went in together, the barn breathing out a smell of sweet hay and old leather that put Maisie's lungs right where they needed to be. She left Eli to his yard and his courage and found the kitchen looking like a woman had lived there all day—flour on the board, beans soaking for the night, a pie tin washed and set to dry with a shine she could see herself in. She tied up her hair again, wiped a child's handprint from the table edge, and rolled dough into neat rounds she'd drop on the hot iron come suppertime.

Minnie arrived with her bonnet tipped back and a paper packet clutched to her chest like it might fly off if she didn't. "I swear, I think Jesse practices his handwriting with angel feathers," she said as she came through the door. "Those lines could cut a man."

"You rode out?" Maisie asked, already reaching for a clean cup. "Coffee?"

"Please and thank you and yes," Minnie said, dropping onto a chair with a sigh that came up from her boots. "Jamie signed. Wife held the baby and cried a little, and then didn't. Tom stood there like a church door. I told the woman to sleep with her windows locked, and I told Jamie to keep his mouth shut in the wrong company. He said he would."

Maisie eased down on the wrap. "Good," she said again, letting the word carry more than one thing. "Did Lane's man pass the ridge?"

"Twice that I saw," Minnie answered. "Lane says he'll stagger it and not tell even himself till he must." She sipped, eyes closing in brief bliss. "Mercy, that's fine coffee. I could almost forgive a man his sins for half a cup."

"Don't encourage them," Maisie said, and Minnie laughed— a bright thing in a house that had learned to hunch.

By the time Minnie rode back with Tom to take the papers to where they needed to be kept until they were read, the shadows had drawn long across the yard. The heat eased. The stove made a small crowd of it where Maisie stood. She rolled hoecakes onto the skillet and watched the edges go dry and the middle bubble. She could cook with her eyes closed now, one hand moving to the tin of salt, the other to the coffee pot, mind like a needle always coming back to Wes.

He came in like a door had been shut on his temper, and it had followed him through anyway.

He did not slam anything. He did not need to. The set of him said the same. Hat still on, dust darkening the denim where sweat had salted it and then dried, jaw drawn taut. He paced once, twice, the length of the stove to the sink and back again, the boards knowing his measure and complaining for form's sake.

"Something happened?" Maisie asked, careful with the words and with her breath. "Or nothing did, and that's worse?"

He pushed a hand over his mouth like he meant to rub the taste of the day away. "Bells chimed near willow," he said, voice sanded down to even. "Not a cut. A touch and a test. Lane's man came through ten minutes after they cleared. He's doing what he said. Not his fault the night don't hold still for him." He stopped pacing, stared at the coffee like it might talk back. "Jesse's count holds. We're still down five. Grayson signed, and Lane's clerk stamped it. Good as we can make it until the judge sets eyes on it. I keep feeling like I should be three places at once and a mile tall in each."

She set the spatula down too hard, and it clanged. "You think I don't feel that?" The heat that climbed her throat surprised her, or maybe it didn't. "Every man here walking around bent with work and worry because of my trouble. I cook and mend and make a house look like a house, and it doesn't touch a fence line. It doesn't keep a bell from chiming."

His head came up at that, eyes already tired and now sharpening. "Don't be foolish," he said, and the word didn't land where he meant it.

Her palm found the edge of the table. "Foolish?"

"The best use of you is exactly what you just called 'only'—a lit kitchen and a quiet baby and a list in Jesse's neat hand made right by yours." He took off his hat and put it back on again like he'd reached for a handhold and found the air. "If I have to worry where you are while I'm in a willow brake with riders who like to cut wire after midnight, I split my mind where it can't split."

"And what am I to be then?" The words leapt, too quick, but they were true, and she let them stand. "A house saint we set up on a shelf? Something to be kept safe, like a jar of peaches put by for winter and never opened?"

His jaw worked. "You want to stand in the dark with Tom and a whistle while men who chew cigars and spit like they're angry at the earth measure our line?"

"I want to be part of the answer," she said, soft and fierce together. "Not the problem wrapped up in a shawl."

"Lord, Maisie," he said, and the name came out both a prayer and a swear. He turned away from her, then back, as if he could pace the argument into sense. "You are not a problem. You are the reason we make an answer that isn't just fists."

"My being here brings trouble," she said, and the old, old ache came with it. "My being here always does."

He went still then in the way that meant he was holding himself between two edges. "Your being here puts a spine in men who already had one and makes them use it." His voice stayed even, but she could hear how close it stood to breaking. "Don't take my choice from me by saying this is something that happened to me without me. I choose you here. I choose the fight that comes with it."

The room did that thing a room does when truth walks through and takes a chair—went a little quiet at the corners, even with the skillet talking and the kettle fretting and the baby shifting in sleep near the stove. Maisie felt her throat pull tight and hated that it did. "Then don't speak to me like I'm a woman who can only set bread and pour coffee."

"I didn't," he said.

"You did," she said back, not cruel. "Maybe you didn't mean it, but you did."

He opened his mouth, shut it. The muscle in his cheek jumped. He took off his hat again and set it on the peg so careful it was almost comic. "All right," he said. "All right. I said it wrong." He let out a breath that made his shoulders drop. "I can't do the day twice. Sometimes I come in carrying the whole of it and pour it on whatever's near." He looked at her then, properly, the way a man looks when he's decided to accept the part that is his. "That's not where I want to set it."

She stood with her hand still on the table and wanted two things at once—to stay and argue it all the way round until both of them found the bottom, and to take herself out of the room before the hurt in her voice made the hurt in his face worse. She chose the kinder of the two she could manage. She took the hoecakes off the iron, set them to the side, wiped her hands on her apron, and picked up the kettle as if there were something else in the kitchen that needed her attention on the other side of the doorway.

"I'm going to sit with Junie a bit," she said. "Beans are ready when the men come in. Coffee too."

"Maisie," he said, and the word stopped her, but did not turn her.

"Yes?"

"I'll say it right next time." He meant more than grammar, and they both knew it.

She nodded without letting herself look. "All right."

The back hall was cooler. The stairs tightened underfoot and made her ankle mindful. She took them with care, and the little tug she could never entirely smooth shot up her shin and then faded. At the landing, she stopped because the house told her to.

Out past the cottonwoods, beyond the ridge where the willow kept its low counsel, a bell chimed once. Just once. The sound hung in the air like a bright bead on a dark string and then went quiet. She held her breath to make room for the next sound. It came, soft and sure—the two short, one long whistle Tom had chosen as their sign that a watcher wanted eyes, not alarm.

Below, Wes had already moved. She could hear it in the boards—the quick hush of a man crossing with purpose. Eli's boots thumped from the yard, then found quiet, too. Jesse's chair scraped back. Rhett let out a word he shouldn't and then swallowed it whole. Across the narrow night, another whistle answered—Eli's, by the sound—and then the small talk of men readying themselves for the kind of patient listening that catches more than noise.

Junie stirred and sighed, not waking. Maisie set her palm on the doorjamb and steadied herself on that small piece of the house, on the knowledge of men outside making a thin line thick with bodies and law, on a promise said wrong and then said better. Lord, keep them, she thought with the brevity of a woman who had learned not to argue with heaven. I'll do my part.

The bell did not ring again. In the silence that followed, you could hear a ranch remember itself—the wind tucking itself around the corners, the last bird scolding the dark, the kettle below beginning to talk again as if it knew its part in a war without shouting. She picked up the thought she had laid down when she took the latch for Eli: I will be useful, and not only in ways that can be washed and put away.

When she went back down, the kitchen was emptying into the yard. Wes paused in the doorway, rifle slung easy, not eager. "Stay inside," he said, and his voice had none of the edge left, only care. "Lamp turned low. If you hear two bells together, take Junie to the cellar and wait for Tom's voice or mine."

"I know the drill," she said, mouth wanting to twitch toward a smile and not quite daring it. "Bring your shirt back without holes. I'm tired of mending."

His mouth did the twitching for both of them then, quick as a skipping stone. "Yes, ma'am."

It was nothing—these small edges smoothed, this making room for humor in a day that had had none. It was everything. He stepped off the stoop and into the night that had its measurement taken, and Maisie shut the door soft and set her hand flat against it for a heartbeat longer than needed, as if steadiness could be passed through pine.

Only after she turned the lamp down did she catch the faintest scent under coffee and flour and soap—cigar leaf gone stale, carried in on a boot heel or a cuff. She went still, not from fear, but attention. "We see you," Wes had said to the trees the night before. "And the judge will too." She tucked the scent away for telling when the men came in.

Junie sighed again and turned her face toward the wall, palm tucked like a cat's paw under her chin. Maisie crossed to her and laid the back of her fingers to the baby's cheek, a quick benediction.

She would keep the lamp low and the coffee hot and her ankle wrapped and her voice ready to be one more true thing on paper when the time came. And when Wes came back through the door, she would hear him out before her temper found the pan again.

Outside, a low whistle rose and fell. Answered. Held.

The house breathed.

Chapter Twenty-Five

By noon, the day had soured in a way a man feels in his teeth before he tastes it.

Wes spent the morning tracing small failures through town—nothing to put a hand on, everything to bruise a knuckle against. At the livery, the feed order was "on its way," though the clerk wouldn't meet his eye. At the mercantile, a bolt of canvas he'd paid for last week seemed to have gone walking. Burke swore he hadn't seen the cigar-chewing stranger in three days and swore it like a man who'd been practicing swearing before a mirror.

"Folks say the Calder spread's running lean," the feed driver muttered at last, kicking at a splinter on the dock. "Just talk, you know how talk goes. Boss told me to collect in advance till things… settle."

"Since when do we settle with rumor?" Wes asked.

The driver shrugged inside himself. "Since it spends like coin."

Minnie cornered Wes on the boardwalk with her bonnet tipped back and a look that could cut thread without shears. "There's a word being passed—quiet and careful, like poison in tea. 'Mind your risk on the Calders. They're overextended. Don't let their trouble become your trouble.' It ain't God's word; it ain't even smart. But men like not to be the last fools buying when others have stepped back." She touched his sleeve and dropped her voice. "This is the work of that Eastern man without him setting a boot on your porch."

Wes thanked her and went on, jaw set. It was there at the bank, too: the clerk's new habit of clearing his throat before every sentence, the way he put an extra pause between *We* and *appreciate your custom,* a space big enough to drive a herd through. The manager was "in conference." The conference, if Wes had to guess, had his name in it.

By the time he turned Jeremiah toward home, the sun was high and brassy, the road kicking dust up into his mouth. The world didn't look any different, but it wore a new weight.

He passed Sheriff Lane on the road south of the ridge. The sheriff tipped his hat and drew his horse up to match Wes's step for a span.

"I hear your bells are keeping time," Lane said without preamble. "My man saw a sign at the willow and nothing more. Whoever's testing you, don't like being seen. It'll make them sloppier or meaner. I can keep riding by. I can't arrest a whisper."

"I didn't ask you to," Wes said. "But if a whisper grows a hand and steals in daylight, I'll want a name on it."

"You'll have it," Lane answered, and wheeled off toward the north line.

The ranch breathed like it had held itself too long. Bells hung dull and quiet where they should. White rags winked in the willow. Jesse's laundry snapped on the line—Maisie's steady knots, neat and square. Junie's laugh carried from the porch, and the sound cut a notch out of the hardness in Wes's chest whether he liked it or not.

Inside, the kitchen had the good end of noon about it: coffee dark and ready, bread cooling, beans thinking on it. Jesse sat with the ledger open, pen squared, calm gone from his face in the particular way that meant he'd been doing sums over and over and the numbers were holding their ground against being wished away. Eli was turning an apple by its stem like he meant to unwind it back to blossom.

Rhett came in last, hat pushed back, dust at his cuffs, temper chewing on a bit. "Feed man turned squirrelly," he reported, not waiting for an invitation. "Said he needed payment on the barrel. I told him if the barrel was full, I'd surely pay for it. He did not appreciate my poetry." He threw his hat onto a peg and missed. It hit the wall, slipped, and hung on a nail that looked surprised to have earned such use.

Jesse didn't lift his head. He drew a line under a column and then another, as if ink could build a fence where wire was losing ground. Finally, he said, "We've coin for three weeks of feed at present rate if nothing else bleeds. If buyers keep 'postponing,' that becomes two. If a calf pulls through that colic Tom's fretting about, that buys us half a week. If not, we lose the calf *and* the milk we wanted for the hands. There ain't a number on this page that likes the weather."

"Blackwell's working town," Eli said, apple stem finally surrendered and set beside Jesse's pen. "He's got men whispering and men listening. He can rot a place without touching it."

"Rot's still a thing you can cut out," Rhett said, too quick. "You just need a sharp knife and a good grip."

"Do we have both?" Jesse asked mildly, still not looking up.

The quiet after that wasn't empty; it was full of the things men don't say because saying them would make them heavier.

Maisie came in from the porch with Junie on her hip and a cloth over her shoulder. She set the baby on the quilt near the stove, put a tin cup within reach, and then crossed to Jesse's side like she belonged there, which she did. "Tell it to me in plain words," she said. "So I can carry the true of it upstairs and not the fear of it."

Jesse's hand paused. The set of his mouth eased, the way it does when a man is seen without having to ask. "Plain," he agreed. "We need our buyers to do what they always do—show up and pay fair—and our suppliers to do what they always do—trust we will. One man's talk is making ten men stall. If the stalling keeps on, we go lean by the time the judge takes our paper." He glanced at Wes then, the first look since Wes had stepped through the door. "We might have to consider other options to keep the wheels turning."

"Such as?" Rhett asked, bristling in advance.

"Negotiation." Jesse let the word sit like a hot coal. "Not giving over *anyone*, and not admitting any wrong we haven't done. But something that buys time. A public truce. An agreement that he leaves the ranch's business alone until the hearing, we leave his pride alone until then. It would calm town. It would keep feed coming." He lifted his eyes to Wes's. "I'm not saying I like it. I'm saying a ledger don't give a man pride to eat."

Eli's chair scraped hard. "No," he said, flat as a slammed door. "You give Blackwell the smallest inch, he puts a train track through it and rides in smiling. 'Public truce' sounds like 'we agree he has a say.' He don't. This is our land, our name, our people."

"I know what it sounds like," Jesse returned, still calm, still careful. "I also know what it sounds like when a man tells a hand he can't pay him. Or when a supplier turns his wagon because a rancher was too proud to buy time."

"So we make another plan," Eli shot back. "We sell a few culls to Harlan Tate ahead of schedule. We ask Cartwright to extend credit for thirty days—he owes us from the spring flood. We pick up hay from the east meadow early. We go to Pastor and ask him to host a meeting with suppliers and buyers in the church yard, with him, Minnie, and Lane standing by to witness. We show our books. We remind them who we are."

Rhett brightened with that, quick as he always did when a plan had something he could carry. "I like the church bit," he said. "Men act right when God's watching."

"God watches your poker games too," Jesse said without heat.

"I play cleaner when Minnie's watching," Eli muttered, and Minnie wasn't even in the room to reap that harvest.

Wes had listened without cutting in, weighing each word the way he'd learned to weigh a steer with his eyes: quarter by quarter, not fooled by showy shoulders. He could hear the sense in Jesse's caution. He could hear the right in Eli's refusal. Both were true, and the line between them was where a man's choices got heavy. He looked at Maisie then—at the steady way she held her jaw, at the wrap peeking above her stocking where she'd forgotten to tug the hem down because she'd been seeing to everyone else before herself. The idea of anything "public" that gave Zeke Blackwell a place to set his boot on her life made something cold move behind Wes's ribs.

"No truce," he said, and put his hand flat on the ledger. "Not with a man who buys his reputation by pawning other men's names. We'll not give him a taste of this house in exchange for quiet. We will make our quiet with work and law." He turned to Jesse. "That doesn't mean we do nothing. Draw up a circular—simple, signed, witnessed by Pastor and Sheriff Lane—inviting buyers and suppliers to the ranch on Saturday. We open the books enough to show solvency. We set coffee and bread on tables and put Tom at the gate so no one turns this into a spectacle. We tell them what we're doing—bells on the fence, statements gathered, hearing set. We ask the men we've stood for to stand for us."

Jesse blew out a breath that was not relief and not defeat. "That buys time," he admitted. "It also risks making us look like we're begging."

"Begging's hat in hand on a porch," Wes said. "This is a rancher showing his work to the men he does business with and saying: we carry our weight; don't be fooled into letting another man set it down for us. If that fails, we go to Harlan Tate with the culls, quiet as you said. Tom can ride to Cartwright tonight and lean on his memory of where he kept his cattle when the river came up in May two years back."

Rhett nodded, already halfway to the door in his mind. "I'll set boys to freshen the yard. Bells are holding. We'll rig benches by the cottonwoods. Minnie'll help with the tables." He glanced at Maisie and grinned. "And Maisie will make bread enough to feed a jury."

"Then the jury will behave," Maisie said, dry, though her eyes were not.

Eli leaned forward, elbows on his knees. "And Burke?" he asked. "He's letting the whisper live in his place because it fills his tables. You want I should go convince him his whiskey tastes better when he minds his mouth?"

"You'll talk to him," Wes said. "With Lane there. In daylight. Words only. Let him know we'll remember who backed away and who stood by. No threats. Not even the kind you think don't sound like threats."

Eli affected innocence so poorly it was almost sweet. "Me?"

"Exactly you," Jesse said.

The talk went on in the steady way of work: names assigned, times set, letters to be drafted and delivered, the small thousand things that make a plan into something a man can stand on. Tom came in from the yard and took it all in with one glance, then nodded once and said, "I'll ride to Cartwright. If he plays hard, I'll tell him I remember his wife's blackberry pie the spring after the flood and how she asked us to take a second slice."

"That's blackmail," Eli said.

"That's manners," Tom returned.

The light slid lower, honey over the cottonwoods. The bells told nothing. Men drifted to their chores with a look in the eye that matched Wes's—the look of a man who knows he cannot carry a whole day but can carry the next ten minutes and then the ten after that. Jesse shut the ledger gently as if it were a sleeping thing and went to his desk to write, dipping his pen slow, making those letters that made Minnie shake her head and call them needle-work. Rhett took two hands and a hammer to the benches. Eli stuck his hat on and went hunting Pastor on the far road where he liked to walk before supper.

Wes stepped onto the porch because he needed open sky to square up his thoughts. The yard wore the long day like a shirt that still fit, though the sleeves had been rolled and the collar loosened. Smoke rose from the kitchen chimney in a blue ribbon. Somewhere beyond the barn, a hawk called the last of itself into the evening.

He put both hands on the rail and let the roughness of it scrape his palms into knowing. Blackwell's new trick was meaner than cut wire because you couldn't mend talk with staples. You could only outlast it with something louder and truer. Work. Law. Community that remembered what it owed itself. He could do that. He had done harder.

Bootsteps sounded behind him, light and even. He didn't turn. Maisie came to stand with her shoulder just brushing his arm, close enough he could feel the heat of her. Junie was asleep; he could tell by the way Maisie's voice came low and unhurried when she used it at night.

"Minnie says Pastor will witness," she said. "She also says she intends to bake until the men who come can't help but believe in goodness again."

"That sounds like Minnie," Wes answered.

"And like sense," Maisie added. She set her forearms on the rail the way he had. The wrap on her ankle peeped above the stocking again; she didn't fuss with it. "Jesse's right and Eli's right, both," she said after a beat. "But I'm glad you chose as you did."

"I won't give you up to buy quiet," he said, and the simple truth of it clicked into place between them like a rifle bolt seated. "Not to him, not to town, not to any man breathing. If this ranch is to fail, it won't be because we traded our souls for another week of feed."

"I know you won't." She didn't look at him. She looked out across the yard, where Tom was tightening a cinch like he meant to ride through the night and back. "But I need you to know I know what it costs to keep me here. If leaving would make it easier—"

"No." The word came out faster than he intended. He forced his voice gentler. "Don't start the sentence if it ends with you walking out that gate." After a beat, softer still, "Please."

Her breath left her in a small, unguarded sound. She turned her hand so her fingers found the edge of his sleeve and rested there, not clutching, just saying what her mouth didn't. "All right," she said. "I won't start it."

The quiet after that wasn't heavy. It held. The two of them stood like that, shoulders near, hands honest, while the yard shifted toward evening. Somewhere in the willow, a bell spoke once—sharp and clean—and then went still. Wes counted ten heartbeats and heard Tom's low whistle answer two short, one long. A test only. The kind of thing you outlast by refusing to flinch.

"Lane stopped me on the road," Wes said after a time. "He's doing what he said. There's only so much a badge can hold back when talk's doing the cutting."

"Talk cuts," Maisie agreed. "So does truth. You've got more of the one than he does of the other."

He glanced at her. "You always talk like that, or did you learn it when I wasn't looking?"

"I learned it the hard way," she said, and did not add the rest. She didn't have to. The air between them knew it.

Junie stirred upstairs, the small restless sound of a child circling the edge of deeper sleep. Maisie tipped her head toward the door. "I'll go sit her down in it. Then I'll come back and make the coffee you'll need when you start worrying in circles again."

He huffed something that wanted to be a laugh and failed halfway. "You know me too well already."

"Not yet," she said, and the promise lived right there in those two words if a man had ears for it. "But I'm working on it."

She went inside with that particular grace of hers—the one that made a room think it had always been meant for her—and Wes stayed a while longer, making himself look at the things he could carry and setting down the things he couldn't. He could not stop Zeke Blackwell from buying himself an echo in the mouths of weak men. He could call those men to his yard, put coffee in their hands, and make them look him in the eye while he told them who he was. He could not make a judge move faster than ten days. He could put paper in that judge's hand, clean and witnessed and free of heat. He could not be in three places at once. He could put men he trusted where he could not be and pray they'd be enough.

He turned from the rail and went back in. Jesse had three drafts folded and sanded, edges squared; one for buyers, one for suppliers, one for men who owed favors and might have forgotten. Rhett had a boy sweeping the yard like it was a church porch. Eli slipped in with dust on his boots and the look of a man who had gotten *some* of what he went for. "Pastor says yes," he said. "Burke says he don't pick his patrons' souls, but he'll pick his words more careful till the hearing. Lane stood there and didn't have to say a thing."

"That's a thing," Jesse said.

"It is," Wes agreed. "Small things in a row make a fence. Get sleep where you can. We start early."

The house set itself to night. The bunkhouse spilled laughter and a harmonica tune that couldn't quite find its key. The kitchen lamp went down to a low, faithful eye. Maisie moved like a prayer between stove and table, wrapping loaves in cloth and setting aside a plate with a note in her careful hand—*for Tom when he comes in.* Wes watched her a moment because a man's allowed that much watching in his own house, then took himself upstairs to put his body horizontal before his thoughts could get ideas.

In the dark, he listened for the sounds that told him whether a day had ended right: the soft click of the latch when Tom came in from last watch, the hushed run of water at the pump, the tiny countermelody of Junie's breathing beneath the low talk of the wind. He said the short prayer he had promised himself he'd keep plain, the one that had only two parts: *Lord, keep them. I'll do my part.*

From the north line, a bell lifted once, like a question. It did not ring again.

Wes smiled into the dark—a small thing, but a thing—and let sleep take him by the collar as if it knew who it had and was glad of it.

Chapter Twenty-Six

Maisie could not make her mind lie down, no matter how she smoothed the sheets.

The house had the hush of a place holding its breath. In the stove, a banked fire gave off a soft animal warmth; the lamp on her washstand threw an amber coin on the ceiling that trembled whenever a draft found a seam. She lay and counted heartbeats until she lost track, turned her pillow, turned it back, and finally gave in to the old habit that had carried her through a hundred fretful nights: check the child, touch the latch, make sure of the world with her hands.

Her ankle grumbled when she swung her feet to the floor— no sharp heat anymore, just the deep ache of mending. She unwound the linen, rubbed in a whisper of comfrey and marigold salve, then rewound it snug. Junie slept in the crib by the window, one fist tucked under her cheek like a cat's paw, mouth parted on a damp sigh. The night had kissed her hair into a dark curl at the nape; Maisie smoothed it back.

"I'm here," she whispered, though the little one needed no telling.

She turned the lamp lower and eased the door until only a finger's width of light bled into the hall. The stair gave up its old note under her careful weight—the same board always spoke on the fourth step from the top—and she paused, listening past the muted thud of her own blood. From the front room came voices. Not raised, but tight as wire pulled past prudence.

Jesse's first—measured, softened for the hour and the walls, but with an edge under the soft. "...not about pride, Wes. It's numbers. We can't pay men on principle."

Wes answered lower. "We won't buy quiet with our name. He's not getting an inch."

"If suppliers keep stalling, there won't be inches left to keep," Jesse returned, quieter. "We've three weeks' cushion, maybe. Zeke does more than talk."

Maisie should have walked on. These weren't words for her, though they bore on her life. She told herself she'd go fetch water and put her where she ought to be. Only her feet didn't take her, and the house carried one more sentence up the stairs:

"I'd fight him till frost, Wes," Jesse said, thread-thin. "I can't ask the hands to do the same if I can't tell them how they'll eat. There's a line between standing firm and starving stubborn."

A scrape of chair legs—Wes rising, she knew the sound—and then his voice, steady as a post sunk true. "There is. Saturday, we call the men to our yard. We show the books. We set coffee and bread. Tom at the gate. We take Cartwright's grace and Harlan Tate's early coin if we must. But I won't go hat in hand to Blackwell. That door don't stay on its hinges after it's opened."

Maisie's palm had gone damp on the rail. She could feel the truth of both men and the harm in each way.

Jesse added, softer still, "If he wanted only money, he'd be gone already. He wants her."

Maisie flinched so hard the newel kissed her shoulder. She had told herself it was only business. That had been a lie to make living easier. Jesse wasn't speaking cruelty; he was naming the thing plain, as he always did. Still, heat climbed her face.

Wes's answer came without a breath between. "He can want the moon. He won't have her. That's not the line we move."

They sank into quieter talk after that—bells and white flags on the north run, extra watch toward the willow swale, Sheriff Lane sending a deputy by at odd hours, Judge Markell hearing in ten days with Grayson's statement ready for Minnie to witness. That plain, practical sound should have steadied her. Instead, a slow guilt slid up under her ribs, cold as a shaded creek.

If she weren't here, would the feed man still be a friend? Would the ledger keep its neat columns without those rude slashes Jesse had inked and then gone over, careful and futile? Would men in town stop weighing a Calder coin, like it might turn to pine shavings on their palm?

She took the last stair and slipped by the parlor on the far side, keeping the hall table between herself and light. In the kitchen, she set a kettle over a whisper of blue flame and leaned her hip against the counter while the water thought about boiling.

Fear had been an old companion—useful as a sharp knife, dangerous as one too. It could cut a woman loose from a burning rope; it could cut her adrift from good land. Junie stirred the way she always did when the house went quiet—as if she kept a sheepdog's sense under her small ribs. Maisie took the kettle off early; it hissed like a scold. She climbed again with a warm mug, paused by the spare room to listen (only the child's small tide of breath), then sank to the runner outside her own door, the mug cooling between her palms.

You could leave, the old voice sneered. Take the child and slip before dawn. Find a wagon headed anywhere. A woman can vanish if she makes herself smaller than a stove and quieter than a door that needs oil.

And then what? her own voice—at last—answered. Run until your soles are bells and never ring? Let him set you down like a card and turn you to his use? Let Ivy's last breath be for nothing?

Footsteps came in the hall—light first (Eli when he was trying not to wake anyone), then the set step she could have picked out from a dozen men. Wes.

She swiped the heel of her hand under both eyes—some things were better done before a man saw them—and he was already folding himself to the floor beside her, as if he'd expected to find her at midnight against a wall all along.

"Couldn't sleep?" he asked.

She shook her head and looked at the baseboard as if it might answer for her.

He didn't fill the quiet. He set his shoulder to the plaster and rested his hands loose on his knees. In the thin spill of light, his face had fewer angles. The years sat quieter on him when the fight in him was put to bed for the night. He smelled like clean sweat, saddle soap, woodsmoke—the scent her body had come to file under *home* before her mind allowed it.

"I heard some of it," she said, because she had to say something or drown in not saying. "Not on purpose. I was—" She lifted the mug and let the rest live there.

"Walls carry what they please," he allowed.

"I know it isn't my business." She drew breath and went on before her nerve could leak away. "But it is my fault. The talk. The men turning skittish. The feed coming late unless coin's put down first. That all walked in with me."

"No," he said at once—so quick it stung her eyes. He set his palm flat on the plank between them, not touching her, but near enough the warmth of him reached. "It came because a small man with coin and no God in him wants what isn't his and found we are not offering. This ranch would still have teeth without you in our kitchen of a morning. He'd tell a different lie to make men wary."

"That makes me feel marginally better and no better at all," she said, and his breath huffed—agreement.

A bell on the north run spoke once—clean, thin, only wind in it. After three beats came another sound: two short whistles, one long. Tom's answer. All well. That simple exchange steadied her more than any speech.

"Jesse is right about some things," Wes said after a time, choosing each word like setting a stone not to wobble. "We can't eat pride. We can't ask hands to work on principle. So Saturday, we meet. We show figures. We ask men who've known our name longer than they've known Zeke's to remember. We take help that isn't poison. But I won't sign away what's not mine to give."

"The other?" she asked, though she knew and wanted it said to her face so she could tie it to herself.

He turned fully, met her eyes. "No truce with him. No paper that sets his hand on you or the child." He shook his head, small and final. "I'm not asking you to be brave for my pride, Maisie. I'm telling you what I can live with and still be the man Tom thinks my father raised."

Her throat went tight. Small words were all she had. "Thank you."

"And you," he added, as if the ledger wouldn't balance until he wrote that line. "You've been walking around like you were made of apologies. I won't have it. Having you here—" He stopped, took the sentence up careful. "I don't know that I deserve the sound this place makes with you in it, but I won't pretend it hasn't made the days better. For us all."

She took that in slow, as if it might spook if she moved too quick. "Eli told me today you needed something to come home to," she said. "I thought he meant a hot pot and a clean shirt. I think he meant something else."

"He meant not walking into a room and hearing nothing but my own footsteps," Wes said. He glanced toward the spare room—the narrow slice of lampglow, the small crib's shadow. "It's a mercy, that small hand in a cradle. Your tread on the stairs. Jesse cussing ink from his fingers. Rhett pretending not to laugh when Eli's joke is poor. Tom humming off-key on watch. Makes a place feel like God's taken up a chair."

A tear jumped her lashes and slid before she could blink it back. She scrubbed at it and let the foolishness stand. "I can't promise I won't have days I want to run anyway," she said. "I've been running a long time, Wes. It's a habit, like a limp you forget you've picked up until weather changes."

"If you run," he said—his voice rough at the edges—"tell me first. So I can put my boots on and go with you." He held her gaze until she stopped looking for a joke and found none. "I'd rather you stayed."

Her hand—traitorous, sudden—went to his sleeve. Cloth under her palm, warm man beneath. He didn't start or still; he let it be.

"I want to," she said. "Most hours. Then a horse throws its voice wrong, and I think about leaving every stitch behind. I feel a coward twice—once for wanting to go, again for wanting so badly to stay."

"Only men who've never watched a door all night think fear is cowardice," he said. "You've done braver things before breakfast than most do in a year, and no one saw to pin a ribbon on it. If there's a coward in the house, it isn't you."

"You're wrong," she said gently. "But I'll take the comfort."

The hall lamp made a small thrumming when its mantle shook. From below, the stove sighed the way a stove does when a man has treated it right. Junie rustled and settled; the world tugged her deeper.

"When my sister died," Maisie said, surprising herself, "I thought I'd used all my courage. I don't know when it started coming back. Maybe the first morning you made coffee like it mattered. Maybe when Tom carried the crib downstairs and Jesse pretended he did it for his own comfort. Maybe when Eli made Junie laugh so hard she hiccupped and I forgot to be afraid for a whole minute."

"Maybe when you decided to stay and told me on the porch," he said, and the memory of that breathy almost warmed the space like a second lamp.

She became aware of his nearness again—the breadth of him beside her, the steady in-and-out of his breath. Her thumb had gone to moving against his cuff without permission, a small back-and-forth like a hand that remembers rocking long after the baby sleeps. When she noticed, she meant to stop. She didn't.

"Maisie," he said, and he said her name like a prayer a man keeps short and plain.

She turned her face up and found his already turned toward hers. Respect in him was a live thing—you could feel it like heat before flame. He didn't come at her like a man takes; he waited like a man asks.

"If I'm wrong," he said, low, "tell me."

"You're not," she said.

There was no rush in the first fit of their mouths. He came that last small distance with a care that put a sting behind her eyes—one hand braced on the floor, the other a breath from her cheek, settling only when she leaned a fraction into it. The kiss was simple and steady. No lightning. The soft press of his lips, the way his breath hitched once as if the world had surprised him. She opened enough to tell truth without words. He answered the same.

When he drew back, it was by a small measure, just far enough to look, as if he needed to see what he'd done and who he'd done it to. His thumb—warm, careful—moved at her temple once, a stroke no one would ever know about but the two of them and God.

"All right?" he asked.

"Mm," she managed, too full for yes. She found herself smiling like a fool and let it be.

They didn't talk more. Sometimes language makes a thing smaller. They sat with their shoulders touching, and the part of her that had been hard as fence wire all winter softened around the edges. She set her head against his upper arm— not a surrender; a rest. He turned so the fit was better and leaned the whole of his weight into the wall so she could borrow it.

After a while, he said, "I don't know what comes next," and sounded more grateful than worried.

"We bake," she said, because she had to put her feet on something she knew. "Minnie will bring half the county if we ask. Jesse'll stand men at the table with his cleanest figures. Eli will charm those who don't want charming. Tom will sit where the willow opens and win at chess against himself."

"And you?" he asked.

"I'll make coffee till my hands smell like it a week. I'll hold the baby when talk turns sharp. I'll stand with a cloth ready for the spill that always comes when men decide they're not nervous anymore." She lifted her chin, set it in a way he'd come to know. "And I won't run."

He let out a sound that was not a laugh and not a prayer but a piece of both. "I'll take that."

From the fields, the cattle shifted like a sigh thrown wide. Far off, a bell jingled once as if a bird had lit and gone. Then the willow whispered and stilled.

Her ankle reminded her it was still a mending thing and not a miracle. He noticed before she spoke; of course he did. He rose first and set his hand out. When she took it, he drew her up slow, easy as water lifting a leaf. He didn't let go at once; she didn't ask him to.

"Sleep," he said—not an order, a kindness.

"You too," she returned, a woman allowed to pay kindness back in the same coin.

He saw her to her door and stood while she set the mug on the washstand. She looked once and found him still there, brim low, eyes steady. She raised a hand—good night, thank you, I'm here, all of it in a small motion—and he tipped his hat and went down the hall to the room he kept like a man who expects to leave in a hurry and hopes he won't.

Maisie eased the crib from the draft and tucked the quilt along Junie's side. Then she lay down and did a thing she hadn't managed in months: let her teeth unclench and her hands go still. The guilt was still there—guilt is a faithful dog— but it lay at her feet and didn't pace. Somewhere, a watcher's boot scuffed and paused. A low whistle—two short, one long— threaded the dark. Answered. All well.

"I won't run," she said into the quiet. If no one heard it but God, it was enough.

Sleep took her like a friend she'd been putting off, and the house, having held its breath long enough, let it go. The bells stayed silent. The night held.

Chapter Twenty-Seven

Wes came into the kitchen to the sound of a spoon against a crock and the soft murmur a woman makes to a child when the house isn't ready for talking yet.

Maisie stood at the table with her sleeves pushed to the elbow, hair braided and knotted low, ankle wrapped neat beneath her stocking. She moved careful, not favoring it so much as remembering it. Junie banged her palm against the table leg, pleased with the noise. The sight went through Wes like bread goes through a hungry man—quiet satisfaction, and something more.

Last night refused to be only a memory. It lived where a man keeps his breath: the feel of her hand finding his sleeve, the steady give of her mouth, the way she'd rested her head against his arm and let herself lean. The newness of it and the rightness, both at once. He'd slept short and deep after, like a watchman who trusts the next man on the line.

"Sit," Maisie said, catching his eye and not looking away, not pretending the night hadn't happened. She slid a plate toward him—hoecakes and a wedge of Mrs. Gable's pie that had somehow survived two days, a piece set aside like she'd known he'd need the sweetness. "You're riding the west line this morning?"

"Tom's got it," he said, taking the chair where he could see the door and the yard both. "I'll go later. Thought I'd give Jesse a hand with orders, then..." He let it trail. The shape of his day hadn't settled yet, but the part that mattered had. He couldn't stand still and let another man write the story of his house.

She read something of it on his face—she was getting quick at that. "You'll be careful," she said. Not a question. Not a rope. Just a truth she wished to nail to the day.

245

"I'll be careful," he returned, and the words didn't feel like a lie.

After he ate, he took Junie out to the cottonwoods and let her fist his shirt while he walked slow between the rows of drying harness. She had taken to him as if she'd been born for it, smiling around the thumb she never kept in her mouth long, reaching for the brim of his hat and missing it on purpose to hear him make a mock growl. When he set her down, she made for a sun stripe on the plank like a chick chasing a beetle. He scooped her back up before splinters could make a lesson of her hands.

"Give your aunt a quiet hour," he told her, and the child burbled as if she agreed.

He carried Junie in and passed her to Maisie. The touch that had been careful at first—always asking—is now the practiced pass they'd learned. Their fingers met and slid, and it was all he could do not to lean and take a second that wasn't his.

"I'll be an hour," he said, and caught Jesse on his way through the office. "You need anything from town?"

Jesse had ink on two fingers and a crease in his forehead that meant numbers and not headache. "Harness rivets, a box of twelve-penny nails, and—" he scanned his list "—liniment from Minnie's. We're down to the dregs. Tell Burke I meant what I said about the company a man keeps at his tables."

Wes tipped his hat. He didn't say he was already headed there before the words were spoken. "I'll keep it clean."

"Wes," Jesse said, as if stopping a wagon on a downhill would be easier than stopping his brother. He didn't add more. His eyes said it: lawful, steady, remember the hearing. Ten days. Grayson ready to sign. Minnie to witness. Sheriff Lane in the loop. Bells and white flags holding on the north run.

Wes rode in alone.

The road wore its usual summer quiet—grass high enough to whisper against the stirrups, meadowlarks throwing their bright little songs into the wide. In the willow swale, the lowest bell chimed once at his passing, then hushed. Down by the dry creek, a white rag caught and released the light like a fish turning. He breathed easier for the sight of them—signs that said *we see you* to friend and enemy both.

Twin Forks showed itself around a bend: false fronts catching sun, Burke's place wearing its fresh red paint as if the man hoped respectability could be nailed on like a trim, the smithy a square black mouth blowing honest smoke, Minnie's apothecary neat as a prayer. A freight wagon rattled past with oats for Tate's place; the driver touched his brim and didn't smile. Men took their cues from weather and talk both. The air had been wrong for days.

Wes tied Jeremiah at the rail before he thought about it and checked the Colt at his hip the way a man checks a latch he trusts—two fingers, a look, then hands down. He crossed the street with his hat pulled low enough to keep the worst of the glare and not so low he'd miss a face.

Sheriff Lane stood in the shade of the gaol porch, talking to Deputy Cole over a folded broadside. The sheriff's mustache twitched when he saw Wes, the nearest he got to surprise.

"You come to tell me you're keeping it clean?" Lane asked, dry.

"I come to tell you I'm going to speak to a man who's been soiling my name," Wes said. "I'll keep my hands where a judge would like them. If he doesn't."

Lane's eyes narrowed. "You've built sense enough not to give a rattler your ankle. Keep it that way. Cole'll be along a circuit in a bit. Don't make me wish he'd started with Burke's."

"Wouldn't dream of increasing your regret," Wes said, and that pulled an actual breath of a laugh from the lawman.

Inside Burke's, the light angled low and yellow, hanging dust cut by the piano's flat A that never held a tune. Burke polished a glass that didn't need it and watched everything without moving more than his wrist. Two card tables held cowhands trying their luck with small money and smaller chances. At the far end, in the corner where men drank to be seen drinking, sat Zeke Blackwell.

Eastern cloth, city cut, hat too new by half—Wes didn't need a tailor's eye to read a man. Zeke's vest was dove-gray, his necktie neat and small, his collar too stiff for a place like this, his boots unscuffed where it mattered. A ring flashed once when he lifted his glass—plain gold, not gaudy; money that didn't need to shout. Roy Danner leaned a hip at the bar with his face turned just so, letting the room catch enough of his profile to spell *danger* without having to hear it. The smell of cheap cigar lay around him the way a skunk lays claim to a ditch. Burke's gaze slid off Danner like water off old oil; a man has to pick his battles when his mortgage isn't paid.

Zeke saw Wes see him and smiled like a host greeting a guest at a supper he hadn't been invited to.

"Mr. Calder," he said before Wes could decide whether to stand or sit. "To what do I owe the pleasure? Do sit. We'll have Burke bring coffee so our tongues don't grow loose."

"I'll stand," Wes said. He put his hands on the back of the chair opposite, not to grip it, only to give them something to do that wasn't what they wanted.

"Have it your way." Zeke lifted his glass and sipped, the sort of pretend whiskey a man orders when he means to look like he belongs in a room and not lose the day to it. "How is the ranch? I've heard tell it's... stressed." He let the word sit on the table like a snake that might be a rope if a man squinted. "Many enterprises are these days. Hard to find good help."

"We've got the help we need," Wes said. "What we don't need is talk. You'll let it lie. The men you've bought to do your dirty work will take their pay elsewhere."

"Tsk." Zeke put down the glass so the ring would catch a slant of light. He didn't look at Danner, but the air swung toward him anyway. "Rumor is a wild thing, Mr. Calder. Can't be haltered once it finds a gap in the fence."

"You cut that gap," Wes said, voice even. "You set men to it. You told Burke's regulars I'd be late with coin. You told the feed driver to carry his load past my gate unless he saw money first. You told a buyer we weren't moving cattle this season when you know full well we've stock sound enough to pick and choose. You'll stop."

A card slapped too hard at the nearer table. Then the flat A from the piano. Life in a room goes on even while men throw down lines on the floor. Burke drifted nearer, not so near it would look like he was listening.

"My goodness," Zeke said, lightly. "You give a stranger a long list of misdeeds for a man you claim not to know." He reached to his waistcoat, drew out a watch, clicked it open, clicked it closed. "I am here on personal business. I have made no secret of that. A relative has gone missing—stolen, some would say— from her proper station. A child with her. A child I am... fond of." He settled on that word like he'd tried others and found them too much effort. "A man would do many things to see his family restored."

"You did many," Wes said. He didn't put Ivy's name in the room. That belonged to graves and kitchens, not to whiskey and dust. "You'll do no more here. You've got a judge to face in ten days' time if you care to make your case before someone who wears the law on his back and not just in his pocket. We'll have statements. Names. Dates. I wouldn't advise pushing your luck."

Zeke's smile slackened at the edges and sharpened in the middle. "You threaten me with *law*, Mr. Calder?" He made the word sound like something a man tracked in on his boot. "How quaint."

"Advice," Wes returned. "Threats make a mess of a man's life and the floor beneath him."

Danner's cigar hit the spittoon rim and clanged. He didn't look sorry. "Funny thing about threats," Danner said to no one and the whole room. "Men hear them even when you plain-spoken it."

"Roy," Zeke said, without moving his head. The single syllable held the leash tight.

Wes let his eyes pass the length of Danner's coat and back, slow, neither rising to it nor letting the bait settle. A deputy's badge flashed quick in the mirror behind the bar—Cole had stepped in, quiet as he could make a boot.

"You're a long way from Albany," Wes said to Zeke. "Why now? Why this?"

Zeke spread two fingers, gentle and useless. "I am, as ever, a concerned man. A husband put in a poor light by rumor, a father seeking the return of a child. Some of us care for our name."

"You can leave mine out of your mouth," Wes said. He kept it calm; he kept it clean. "You carry on your talk and the feed comes late again because of it, I'll bring it to Lane and Markell both. And I'll bring it with proof."

"Proof?" Zeke set his elbows on the table and made a church of his hands. "What proof does a—" he swallowed a word, chose another "—rancher have that the wind blew ill from a particular window? Men decide what they think of a family. Nothing to do with a gentleman like me. I am, after all, only inquiring after a little girl whose aunt has... confused matters. I'm sure you know how a woman's judgment can go sideways under stress."

Wes felt his jaw want to set. He let it, a little. "I know a woman who's carried more than most men could lift and not lost her judgment once."

"Stolen property makes a poor weight to boast of," Zeke said softly, and that turned even Burke's head.

Cole took a step, slow. Burke's hand closed around the glass he'd been polishing. Danner smiled like he smelled a fight a mile off and had been jogging to catch it.

Wes straightened his hands on the chair back until his knuckles remembered their work and not their wanting. "Say that again," he told Zeke. Not loud. Not a dare. A request a man makes so he can be certain what needs doing.

Zeke's eyes glinted with something that made the hair along Wes's arms take stock. "A child belongs to her father. If you've taught the county to call a thief 'aunt' and a stolen thing 'daughter,' that is your misfortune, not mine. You are harboring what is mine. You are interfering with my household. You are a trespasser, Mr. Calder, and a bully besides."

The room held the words the way a barn holds heat. Wes let them be what they were—lies dressed as law. He pictured Judge Markell's neat hand on a docket, Sheriff Lane's slow pen scratching, Minnie's witness signature precise as stitching. He pictured Maisie's mouth soft in the lamplight, the trust she'd put in him a few hours back, the small weight of a sleeping child in a crib by the stove.

"You're done," he said. "You stop the talk. You call your dogs off our wire. You keep your boots off my dirt. You bring whatever paper you believe you have into Markell's hearing, and we'll meet you there. You come by my place between now and then, and you'll find more law than you care to carry."

Zeke rose, enjoying the stage. He set his palms flat on the table as if he'd push it through the floor. "Listen to yourself," he said, louder now, for the room. "A man of the soil playing at court. You've had too much dust and not enough sense. You think this town will choose *you* over a father? Over money? Over—"

"Over truth," Wes said.

Zeke's smile went thin as wire. He leaned in until the starch in his collar creaked. "A word of advice, rancher: a wise man counts his losses. You've got cattle going light, fences getting thin, and neighbors who don't want trouble. Give me what's mine, and I'll stop tapping your ledger until it sings."

"I'll see you in ten days," Wes said, and loosened his hands from the chair. "Or not at all."

He turned because he meant to keep his own word to Lane. He had made his line and set it in front of witnesses. There was nothing to gain by letting a man like Zeke pull him into a dance he'd practiced all his life.

"Running already?" Danner called, cheerful as a coyote. "Why, we were just getting friendly."

"Roy," Zeke said again, a leash tightening.

Wes put a shoulder to the swing door and let daylight find him. The street had the ordinary noon of a small place—two boys knotting rope for a trick they'd never tie right, a woman shading a jar of penny candy in her apron as she crossed from the mercantile, a team backing a wagon at the livery with more noise than need. He stepped clear of the threshold so he wouldn't be a silhouette a fool could shoot for sport.

Cole's reflection in Burke's window showed the deputy angling to take the corner where he could see both room and street. Lane, across the way, had put a hand to the butt of his revolver in a way that wasn't yet a draw.

A single sound split the day:

A gunshot.

Chapter Twenty-Eight

The bell on the north run chimed once—sharp and out of season—and a heartbeat later, the yard filled with the hard thunder of hooves.

Maisie was out of the chair before her breath caught up. The shawl slid from her shoulders and fell, forgotten, across the rocker's arm. She made the porch in three careful steps despite the tug in her ankle and arrived in time to see Jeremiah's dark shoulder lunge into the yard and check. Wes was in the saddle, pitched forward, his hand sunk into the mane like a man hanging on to the side of a river.

Blood streaked down his trouser leg, dark where it had soaked, bright where fresh. Jesse and Rhett rode hot behind him, pulling up sharp and spilling dust. Eli came from the barn at a run, caught Jeremiah's reins, and set his shoulder to the gelding's chest to steady the animal.

"Kitchen," Jesse snapped, already off his horse and reaching up. "Get him down."

Wes tried to shift on his own and nearly slid to the ground. Maisie was already there, hands up. "Lean," she said—no tremor in her voice, only instruction. "On me. Now."

His weight found her forearm. For a second, they were cheek to shoulder, the heat of him and the wild pace of his breath across her temple. His jaw was tight as a cinch. He didn't swear. He didn't make a sound beyond that breath. Rhett got under the other arm. Between them, they made the door.

The room took them in—table cleared with one sweep, lamp turned up, kettle dragged to the hearth for boiling. Tom's boots hit the threshold a beat later; he'd been on patrol between pump and gate and came at the bell's single note like he'd been called by name. He shut the door behind them with the heel of his hand, cut the yard off, and the kitchen became a place for work.

"Lay him out," Maisie said. "Jesse, fire high under the big kettle. Eli—clean rags. Anything white. Rhett, knife from the drawer, the one that holds an edge. Tom—hold his shoulders if he kicks. We'll need whiskey if there's any left."

No one argued. No one asked who'd put her in charge. They moved the way men move when a woman's voice carries the right sense in it. The table took Wes's weight with a groan that made Maisie's teeth set. She shoved her sleeves to the elbow. The cotton slid and stuck to her forearms. Heat pulsed in her ankle; she planted the foot and forgot it.

"Through-and-through?" Tom asked, voice level, like he was asking after the weather.

Wes's mouth twitched. "Flesh," he got out. "Thigh. Caught me stepping off Burke's. Cole answered. Not—" He hissed once. "Not deep."

Maisie's gaze cut to him, then down. She slit the trouser leg with the knife Rhett slapped into her palm and folded the cloth back. The wound sat high on the outer thigh, a mean groove dug along the muscle, bleeding fast but not jetting. No arterial pulse. The back of her neck cooled. Not clean, not small—but not the kind of red that pumps a man empty before you can fetch a prayer.

"Boil the needle," she said. "Thread. My pouch—top drawer by the flour, blue cord. There's strong linen in it. The needle case is wrapped in red."

Jesse went for it. Eli dumped a heap of rags across the table and knocked a mug into the basin with his hip. It shattered. No one flinched.

Maisie pressed the heel of her clean hand above the worst of the bleeding and leaned in with steady pressure, counting to ten and then to ten again, letting the cut weep and then settle. Heat slid against her skin and ran down to her wrist. She closed the sight of it off and made her world smaller: the press of her palm; the slow give of the vessel beneath; the rise and fall at Wes's ribs under his shirt. He stared at the ceiling, jaw locked, tendons in his neck standing.

"Easy," she said, not knowing if she meant him or herself. "Easy there."

Tom slid a folded towel under Wes's head, his big hands light on the shoulders that had carried more than their share. "Who fired?" he asked, not to pry, only to set the shape of things.

"Not from inside," Wes said through his teeth. "Rooftop. Alley angle. Cole was quicker. I rode while Lane kept the peace."

"Good," Tom said. "Let the law carry its end."

The kettle rattled to a boil. Jesse held the needle in the steam with tongs, turned it, held it again until it shone. He fed the linen through with careful fingers, his ink-stained hand steady as a scribe's. Eli found the bottle of whiskey and broke the wax with his thumb. That clean, hard smell cut the room.

Maisie washed her hands in water so hot it made her bite her lip, then poured whiskey over them and over the wound. Wes made no sound, but the muscle under her palm jumped.

"Sorry," she murmured, and meant it.

"Do it right," he said, the words shaped around breath. "Don't be sorry."

She took a breath and set to it. The first stitch is always the hardest—first bite through skin, the tug, the way the flesh answers and says *you're here*. She bit clean, set the knot snug, and kept the line near. She'd mended split palms and barked knees, one neighbor boy's cheek after a mule took to him, but not this. Not a man she knew by the sound of his step and the curve of his hand at a child's back. Her fingers did not learn new work; they remembered what matters.

"Talk to me," she said to anyone who wasn't the needle. "Say anything."

"Burke claims ignorance," Rhett offered, voice low. "Says he don't hire the souls of men who sit their tables."

"Lane sent Cole after the roof," Jesse said, as if to the ledger. "Said the livery's boy saw two men split. One limped, one laughed. If there's justice in the world, that one's tongue rots."

Tom shifted his grip at Wes's shoulder and gave a slow count under his breath, not to ten, not to any number a man might break on—more like a hymn's measure.

The bleeding slowed under her hands as the edges came together. The groove was angry and ragged at one end where the bullet had kissed hardest, but it was honest muscle and not a gut, not an artery. She set the last knot flat and clean and cut the thread with the quick pinch of her nail. The back of her neck went cold again, this time with relief. She rinsed the whole with whiskey and then with cooled water, pressed a clean cloth, and wrapped the thigh snug in fresh linen, firm enough to hold, not so hard it would throb more than it had to.

"Done," she said, and only then did she feel the tremor in her own fingers. She set the bloody cloths in a basin, more by feel than sight.

Wes let out a breath that had been sitting in him since the door. His eyes found hers, blue gone dark, steadier now that the worst was tied off. "You do good work," he said, voice roughened by pain and the bite of whiskey.

She wanted to laugh and cry and hit him for riding home with all that blood—wanted to put her mouth on the line of his jaw and tell him not to be brave for her sake ever again. Instead, she wiped a streak from his knee with the corner of a clean rag and said, businesslike, "You'll keep off it or you'll split every stitch. You hear me?"

"Yes, ma'am," he said, and the corner of his mouth tried to make something like a smile of it.

Eli uncorked the whiskey again, but Tom shook his head. "Small," he said. "He'll need his wits if Lane comes to ask where to write his report."

"Small," Maisie echoed. "And only if the pain shoves."

Wes swallowed a token mouthful and coughed once, the sound quickly swallowed by the pulse that still thudded in the room—the kettle's soft rattle, the lamplight's hiss, the breath of men turning from fury to steadiness.

"More water," she said. "And—Jesse—if there's any laudanum, a thumb's worth. Not more." She met his eyes. "He'll need sleep to heal."

Jesse nodded and went to the cupboard where they kept unlucky medicines. He brought the small dark bottle like it offended him, and poured the careful measure into a spoon. Wes made a face but took it without argument.

Tom eased his grip, testing, and when Wes didn't thrash or stir, he let his hands fall away. "Whoever shot didn't follow," Tom said to the room at large. "Bells had only the one note—arrival, not chase. I'll take another loop. Rhett, trade with me at the willow in an hour."

"I'll take two," Rhett said, bristling for a fight he'd been told not to have. "Then wake Eli."

"Lawful," Wes said without lifting his head. The one word leveled the room. "Keep it lawful."

"We hear." Rhett planted his fists on his hips like he could keep them from balled into the next thing.

A knock sounded quick at the back door, then a voice, woman-clear. "I brought what I had." Minnie didn't wait to be invited. She slid in, bustle and bottle, hair a little wind-fussed beneath her bonnet. She took the room in at a glance: the blood, the basin, the man on the table too pale by half, the woman with whiskey on her hands and linen threads stuck to her sleeve.

"I was on the square when Cole ran past," she said, setting a satchel on the counter. "Thought I'd be needed. Hello, Eli." She did not look at him again. He colored anyway, caught in the act of feeling relieved to see her and ashamed to be relieved.

Maisie's shoulders let down a fraction. "I cleaned and stitched," she said, the words coming out as fact, not apology. "Through-and-through along the outer thigh. No pulse. Bleeding's slowed."

Minnie's gaze went warm. "You did fine." She had a way of making those words feel like a benediction. "Let's add what I can." She drew out a brown-glass bottle and a folded packet. "Carbolic." She wrinkled her nose. "Smells like a sin, but it saves stitches. Calendula for the outer edges—later, not now. We'll keep it simple. Clean dressings twice a day. Cool water if it swells. No salves on the fresh wound. Not yet."

She dabbed carbolic around the sutures with a bit of lint, quick and precise. Wes hissed once; Maisie set her hand near his elbow, not touching, only there. Minnie's hand was sure and light. She had a nurse's calm and a shopkeeper's speed.

"Sheriff Lane?" Maisie asked without lifting her eyes from the work.

"In his office when I left," Minnie said. "Sent Cole to fetch a name. Burke swears he knew nothing. He swears too much. But this—" she glanced at Wes's leg "—this will read better than all his swearing. The judge will want to see the mark."

"The judge will see it," Wes said. The laudanum was starting to sand his edges. "Ten days."

"Ten days," Minnie echoed, binding the clean wrap with a neat tuck. "You'll keep your stitches that long if you do as you're told."

Eli coughed like a man who'd swallowed dust. "He can be taught."

"Can he?" Minnie arched a brow. "You can set a bell on his boot if you like, and I'll listen for every time he puts it down where it doesn't belong."

Rhett snorted. Jesse's mouth quirked. Even Tom let a corner of his beard hide a smile.

"Out," Maisie said, soft but with a pointedness that had every man in the room hearing a broom behind it. "All but Jesse. I'll need a hand moving him to bed. Minnie—thank you for coming. Will you...?"

"I'll leave what you need." Minnie tucked the bottle and packet back into her satchel and set a smaller roll of bandage beside the lamp. Her hand brushed Eli's sleeve as she passed him; the touch lasted no more than a breath and carried a book's worth of quiet. "You send for me if the fever so much as thinks of starting," she told Maisie. "I'll be back by sundown."

The door took her and her rosewater with it. Eli ran a hand over his hair as if he could smooth the feeling she left. "I'll spell Tom first," he said, voice brisk in a man's effort not to sound like anything else. He went.

They moved Wes with care—Tom under one shoulder, Jesse and Rhett at the hips and legs, Maisie walking backward to keep the bandage from catching on the table's rough edge. It took time and the kind of patience you only find when there's no alternative, but at last they got him to the spare room where the crib had sat since Tom hauled it down. They settled him into the bed he'd turned down himself a hundred nights without thinking it would ever hold him as a patient.

"Up," Maisie said. "Just enough to set the bolster." He obeyed without argument, and she slid the extra pillow beneath the thigh to keep it above the heart. She smoothed the sheet and the light blanket and counted the stitches with her fingers through the cloth, not because she doubted the number, but because the counting steadied her.

The men went out by unspoken agreement, one by one, taking the noise of boots and breath and worry with them. Jesse lingered at the threshold. "Lane'll be by," he said. "I'll meet him at the yard and keep it short."

"Tell him I'll talk," Wes said, eyes half-lidded. "Not now. Later."

"We'll keep it lawful," Jesse returned, and clicked the door nearly shut.

The quiet that fell wasn't empty. It held the kettle's low hum from the kitchen, the faint baby-breath from the cradle tucked near the warm of the stove down the hall, the yard's small noises coming in under the sash. Maisie sat on the edge of the bed and looked at the man who had ridden home bleeding and tried to stand under his own power so she wouldn't have to see him fall.

"You should be horse-whipped," she said, and her voice wanted to shake. It didn't.

"For coming back?" He tried for that corner-smile again and didn't make it.

"For being shot in town like a fool when you promised me careful."

"I said I'd be careful," he said. "Not charmed."

Her eyes stung sudden and stupid. She set her hand on the sheet near his and flattened it so the shake wouldn't show. He turned his palm and covered her fingers with his own, warm and too steady for a man with stitches.

"Wasn't inside," he said, softer now that the work was done and the laudanum had loosened both tongue and guard. "Door swung, light hit wrong. Man on a roof somewhere behind Burke's misjudged his hurry. Cole was quicker. I left before the room learned to lie about what it had seen." His thumb moved once against her knuckle, absent, a man remembering that a hand in his needed answering. "I told him I'd keep it clean. I kept it as clean as a bullet will allow."

"You told me you'd come back," she said. The shaking had gone from her voice, but she heard it in her bones. "You did. But if that bullet had caught higher, or deeper—" She stopped. Words weren't big enough to hold the shape of that fear. She breathed it instead.

"I'm here," he said. "Because you set your hands where they needed to be and didn't blink."

"For that, thank the Lord," she said, and meant it plain. "And a little for Minnie's stink-water."

"That too."

They were quiet a long breath. The lamplight painted the line of his cheek and the worn place at his collar. He looked younger like this, and older, both at once—youth in the slack of his mouth when pain wasn't pulling at it, age in the set of his brow that said a man has made choices and intends to stand by them.

"Wes," she said, and the name made something tender in her chest ache, "they aimed to hurt you. Not scare. Not warn. Hurt."

"Then we were right to set bells and flags and paper besides," he said. "Right to keep to the law and not the fist." His fingers tightened over hers, the only sign that the thought of not being able to stand up to the next thing had crossed him and been told to wait. "Lane'll write. Markell will hear. Grayson will sign. Minnie will witness. We'll stack truth higher than talk and higher than money if we must. And we'll keep the watch."

"We," she repeated. The word felt like a tether thrown into good hands.

"You," he said, and his voice went rough again, not from pain. "You keep being here when I walk in the door."

She didn't trust her mouth for that answer, so she gave him her other hand, the one she hadn't known what to do with since he'd been carried through the door. He took that, too, and held both as if the act held weight equal to stitches.

Junie fussed down the hall, the small cat-sound she made when a dream jostled her into the edge of waking. Maisie rose half an inch, and he tightened his hands in answer. "Go," he said. "I've got practice at lying still."

She hovered long enough to tuck the sheet at his hip and to set the water glass where his hand would find it without hunting. "I'll be back."

"Count on it," he murmured, already slipping toward the kind of sleep a man falls into when the danger is over and the cost starts to be counted.

She found Junie blinking at the ceiling, astonished to be a person again. Maisie scooped her and pressed her face into the warm curve of the child's neck, breathing in the milk-sweet, clean smell that had anchored her to this house from the first day. Junie patted her cheek with a damp palm and then stuffed those fingers into her mouth like the world would go quiet if she filled it.

"Your uncle is ridiculous," Maisie whispered, rocking without thinking near the open stove where the lamp made a low gold. "But he is ours. And he is staying."

By the time Jesse came back with Sheriff Lane in his hat and Cole behind him in his dust, Wes slept. Lane made his voice small in a large man's body. "We'll take it later," he said at the sight. "I'll set it down clean. You tell him I expect him to put words to it tomorrow. Not today."

"We will," Jesse said.

Cole's gaze landed on the strip of trouser that had been cut away. He reached without asking and picked it up with two fingers. "May I?" he asked then, because he remembered whose kitchen he stood in.

"Keep it," Maisie said. "He bled enough into it a judge might feel the weight."

Cole nodded. "We have a mark on a roof rail and one on a rain barrel. Burke's porch post caught a splinter that looks like a second shot hit wood. We'll bring what we have."

"Bring it," Jesse said. "We'll have papers of our own."

Lane tipped his hat to Maisie in a gesture that amounted to respect. "You did good," he said simply, then took his deputy and his dust back out.

The door shut. The house took in the new quiet and made it part of itself.

Rhett came in from the willow to trade watches with Tom and paused at the threshold to look toward the spare room where the lamp still made a square of light on the floor. "He breathing?" he asked, hushed like a church.

"He's breathing," Maisie said. "He'll live to be more trouble."

"Good." Rhett grinned without showing teeth, a flash of boy in the man. He held up something that looked like an insult to the nose. "Eli said we ought to leave these near the worst breaks." Two cheap cigars sat in his palm. "Bait. Stink might carry farther than a bell."

"Don't smoke them near the baby," Maisie said, which made Rhett laugh outright and go back out into the dark, the smell trailing him like a challenge.

She saw to the last of the bloody water, added a log to the fire's low blue, and set fresh bandage rolls where her hand could find them if the night asked. Her ankle reminded her of itself when she straightened. She moved slow up the stairs, Junie heavy and welcome on her shoulder.

At the landing, she paused and looked back. Somewhere by the willow, a bell ticked once against the moving air and then went dumb again. Tom's tread came and went, came and went, solid as his word. In the room below, Wes slept with laudanum's help and the knowledge of being kept. The map Jesse had sketched lay on the table with Xs where bells swung and white flags would show new cuts by lantern.

She pressed her mouth to Junie's hair. "We will not run," she said into the curls, making it a promise older than fear. "We will stand up straight and tell the truth."

It wasn't an oath shouted in a yard or hammered into a table. It was the kind a woman makes in a warm kitchen with a sleeping child and a man she has just sewn back together under her roof.

By the time the moon lifted clean over the barn, Maisie had washed her hands until the water ran clear, mended two shirts not because they needed it but because her fingers did, and written, in a small, neat hand Jesse would approve, the names and dates the judge would want when he asked who had seen her with the child and when. She set the paper on top of Jesse's stack so it wouldn't be lost.

Then she went back to the spare room. Wes lay where she'd left him, breath even. She sat again on the edge of the bed and listened to the sound of being alive—the small catch at the end of an inhale, the release that followed. She slid two fingers under the blanket and found the pulse at his wrist. It beat steady against her touch. She whispered thanks for it without dressing the prayer in words.

His fingers curled, even in sleep, and found hers. He didn't wake. He only held on, the way a man does when he knows what he'd almost lost and what he still means to keep.

"Rest," she told him.

Chapter Twenty-Nine

Zeke Blackwell had not come to Twin Forks to drink with ranch hands.

He sat where a man of means sat—back corner of Burke's, facing the room, mirror behind the bar giving him the door and the street in one glance. Fresh shirt. Plain knot at the throat. Coat brushed by noon. The coffee cooling beside his elbow was for posture, not thirst. Respectability took tending.

The room moved around him—cards slapping soft, Burke polishing his conscience into the walnut, talk rolling like a lazy creek. Zeke let it pass. He had set a better current in town: whispers about unpaid bills, a buyer who found reason to ride south, a feed wagon that came late and shrugged. Rumor cost less than men and traveled farther. He hadn't needed a fresh cut in fence wire in days.

Only one thing had gone crooked—the shot that nicked Wes Calder. He had not ordered that. He gave aims, not noise. Now the sheriff's attention had woken, and the law, once alert, had a habit of writing things down. Annoying, but manageable. A wounded man bent the house around him. Bend a house long enough, and it broke when you leaned.

The batwings shook and clapped.

She came in on the echo—a small woman for a big room, plain dress, hair pinned to keep, not to show. The light from the street made a square on the floor and set her in it as if a photograph had been framed for him. Zeke had expected some version of this. People like Maisie Ward mistook resolve for victory, as if stubbornness could settle a ledger.

She didn't look around. She came straight to his table.

"Mr. Blackwell," she said.

He might have smiled, but smiles spent coin he preferred to save. He only lifted the cup and let cold coffee touch his lip. "Mrs. Calder," he returned, mild. He liked the new name; it reminded listeners she'd changed hands.

Color rose at her throat and stopped there. "Leave them alone," she said, voice even, as if they were discussing the price of flour. "The Calders did you no harm. This is my quarrel with you, not theirs."

Burke's rag slowed. Cards paused mid-air. Zeke kept his eyes on her and not on the men who suddenly found the floorboards worth studying.

"Strong words," he said. Admiration disarmed; he could sound admiring on command. "You forget yourself. You forget the child."

"I haven't forgotten Junie." Her jaw steadied. "I'm not giving her to you. But you don't have to keep picking at their fences and their business to get what you want. You want me. Say it plain. Then say what leaves them be."

He admired the shape of her logic even as he located where it would break. She believed that because she had put herself between two things, bullets would alter their course out of courtesy. It was sweet in a girl. In a woman, it was tiresome.

"Your sister taught you poor lessons," he said, and let a thread of softness into his tone, the way a teacher corrects a pupil. "She ran. She failed. She died of it. I am collecting what is mine. It is a simple sentence to understand."

At Ivy's name—he never called her *your sister*; he rarely called her *my wife*—Maisie's mouth tightened. Good. He'd found a seam to press later.

He was setting his fingers to it when the batwings banged again.

Pike Hart came in like a wind that had gone stale—too quick, hat shoved back, eyes bright with need. Zeke used Pike for work that could not survive daylight. Men like that were useful until they wanted to be paid for the wrong thing—noise instead of result.

"Blackwell," Pike said, seeing only the corner, only the man in it. "You promised silver."

Zeke didn't stand. He didn't raise his voice. "I promised pay for tasks completed," he said. "You failed me twice. First with a cut that drew the sheriff's eyes. Then with a shot that bought me a deputy's questions."

Pike laughed, thin as a blade. "The cattle moved. The man bled. You got your smoke." He hooked a thumb at Burke without turning. "Ask him. I moved quick. Your kind of quick."

Zeke let silence do the work. It made men like Pike wonder how far they'd overstepped.

"You're not paid for trouble," he said at last. "You're paid for results."

Pike's grin soured. He needed a thing to take; he always did. He closed the space to the nearest body in two long strides. Before she could turn, he had his fingers around Maisie's arm. The room made a noise like a dog thinking about barking—and decided not to. Saloon courage seldom showed up when useful.

"She's my payment, then," Pike said. "Send a man with coin if pride stings you."

Zeke stood.

No haste. He stood the way a man stood who expected obedience. Heat walked behind his eyes—not for the woman, but for the humiliation of being forced to watch someone else's crude theater on his stage. She was leverage. Used well, it lifted a world. Used poorly, it split the fulcrum. Pike had put a dirty hand on a lever Zeke had meant to pull with clean gloves.

"Unhand her," Zeke said, and dropped gentility from his voice.

Pike turned his head just enough to lay a grin across the room. "She came to you," he crowed. "Seems she made up the mind you kept teasing."

Maisie jerked free without a sound. Zeke marked the set of her jaw with a small, bitter appreciation. He had once told Ivy he admired a firm mouth. Ivy had answered with silence then, too.

"Mr. Hart," Zeke said—giving the man back his name, as if admitting him to a parlor—"you misunderstand business and courtesy both." He stepped so the lamplight cast him clean, the boards and the men on them invited to witness. "Take your hand off her and walk outside."

Pike loved a dare more than coin. He squeezed once—enough to leave a mark—and shoved her toward the batwings. "Outside suits," he said. "Less talk."

Zeke followed because there was no choice. Humiliation walked ahead of him, dragging its feet. Burke polished nothing in particular. Cards began slapping again. In the mirror, Zeke disliked the tightness at his mouth. Recoverable, he told himself. Control could be repurchased.

Evening had dropped over Main Street. Dust made a low cloud under the lamps. Men on the boardwalk watched with the small eagerness of those who pay nothing to see and owe nothing to help. Minnie Abbott stood three doors down, bonnet askew, basket at her hip. When she saw Maisie, she took one step forward before twenty years of careful living pulled her back. Useful. Witnesses had their uses.

Pike dragged the moment because dragging made him feel tall. He caught Maisie's arm again. She didn't stumble. That angered him; he preferred prizes that broke easy.

Zeke moved until his shoulder stood slightly ahead of Pike's, his shadow falling where it should, making the smaller man seem to walk in his light. "Unhand Mrs. Calder," he said, pitched for the boards, for Burke's doorway, for every ear not meant to be listening. "She has business with me."

"Your turns," Pike said. "My pay." He spat dust. "She's worth more than silver if the talk's true."

The talk. Once his instrument, now a stick in another's hand. He swallowed the bile the word raised.

"Burke," Zeke said, not turning, "fetch Sheriff Lane and tell him Pike Hart laid hands on a lady against her will." He did not expect Burke to move. That wasn't the point. He wanted the sentence said in public, the kind you could quote later when it served. Appearances were a country a man like him ruled without soldiers.

Pike jerked Maisie off the boards into the narrow between Burke's and the livery. She did not cry out. That more than anything made fury come clean. A woman's courage writing over his script—it offended him.

"Enough," he said, and stepped down after them.

The alley held the day's heat like old breath. One lamp made a coin of light in the dust. Pike had a fistful of her skirt now. He would have torn it if it meant speed. He thought in short, ugly words—cart, rope, pay.

Zeke caught him by the collar and hauled him back hard enough to salt his tongue with his own blood.

"Touch her again," he said low, forcing the man to lean to hear, "and I cut you out of this entirely." He did not say *pay*. He said *this*—the whole enterprise: rumors, fences, bought men, and men who thought they weren't. "You are a tool. Greedy tools rust."

Pike went still, but only to count angles. He remembered he had a pistol. He liked being the first to remember. The cocking made a small clock sound. He didn't aim at Zeke. He wasn't that stupid. He aimed at imagined shapes—sheriff conjured by Burke's name, brothers coming fast, a night watch with a whistle. "Cut me," he said, "after I'm paid."

Maisie eased until the livery wall found her shoulders. Her hands went behind to feel for a rail, a tack box, anything that made the ground more hers than his. The lamplight glanced off the edge of a wrap under her skirt. The ankle wasn't healed fully. Zeke pocketed the knowledge like a small knife.

He also saw Minnie at the alley mouth, small as a wren, eyes burning, hand pressed to her throat. She met Maisie's gaze and shook her head once—women's language for *I see. I'll fetch help. Keep breathing.*

"Properly," Zeke said, gathering the scene back into his hands. "You"—to Pike—"fetch the small buckboard from the back. Mrs. Calder and I will speak where saloon walls don't have ears. You will follow at a distance. If you are seen, you are not paid."

He turned to Maisie then, because men like Pike followed a line of sight like a rein. "Madam," he said, with restored gentility, "you will be treated with respect. I regret this man's rudeness."

"You regret nothing," she said.

"I regret inefficiency."

She looked past him toward the street, toward the line where help might appear. The movement tugged on something in him like a hook. He refused to name it.

Pike brought the buckboard—single axle, a sway to it, the kind livery boys rent cheap. He had the reins and a grin he thought was smart. Zeke stepped as if to offer a gentleman's hand. He intended to take the bench first and let courtesy cover custody.

"Maisie," Minnie said from the alley mouth, voice low and tight. "Hold a moment—"

Pike clicked his tongue and let the horse lurch, blocking the line between the women. Zeke shot him a look worth coin later.

"This is the place you chose," Maisie said, and climbed without his hand.

Zeke followed, set the brake with a neat click, brim lowered so lamplight made respectable angles of his face. "Drive," he told Pike, not looking at him. "Not fast. Not slow."

They came out on Main Street exactly as he'd scripted it if he'd had time: a gentleman with a lady for air, a second wagon trailing. Men glanced and glanced away. Burke stood in his doorway like a toad watching rain. Minnie turned on her heel and moved with a purpose that would outrun fear—toward the one man Zeke did not want in this night's business.

His jaw set. Humiliation had weight; he made a plan out of it, the thing he knew how to do with feelings that refused to be efficiently spent.

"You are very calm," he told the woman beside him.

"I am very tired," she said. "There's a difference."

He almost laughed. He almost admired her. He did neither. Admiration and laughter were waste, and he had learned long ago, under a silver-handled cane, what waste earned.

They skirted the freight yard where wagons slept like hulks. The river to their right told itself its long dark story. Wheels found and left ruts. Pike drove like a man counting his own breath instead of the horse's.

"You will have your audience," Zeke said. "You will say your piece. I will say mine. Then you will put it to paper that the child is better kept by the man who can afford to keep her."

She turned her head a degree. "That man is already keeping her."

He touched the brake, two notches, just to feel control bite. "You mistake a moment's shelter for a life," he said. "One is cheap. The other is dear."

"Sometimes the dear thing is the one you can't put a price on," she said.

He had no tidy answer. He chose to be irritated by the lack of tidiness rather than by the truth under it.

They crossed the little bridge where cottonwoods threw long shadows. Zeke lifted a finger, and Pike turned up an old freight spur toward a storage shed men used when they didn't want questions.

Light moved ahead—lanterns, more than one. Boots behind the light had weight: the sound of men who knew where they were going, not towners trying on courage. Zeke did not turn. He didn't give the lights the courtesy of acknowledging them.

"Keep straight," he said to Pike, calm as a ledger line. To Maisie, under his breath: "If you want your gentlemen to remain gentlemen, advise them to leave the law to the law."

She didn't answer.

The lanterns came on at the jog—two men only, not the sheriff, not yet. One was Burke's boy trying to look useful. The other was a deputy with more shine on his badge than sense in his eyes, likely sent on ahead by Lane while the sheriff gathered a stouter knot. Fine. Zeke could work with that. Appearances again.

"Evening, Mr. Blackwell," the deputy said, breath quick. "You'll step down with the lady."

Zeke set his hands on his knees, feeling the seam's bite. He turned his head enough to show respect without ceding the bench. "Deputy," he said. "Mrs. Calder wished to speak in private about her sister's child. If Sheriff Lane prefers such talk in his office, I'll oblige him next time."

That sentence would read well later.

Pike's shoulders hitched. He didn't like deputies. He liked being the man in charge of his own foolishness. He kept the reins, and his hand slid near the pistol at his belt like a habit.

"Reins on the rail," the deputy said, more bravado than ballast.

Zeke did two things at once. He lifted his hand off Maisie's knee—he'd set it there light as a paperweight when the lanterns appeared, not a threat, a posture—and he turned his face so only the deputy caught the next line. "See to Mr. Hart first," he murmured. "He's the one likely to point iron where he shouldn't."

Pike heard his name and made the mistake men like him make when their names are spoken with authority: he moved. The pistol gave a tiny, idiot click.

"Don't," Zeke said without heat. "We are done with noise."

For a heartbeat, no one breathed.

Then Minnie's voice carried thin from the road, sharp with sense: "Wes is coming."

Zeke felt the night tilt, not with fear, but with the nuisance of a stage gaining actors he hadn't cast. He could still win the scene—win it in the only way that mattered to him: on paper and in the mouth of the judge. But the clean, private abduction had been ruined the moment Pike laid a filthy hand on a lady in a public doorway.

He made the calculation he should have made twenty minutes earlier and cut the loss.

"Drive," he told Pike softly. "Now."

Pike flicked the reins. The horse lurched. The buckboard leapt into the shadow of the spur road. The deputy swore and stumbled. Burke's boy did nothing useful. Minnie's running footsteps took the main track toward the ranch—toward the men Zeke least wanted on this spur.

Maisie's fingers tightened on the edge of the bench. She didn't speak. He did not mistake her silence for surrender. He knew a bridle from a bit.

The sheds swallowed them—black hulks, tar-smell heavy. Pike hauled the horse into a cut behind a stack of freight crates. Zeke set the brake and stood, coat settling neat.

"We are not done," he told her, voice low, even. "You wanted to speak. You will. Then you will write."

Her eyes were dark and clear. "You can force paper," she said. "You can't force truth."

He almost admired the line. He didn't. Admiration was waste.

He lifted two fingers. Pike jumped down to tie the horse. Zeke offered a hand. She ignored it, climbed with care; the ankle slowed her, but didn't stop her. Good. He preferred opponents who understood pain.

From the road came the drum of more boots—the steady, measured kind. Wes Calder did not run loud. He arrived.

Zeke met the sound without turning his head. "Mr. Hart," he said, never taking his gaze off Maisie, "if you so much as breathe like a fool, I leave you here for Lane to spell in his book."

Pike swallowed hard. For once, he understood a sentence the first time.

Zeke took one step toward the shed door and let the night, finally, set its hook where he'd meant to set his.

He had her. Not yet on paper. Not yet in the judge's ink. But here, under tar smell and shadow, with a deputy panting and a rancher coming in on a damaged leg, appearances beginning to fray—he held the only leverage in the county that mattered.

"All right, Mrs. Calder," he said, as the lantern light from the road brightened and the voices he didn't want entered the yard. "Say your piece."

She lifted her chin. "Leave them," she said. "Take your quarrel with me."

He inclined his head, as if receiving a petition at a desk.

"That," he said, "is what I intend."

Outside, a voice he knew cut clean through the dark: "Blackwell."

Zeke didn't turn. He smiled a fraction. The stage was crowded now, the lines messy, the audience larger than he liked. But he had drawn the principal actress to his mark, and for the first time since he walked into Burke's that afternoon, he felt the scene shift his way—not elegant, not quiet, but useful.

He put his hand behind his back like a gentleman waiting his turn, and let the night come on.

Chapter Thirty

Roy Danner didn't ride fast so much as he rode mean—jerking the reins, cutting corners where the ground went slick, letting the iron mouth of the bit do his talking. The world tipped and jarred against Maisie's shoulder with every step of his bay. His arm was a hard bar across her collarbones, the pistol cold against the hinge of her jaw. Cheap cigar stink leaked off him, souring the air worse than sweat.

"Easy," he muttered when she stumbled. The barrel nudged higher. "You don't want me twitchin'."

Her ankle flared, not the old lightning-bolt pain of the first week on the ranch, but a deep, sullen ache where the swelling had come down. She tasted dust. Blood, too, where her lip had split on his coat button when he'd dragged her from Burke's. The saloon's blur—Zeke's pale eyes, the card players gone silent, the door slamming—still rang in her skull. She'd meant to stand there and tell Zeke to quit, to take his poison and leave the Calders be. Roy had ruined even that. He'd gripped her arm and hauled her out like a sack a man meant to sell.

"Calder place," Roy said now, as if she didn't know the line of those cottonwoods by heart. "We fetch the babe, we're square. Then I'm gone."

"You won't touch her." The words came raw. "You won't lay a hand on Junie."

He laughed. A short, ugly sound. "Gal, your man in there stuck his nose in where it don't belong. He'll trade quick enough when he sees you with a hole in your head." He angled the pistol when she twisted. "Don't make me prove it."

She set her teeth. Fear tasted like pennies. Resolve tasted like lye. "He won't trade," she said, though her voice shook. "And I won't let you."

"Won't be up to you in five minutes." His breath brushed her ear. "Walk."

They came off the creek path into the yard, the house throwing a long wedge of shade across the packed earth. The bells on the north run—mule bells Tom had hung low on wire at dusk—didn't carry this far, but Maisie saw the white flags they'd tied at old breaks, little ghosts fluttering in the green of the willow swale beyond the pens. A scrap of normalcy, even with a gun at her throat.

Tom stepped out from between the sheds first, wiping his hands on a rag. He went still at the sight of them. The rag hung in his fingers another beat; then it fell. He didn't reach for his rifle. He didn't shout. He lifted one hand—open, slow—as if gentling a skittish colt.

Behind him, Rhett's head came up like a dog catching a scent. Eli pushed through the barn door at a trot, took one look, and stopped so fast his boots scuffed pale furrows in the dirt. Jesse followed slower, calm in the shoulders but tight at the mouth, eyes moving like a bookkeeper already counting.

"Howdy, boys," Roy sang, lazy. The pistol never wavered. "Let's keep this simple."

"Roy Danner," Jesse said it like a ledger entry—fact and place. "You're trespassing."

"Funny," Roy said, "comin' from folks can't keep a fence." He bumped the barrel into Maisie's jaw until her eyes watered. "Where's the babe?"

"No." She put iron in the single syllable. "Don't you give him—"

"Hush." Roy pressed harder. "You talk when I say."

Eli took a half step, rage quick in him as ever. Jesse's hand came out without looking and landed on Eli's sleeve. It didn't look like much. It held like chain.

Tom's gaze never left Roy's pistol hand. "You get paid," he asked mildly, "or you come to collect the hard way?"

Roy's mouth thinned. "A man shouldn't have to ask twice for what he earned."

"So you grab a woman in broad daylight and bring her to a ranch with five witnesses," Jesse said, voice still even. "You think that earns you anything but a few years at Canon?"

Roy's finger flexed on the trigger. "You ain't the one holdin' the ace, bookman. I am." He shoved the gun harder against Maisie's skin. "You want her head whole? Fetch the baby."

"Don't," Maisie said, and the word tore out of her. "Don't you dare. Jesse, listen to me. None of you—"

"We hear you," Jesse said quietly. "We're not handin' her over."

Rhett had edged toward the low fence by the lot, body angled, eyes cut to Tom waiting for a sign. Tom gave him none. Eli's jaw worked like he had a nail between his teeth and couldn't spit it. The yard held its breath.

The house door opened. Wes stepped down into the sun.

He wore his shirt untucked on one side, where Maisie had slit it to reach the wound. The bandage showed under the hem, bright as new cotton. He walked without favoring the leg until the last two steps; then he shifted, a hitch that would have read as weariness to any man who didn't know what he'd bled on her kitchen table. His rifle hung easy in his hand, muzzle low, stock nestled loose against his palm. No hurry. No show.

Roy's eyes slid to him and flattened. "Well," he said, "look who ain't dead."

"Shame you ain't either," Rhett muttered, too soft for Roy, not too soft for Eli. Eli's mouth twitched; Jesse's fingers tightened fractionally.

Wes didn't aim. He didn't need to. He stopped ten good paces off and set his voice where it would carry without raising dust. "Let her go, Danner."

"Be smart, Calder." Roy's smile showed the brown edge of a tooth. "You pass me the babe, I pass you the woman, and nobody spits blood on your nice clean porch."

"Roy," Wes said, calm as creek water under ice, "we've already got a judge scheduled, statements drawn, a sheriff on notice, and your name on the first line. You're on our land with a gun to a woman's head. You won't walk away from that if you fire. Even Burke'll tell you that."

"Burke'll tell me he wants his money," Roy snapped. "And Blackwell promised me mine for doin' a job he wouldn't dirty his own gloves with. He welshed. So I'll collect what I can." His jaw twitched. "Baby first."

Wes's eyes flicked to Jesse. Just a breath. Jesse shifted, just a hair, enough to angle his body between Eli and the barn. "Eli," he said without moving his mouth, "ride Lane." The words were air only. Eli didn't nod. He simply turned a fraction, spat, and ambled two steps toward the well as if thirst had finally beat temper. The next step took him wider. Another took him behind the corner of the tack room and out of sight.

Maisie saw it and swallowed a sob of something like relief and something like terror. She didn't know if Eli would make it to the gate before Roy twitched. She didn't know if Sheriff Lane would be near or on the far side of town. She knew only this: she would not call for Junie. She would not.

She forced her gaze to Wes's because it steadied her when nothing else did. He didn't smile. He didn't soften. He held her eyes and let her see what she needed—no bend in him at all.

"Roy," Wes said again, "you make this worse with every word you say. You leave now, you meet Lane on the road, you say you were a damn fool, and you're ready to give a statement on fence-cutting and threats, and maybe the judge shows you the mercies of a man your age. You shoot, you don't get a courtroom. You get a rope and a bad hymn."

Roy snorted. "You bluff pretty." He angled his head, scar by his ear catching a glint. "Blackwell told me you'd try a straight face."

"You keep sayin' that name like it's a shield," Rhett said, voice gone rough. "All I hear is a coward hidin' behind a bigger one."

Tom cut him a look. Rhett ground his teeth and shut his mouth.

"Look at me," Wes said, and Maisie did. His voice lost none of its quiet when he turned it to her. "You hold still, Maisie. Don't help him."

"I won't," she said, though her knees had begun to shake.

Roy laughed again, that ugly bark. "Sounds like you got yourself a pet, Calder. Ain't you s'posed to be a married man now? Word in town says so."

If he meant to rile Wes, he failed. He only put a heat in Maisie's face that made her want to spit in his eye. She didn't. She kept her hands where Roy could see them and made herself breathe through her nose the way Wes had done when she stitched his leg—steadily, like a man refusing to faint.

From the upstairs window, a faint sound—Junie shifting in her sleep—touched the room above like a feather. Maisie prayed Roy hadn't the ears to catch it. She would have cut her own tongue out before she called to the child.

"Last time," Roy said, impatience sharpening him. "Bring me the baby or bring me a shroud for this woman. Your pick."

Jesse eased one foot forward. "Roy," he said, and there was an older man's patience in his voice now, a schoolmaster's. "You're talkin' to a ledger more than a man at this point. Hear me. We have witnesses to you cutting fence. We have Grayson willing to sign—Minnie Abbott will witness—that you came at him with offers to let 'a rich Easterner' pay him to let wire go loose. We have Tom's bells and flags set and nicked where you tested them. We have your nippers in evidence. You want to stack a woman's life on top of that and call it a life's work? For a man who won't even pay you?"

Roy's eyes flickered. Not much, but enough: a twitch at the lid, a swallow in his throat. Money had brought him here more than loyalty ever would. Maisie watched that swallow the way a miner watches a vein of gold, fear and hope pounding out of step.

"Blackwell will make this right," Roy said, but some of the swagger had leaked from the words.

"He made it wrong," Wes said. He didn't move the rifle; he didn't need to. He was all the proof Roy could want that a man could stand through pain and speak true. "He's the one will leave you standin' alone when the noose shows. You let her go, we tell Lane you were put to this and you stopped. You keep hold of her, I can't promise you live to see a bench. D'you understand me?"

Maisie felt it then—the smallest slack where Roy's arm cinched her. Not mercy. A calculation. She made herself smaller, as if she were ready to faint. If he shifted his grip to hold her weight…

Tom saw it too. His voice went softer yet, like a hand over a skittish horse's eye. "Mister Danner, you let the lady take two steps, we'll all breathe easier. That makes this steadier for you. No one's lookin' to twitch you."

"Two steps," Jesse echoed, not a command—an invitation.

Roy's mouth worked. He licked his lips. Spit dark on the dust. "One," he said finally, and tugged the pistol back a hair from her skin. "You make me nervous, girl. Don't be stupid."

Maisie moved. One slow step forward, into the open, out from the hook of his arm, but not far enough to give Rhett a lane or Wes a clean shot. It wasn't freedom, but daylight lifted the press at her lungs. She kept her hands up. She could feel the tremor in her fingers and willed it still.

"What's your end of this, Roy?" Wes asked, like two men jawin' over a rail. "You think Blackwell gives you land? A piece of a herd? Or is it coin in your pocket and you ride south lookin' over your shoulder every night 'til some other man takes your boots while you sleep?"

"Coin's cleaner than cattle," Roy said, but his voice was half-distracted now, half-turned inward to whatever ledgers he kept in his own skull.

"Cleaner don't mean safer," Tom said. "Nor honorable."

Roy spat again. "You Calder men and your words." The pistol steadied once more, and Maisie went cold. He'd chosen. "Enough sermon. Babe. Now."

"Don't," she said, without pleading, without terror. She said it like Ivy had said it that last night, quiet and sure. "Don't give her."

"We ain't," Rhett growled, before Jesse shot him another look.

Wes didn't glance away from Roy. "No baby. Not now, not ever. You know that. What you can have is your life, and I'm telling you as plain as I can: this here is the last time I offer you that." He shifted his weight and—only then, only with Maisie already a step clear—brought the rifle up. He didn't aim at Roy's head. He set the sight like a surgeon, low where it would end a fight and not a life.

"Careful," Tom breathed, as much to Roy as to Wes.

Roy's eyes flared. "You s'pose to be the righteous one," he jeered. "Stand there talkin' law and church like a preacher. Then you point iron at a man who ain't shot yet."

"I'm pointin' iron at a man who keeps threatenin' a woman," Wes said. "There's a difference Judge Markell'll know by smell." He didn't blink. "So will Lane."

A faint, far-off drum of hooves reached the yard from the road. Maisie almost sagged. Eli. Please, Lord. Let it be Eli with the sheriff. Let it be time.

Roy heard it too. Panic changed the angle of his jaw. "You brought the law on me?" He swung the pistol wild, away from her, toward Jesse, then back. "You think to box me in, you—"

"Don't," Wes warned, the single word a crack in winter wood.

Rhett shifted. Tom's hand floated a breath from his rifle and held there—visible, empty, a promise not to start a war. Jesse didn't move at all. He only said, "This is a witness yard now, Roy. Every word you say, every step you take, it's already written."

Maisie lifted her chin. "And I'll speak it in the hearing. Every bit." Fear was still in her—it would be a fool's lie to deny it—

but another thing stood up alongside it now, old as a sister's vow. "You won't touch her."

Hoofbeats, closer. A cut of dust at the end of the lane.

Roy bared his teeth. His left shoulder twitched—the tell she'd have missed a week ago. She saw it now. He'd aim to shoot to scatter them, grab her again in the split second after the blast when men flinched. He'd done this before. He'd do it again if he lived past today.

Wes saw it too. She knew by the way his finger settled against the guard, not on the trigger but near it. Ready. His eyes never left Roy's.

"Think," he said, last time. "Be a man who turns back before he kills what's left of himself."

For half a heartbeat, Roy did think. She saw the work of it in his face—the counting, the weighing, the sudden flare of fear like a match cupped in the wind.

The ridge beyond the willow held still as a raised hand.

A glint of metal, high and far, winked once in the late sun.

Tom's head turned a fraction. Jesse's eyes cut to the cottonwoods and back. Rhett's breath hissed between his teeth.

Maisie didn't have time to name the shape on the rise.

She only knew the yard, bare and bright, felt like the inside of a bell just before the clapper struck.

Chapter Thirty-One

The yard felt like the inside of a bell before the strike—thin air, every breath stretched tight. Danner's arm had eased off Maisie a hair when Jesse talked him toward sense; his left shoulder gave that twitch Wes had already learned meant he'd shoot to scatter and grab.

Wes didn't blink. He held Roy's eyes, not the ridge, not the house. Talking bought seconds. Seconds bought lives.

"You know how this ends if you fire," he said, steady as a prayer said over seed. "You end on a rope or under a slab. I'm still givin' you the road out."

Hoofbeats ghosted the lane—far yet, dust still held to earth. Good. Eli had found a horse with lungs.

Roy's jaw jumped like a baited line. "No more talk." He shifted the barrel.

A flash on the ridge cut his right—metal catching a slip of sun. Wes didn't take his eyes off Roy, but he marked it anyway: rifle glass, high past the cottonwoods, one rider sitting a horse like he'd been born to a pew, not a saddle.

"Don't," Wes said again, and in the same breath the ridge answered.

The crack hit the yard like a whip. Roy jerked, the pistol jarred wide. Blood leapt out bright where his right shoulder met shirt; he stumbled with a sound that wasn't a word and went to his knees, shock before pain making his face youngest, then oldest, then something helpless between.

"Gun!" Jesse snapped—a warning, not a panic.

Wes moved the way you do when you've done a thing your whole life: forward enough to matter, not so far you crossed mercy with rashness. The rifle came up now, clean, sight set low. He didn't need to shoot—yet. He needed Roy on the dirt and the pistol away.

"Leave it," Tom said, soft but a command, as Roy clawed left-handed at the iron he'd dropped.

Rhett slid the fence rail like a boy and came in low from the side. His boot scuffed the pistol back two strides. Jesse stepped in and set his heel on it; Tom's fingers ghosted the stock of his own rifle and then released, palms showing. Maisie eased one pace clear, hands still up, breath shaking but steady as a pulled stitch.

Across the creek, the rider on the ridge lowered his gun with the careful flare of a man who liked being seen. He raised his head enough the brim lost his eyes, and the light caught the smooth side of his face.

"Zeke Blackwell," Jesse said, not loud. The name hit the yard like something finally named under a doctor's hand.

Zeke let the echo sit, smiling down as if from a stage. "There now," he called, voice tidy as a pen stroke. "A nasty fellow, that one. Seems you've had trouble with his like before." He set his rifle back into the crook of his elbow like a gentleman shepherding a cane. "I thought I'd assist."

"By shootin' your hired hand," Rhett muttered. Tom's hand brushed his sleeve and rested there; the touch laid a bridle on anger without breaking it.

Wes did not drop the rifle. He did not raise it. He set it in the line that told a man choosing wrong would cost him, and he lifted his chin.

"You step off that ridge slow," he said to Zeke, "gun held by the barrel. Leave it where Tom tells you. Then we'll hear whatever story you've decided on."

Zeke laughed as if somebody had told a good joke and he could afford to admire it. "Mr. Calder," he said, the title dry as a judge's mouth. "You do like your little displays."

"And you like to scare women from a distance," Rhett said louder. Jesse didn't hush him this time. Some words needed air.

Zeke walked his horse down the slope in unhurried half-circles, like a man making a letter right on the first try. Close enough, Wes saw the city make in the cut of the coat, Albany tailoring carried west and stained with trail. Zeke did as told with the rifle: held it by the barrel between two fingers and set it on the ground as if the dirt offended him. He didn't scuff his boots. He didn't look at Roy bleeding under the willow, and he didn't look at Maisie long enough for Wes to call it a look. But when his gaze touched her, something flared and turned cold in it fast enough to burn.

"You don't get to set the stage," Wes said. "Not here."

Zeke clasped his hands behind him like a sermonizer. "This place," he said, eyes drifting over house, yard, wind-lean fence as if he might hang price tags, "has been poorly managed and worse defended. The law will find it admirable that a responsible party finally chose to intervene." He tipped his chin toward Roy without lowering his voice. "Mr. Danner is the one you want. He's the kind who cuts wire and steals cattle." The smile sharpened. "The kind who abducts children."

Maisie flinched like a string pulled. Wes didn't look back. He didn't need to. He felt her, a presence he could set his back to like a rock.

"We've got statements sayin' different," Jesse said. "We've got tools that match cuts on our wire in your man's pocket, witnesses saw him solicit fence work for a 'rich Easterner,' and bells nicked where somebody tested our new ties last night." He hit each point like a nail set right. "Blackwell, your name sits behind every piece of the trouble, and you know it."

Zeke's smile gentled, which is what his did instead of hardening. "Gentlemen," he said, "your... zeal... has turned amusing little misunderstandings into slander. I would be within my rights to sue for defamation." He let his voice carry honey down the edges. "I am a husband whose wife died tragically. I am a father concerned for his child. And this ranch harbors the woman who stole her." He looked past them, toward the upstairs window where a curtain breathed. "I am here to reclaim what is mine."

Rhett's curse was soft and filthy as creek mud. Tom's quiet "steady" pulled it back by the tail.

Wes felt the old understanding settle—the one he hadn't wanted to admit until this breath: Zeke would not stop because sense or shame found him. He would not pause because a good man asked. He would change tactics as often as a fox changed brush, and the only thing that would hold him was daylight and law.

He set that truth in his bones as if he were driving a corner post: You can't out-mean him and still be the man you promised to be. You drag him where witnesses stand and let the law you've prepared do the breaking.

"You fired a rifle at a man in my yard," Wes said, keeping his voice level, keeping the law in it. "You brought a gun to our fence two nights back. You put men on neighbors' lines. You threatened to take what isn't yours." He raised the rifle—not to his shoulder, not yet, but high enough the barrel showed daylight. "Zeke Blackwell, you'll answer for that."

Zeke's nostrils flared. "Answer to whom? To your... foreman?" The contempt he tried to keep from his face stained it anyway. "You think a country judge will choose your word over mine? Do you think your little friends will stand up when reminded what happens to farmers who bite the hand that feeds them?" His voice rose, elegance fraying. "You will hand over what you've stolen. The child. The woman who aided the theft. This land—" he cut his palm through the air, "—may not be mine in ink yet, but it will be. Or I'll see it salted, and you with it."

"Only man I ever saw take salt to ground was one who'd already lost it," Tom said, not loud, and the old soldier in his tone laid a chill on the dirt.

Hooves took the lane at a gallop and skidded where dust lay thick. Eli's whistle—two short, one long—sliced the air. Sheriff Lane swung down before his mare had fully stopped, boots hitting hard. Two deputies—Harkness with the bum hand, and young Mateo with his hat shoved back—fanned without being told. Three revolvers found the same figure with a unity born of long habit.

"Rifles where we can see 'em!" Lane's voice cracked like August thunder. "Hands waist-high. Nobody moves unless I say."

Wes lowered the muzzle a hair and turned his body to show compliance without losing position. Jesse lifted both palms sure and slow. Rhett kept his weight down, but his hands rose. Tom held himself like a man who had made peace with being aimed at many years ago and had never lost the knack.

Zeke did not move at first. He looked at the star on Lane's vest, then at the deputies' steady hands, then at Eli behind them, jaw set and eyes bright with the kind of fury that comes clean as spring water.

"Mr. Lane," Zeke said with a small, practiced bow. "I am delighted to see the law arrive. You'll find a violent criminal there—" he indicated Roy with that same flick of contempt, "—and a ring of men intent on keeping a child from her rightful parent."

Lane's gaze took the yard in a single travel: Danner bleeding, pistol kicked wide, rifle on the ground where Zeke had set it by the barrel, cloth flags white as handkerchiefs on the north line, bells hung low on wire. He had the look of a man seeing a story he knew the shape of before the first page turned.

"Funny," he said, "I got a wire from the Calder place last week asking for more patrol up north. I got a liveryman who says a city fella's been buyin' fine tools for rough work. I got a storekeep, Burke, who told me—after Eli here leaned on him—that a smooth talker he'd rather not name had been inviting fellows with light scruples to play cards and listen to offers. And I got a judge sittin' in two weeks waitin' on sworn statements from Jamie Grayson and one Minnie Abbott." He scratched his chin with the side of a finger, never moving the barrel of his Colt. "What I don't have is patience for a man with Albany shine and neighbor-killin' notions."

Zeke's smile held. It simply lost any warmth it might have once carried. "Sheriff, be reasonable. I am the wronged party."

Roy made a sound—a wet laugh, ugly and grateful and mean all at once. "Wronged," he croaked, left hand clamped to his shoulder. Blood seeped between his fingers slow now, his skin gone the color of old parchment. "You promised me cash and a train clean out. Promised I'd never see a cell." He coughed and swore softly. "Lyin' bastard."

Lane didn't look away from Zeke. "There it is," he said. "Hark, take the gentleman's iron from the ground with two fingers and lay it in my saddlebag. Mateo, see to Danner's shoulder enough he don't die under my badge. He breathes, he testifies."

Harkness moved slow as Sunday. Zeke didn't twitch. He had the sense to know three angles of fire would write the next lines of his story if he did.

"Mr. Blackwell," Lane said, all polite again, "you are under arrest for aggravated assault with a deadly weapon, conspiracy to commit theft, and whatever else Judge Markell decides fits once these men sign what they've told me they're ready to sign." He nodded toward Jesse. "Jesse, you got that paper drawn?"

"Clean as a hymnbook," Jesse said. "Witnessed tomorrow at Minnie's counter. Jamie Grayson'll sign with his own hand."

Zeke's control slipped. Something raw and childlike flashed across his face—the look of a boy told no and not yet by a father who'd never loved him. It vanished almost before it was there. He smoothed his mouth and held his wrists out with the flair of a man offering gloves to a valet.

"Careful," Lane said evenly, stepping in, close enough now Wes could see the flecks in the sheriff's eyes. "These irons are cold. Albany hands ain't used to that."

The click of metal on bone sounded loud as a hammer in the quiet. Mateo knelt at Roy's side, pressing a folded bandanna hard into the wound; Roy hissed and went gray, but he stayed. Eli moved like he meant to stomp Zeke's hat into the dust; Jesse's fingers touched his sleeve and drew him back sure and unshowy. Tom's hand remained a ghost near his own rifle without needing to touch it.

Wes let breath out slow. He felt every inch of the wound in his thigh—an iron line that ran hot then cold—but he kept his weight where it belonged. He turned his head, finally, to check on what mattered more than the sight line.

Maisie stood a pace behind and to his left, shawl drawn up tight as if the wind had teeth. The wrap lay neat at her ankle; she'd moved that one step and no more. The fine tremor in her fingers had calmed to a quiet hum. She met his eyes. There was thanks there, and relief that hadn't room yet to be joy.

"It's nearly done," he said, a murmur meant for one set of ears. "Not over. But turned."

She nodded, once. "I know." It came back soft and true, and something that had sat low in his chest for months rose and settled higher, like a beam lifted into its right notch.

Lane swung to the side without warning and pinned Wes with a look. "You plan on shootin' any more men today, Calder?"

"No, Sheriff," Wes said. "Been tryin' to avoid it."

"Good." Lane holstered with the ease of habit. "Then fetch me the tool you took off Danner and that bell you found nicked. We'll make a neat little bundle for Judge Markell. Hark—walk Mr. Blackwell to the rail. Ride's long. I'd hate for him to fall off."

Harkness's mouth twitched. Zeke's didn't. He took the movement like a man takes bad news from a doctor—some pain in the future loosened his shoulders, not in surrender but in calculation. He turned his head one last time toward the house, toward the upstairs window where life breathed that didn't include him.

"Maisie," he said, voice silk. "Be sensible. Come with me quietly. This little drama only makes it worse for you."

Wes didn't turn his head, only his eyes. He didn't need to answer. The whole yard already had.

"Sheriff," Jesse said mildly, "we've had a long day."

"Yes, you have." Lane tipped his hat a hair toward Maisie without taking his eyes off his prisoner. "Ma'am."

"Sheriff," she said, and her voice didn't shake.

They took Zeke away between horses, irons chiming once against a stirrup, a city man riding like the saddle might stain him. The deputies led Roy after, slumped over Mateo's saddle horn, muttering in pain and bitterness both. Eli walked behind them a few paces, hands empty, shoulders wide.

When the dust settled back to earth, quiet wrapped around the yard in a different shape than the one that had held them all day. Not the hush of dread. The hush after noise.

Wes let the rifle fall to cradle and set the butt gentle to earth. His leg chose that moment to remind him a bullet did not forget just because a man ignored it. The world went white at the edges for a breath; he rode it until it passed.

"Sit," Maisie said low, one hand on his sleeve. He sank to the porch step without arguing. Tom, who had seen more men put on bravado than boots, nodded approval without making a speech. Rhett blew out a breath and laughed once—a sound with no mirth and plenty of release.

Jesse picked the kicked pistol up with two fingers and dropped it into the scuttle, a metal-on-metal clatter like the end of a hymn. "We've got work," he said, which for Jesse was another way to say we're alive.

Chapter Thirty-Two

The note she'd been holding all day—the tight one, the high one that made her chest small—slid down into something she could breathe through. She kept her hand on Wes's sleeve until she felt the tremor in him settle. His skin under the cotton burned with a heat that said the wound would need watching. She made a little list without looking at any paper: boil water, comfrey and marigold, clean cloths, change the wrap, not too tight.

"Junie," she said, the name a prayer and a thought at once.

"I'll fetch her," Jesse said before she could move. "You sit a minute." He didn't wait for argument; he vanished into the cool of the house, footfalls even on the steps, that little hitch board near the landing sounding exactly where it always did.

Rhett leaned his forearms on the fence and pushed his hat back to look at the ridge. "Don't know whether to cheer or spit," he said.

"Do neither," Tom advised. "You'll just dry your mouth more."

Eli's laugh was real this time, small and tired. He tipped water from a dipper into Wes's palm. "Lane about near ran his mare to foam," he said. "You owe me for talkin' him faster than his sense likes." He looked over Wes's shoulder at Maisie then, humor sliding aside. "You all right?"

She took stock like Jesse would: ankle held, lungs working, head clear enough, hands steady now. "I am," she said, and it was true in the way truth sometimes surprised you by being simple. "Thank you for riding."

"Would have sooner flown." Eli sobered. "He'll make noise in a courtroom."

"Let him," she said, and the quiet in her voice was not hard; it was the opposite. "We have the truth."

Wes's head turned a fraction at that. His gaze found hers and held. He didn't say anything fine. He didn't need to. He laid his hand over hers where it rested on his sleeve, big and warm and sure, and the calluses on his palm rasped her knuckles like a sound she'd been waiting on.

Jesse reappeared with Junie newest awake and indignant at being plucked from her crib. The baby took one look at the yard and then at Maisie and flung hers arms wide like a judge awarding custody.

"Hush now." Maisie gathered her in, the weight of her settling Maisie's heartbeat as much as Maisie's arms settled the baby's. Junie's hand went straight to a lock of Maisie's hair and twined as if to anchor the day down.

Zeke looked back once from the end of the lane, a small shape held neat between two larger ones. If there was a prayer in his face, she couldn't see it. If there was hate, she didn't feed it with a second look. She bent and kissed Junie's temple, smelling milk and sleep and stove-warm cotton, and that was the only answer he would ever get from her.

Lane paused at the gate long enough to lift two fingers to his hat brim. "Tomorrow," he called, meaning statements, meaning Minnie's neat script and Jamie Grayson's careful hand and Jesse's ledger cleaned of fear. "Don't sit up all night waitin' on trouble. If it comes, your bells will sing."

"They already did," Tom said. "We just finally heard the tune."

When the law rode off and their dust went to haze, the men turned to what men turn to when they can—small work that puts the world in order. Rhett picked up the coil of wire he'd dropped and carried it to the shed. Eli reset the gate latch that had rattled when the hooves beat past. Jesse took the pistol from the scuttle with a towel and set it on the high shelf they were keeping for the judge, beside the nippers and the bell with the fresh nick, as if a small, ugly altar could be made to the truth.

Maisie sat with Wes on the porch steps and let the last of the light draw thin lines on the yard. The house breathed around them. The cottonwoods made their soft, river-sounding talk. Junie patted Wes's cheek solemnly like she'd chosen him again and would have to keep choosing him forever. He obliged by making a face until she laughed—short and tired and perfect.

"It turned," she said, not to convince herself, but to put the day into words so it didn't float.

"It did," he said. He looked down at the bandage peeking white where his shirt hid it and made a wry shape with his mouth. "Doesn't mean easy."

"No." Maisie smoothed the baby's dress, the habit of straightening what she could never leave. "Just means we're not hiding." She glanced toward the kitchen, where Jesse's pencil would be making its calm rows. "Not in the yard. Not in the town. Not in court."

He breathed something that might have been a laugh if it had had more strength. "That's the truth that kept kickin' us," he said. "I can fix fence and hang bells and sit a watch 'til my bones forget sleep. But a man can't out-crook a crook without turnin' crooked. You haul him into daylight, or you become him." His thumb brushed the back of her hand once, a small pass that felt more like a vow than any words. "We'll do it in daylight."

"We will," she said. For a heartbeat, the porch boards under them felt like the only ground that mattered.

Junie yawned so big it seemed it might turn her inside out, then folded into Maisie's shoulder like the day had finally spent her. Maisie stood careful, ankle reminding her to be sensible, and Wes rose slower, the two of them moving in that unspoken coordination they'd found without talking about finding it.

Inside, the kitchen light lay warm on the scrubbed wood. She set Junie back in the crib, laid a hand on the little belly that rose and fell, and came back to the table where the jar of comfrey and the ribbon-tied marigold already waited. Wes sat and undid his cuff so she could reach what needed reaching. She pressed heat into the angry line of the wound and felt him let his breath go the way a man lets a sorrel take the bit and lower his head after a long pull.

"Mercy," she said, quiet, because the word had earned its place in her mouth again.

"Simple as a hand where you need one," he answered, almost smiling, and she did this time.

From the porch, Tom's step crossed and recrossed like a metronome set to ease; from the bunkhouse, a low tune—Rhett, likely, wasting no opportunity to be loud now that loud didn't get a person dead. Jesse's pencil scratched on. The house wore those sounds like a shawl.

Maisie wrung the cloth and laid it again. "When this goes to court," she said, not asking, "I'll speak. I'll say what Ivy told me to say if I ever got the chance."

"You will," he said. "And I'll stand next to you."

She tied the linen off neat and looked up, the words she had been holding coming without ornateness or apology. "I'm not afraid to be seen anymore."

Wes's gaze didn't shy. "I'm not afraid to be yours," he said, as plain as a man could and still make it a poem.

Outside, somewhere along the north fence, a mule bell chimed once and quit. Not a warning. A neighbor riding past, maybe, or the wind deciding to show its small strength. Maisie didn't flinch. She only reached for his hand, and he gave it. The house, the yard, the line of cottonwoods—all of it felt held, not by walls or wire alone, but by the choice they'd finally laid down like a beam on stone: daylight over shadow; law over fury; family over fear.

The danger wasn't burnt out. It had simply been drawn into view.

But that was enough to end the day.

They sat there in the soft, honest tiredness that comes after you've done what you could and what you ought in the same hour, and when the lamp guttered, Wes rose to trim it, and Maisie let him, and neither of them looked over their shoulder.

Chapter Thirty-Three

By noon, the ranch sounded like itself again—wire rasping true, staples set home with short, clean blows, a team leaning into the trace with the creak of honest leather. Mule bells on the north run kept their small watch; the white flags Jesse had tied at weak posts hung still. Sheriff Lane had ridden out with Blackwell in irons and Danner cussing on a deputy's horn. Burke had cleared his back room of city men and cheap cigars. Buyers who'd spooked on rumor nosed back with careful questions—weights, dates, numbers—as if a river that forgot itself had found its old channel.

On paper, the worst had passed.

Wes could not make his shoulders believe it. Not with the way Maisie moved through the house.

She kept to the work the way a woman does who's learned it can steady a mind—bread and beans, a sweep for a floor already clean, little repairs set right with Ivy's thimble bright in her palm. She laughed when Junie did something plain foolish and sweet, scolded Rhett for tracking mud, thanked Jesse for hauling water. It all looked right, sounded right. But her silences were a shade longer than they'd been two days ago. When a man turned his head, he could feel them, faint and cool—the draft that sneaks under a door that looks shut.

Her ankle still wore the wrap he'd tied; her step off the porch was careful but sure. She kept Junie close in the yard. Now and then, he caught her looking at the horizon, not with dread but with the old habit of measuring distance.

He knew the feel of a thing thinking about leaving. He'd learned it the hard way—once in a cemetery where earth shut over what he couldn't keep, once at a kitchen table with a ring between two hands and no way to make it mean what it ought.

That knowing pressed behind his ribs until he went out and tightened a wire that didn't need it.

He lasted until noon.

Jesse sat at the table with a clean page and three new columns ruled straight as fence line. Eli rasped a foundered mare's hoof to even, talking soft nonsense to keep her honest. Rhett took Tom's first watch in the willow, mule bell tied low. The ranch held.

"Quit walkin' a groove in that dirt," Eli said at last without looking up. "Go say what you need to say."

"What if it's wrong to ask?" Wes asked, meaning more than he said.

"Wrong not to," Jesse answered, pencil stilling. He didn't lift his eyes, which was his way of kindness. "Some truths don't hitch easy. You still got to put a hand to the halter."

Wes tipped his hat and went around the house.

Behind the kitchen, a washline stretched between two cottonwoods, high as a man's shoulder, heavy with the day's honest business—two of his shirts, one of Rhett's, a row of dishcloths, and a parade of Junie's things that looked like prayer flags for a domestic faith: little socks, a white chemise, the muslin dress Minnie had refused coin for. Maisie stood with a basket at her feet, clothespins looped on twine around her neck. Her hair was braided and looped low; sleeves rolled; the hinge of her throat caught sun where her scarf lay open. Junie sat in a square of shade, serious over a wooden rattle as if composing something the adults were too dull to hear.

"Afternoon," Wes said.

"Afternoon," Maisie answered, reaching for a sheet, snapping it once, pinning a corner. Her voice didn't run; it didn't invite.

"I'm not going to ease into it," he said.

"All right."

"I don't want you to go." His best luck had always been with plain. "I don't want to wake in a house without you in it—no step on the stair, no hum at the stove. I don't want a yard without you settin' Junie on the step to see if the dirt looks friendly. I don't want to be a man who's grateful you were here and content to let you walk on."

She didn't look away. "I hear you."

"I don't want to be grateful," he said, and then made himself finish. "I want you to stay. Not because you have to. Not because a judge could order it or a fence could promise it. Because I want to live a life with you in it. Because that near-kiss on the porch feels like a promise I mean to keep with the rest of me. Because when I hold that baby, I don't see a burden that belonged to someone else. I see my daughter. And because every morning I find I've made a place in my head for your voice, whether you speak or not."

The pins clicked against each other where they hung. A breeze lifted the sheet between them and set a ghost of it against his shoulder before it settled. Junie thumped her rattle once, approving of the wind.

"You haven't said love," Maisie said—careful with a word that bruised if it fell wrong.

"I won't waste it," he said. "I used it once and wasn't fit to keep it. I've gone a long way without puttin' it on anything that couldn't stand it. I can put it on this." He swallowed like a man with dry bread and no water, then said it because a thing that true ought not be hoarded. "I love you, Maisie. I love the way you make a quiet room into a roof in a storm. I love that you don't let fear set the table. I love that you were brave enough to run and braver to stop. I love how you see to everyone's hunger before your own and still let me catch you when you need it. And I love that baby like I made her with hammer and nail and God's own breath."

June light made her eyes bright and gentle both. He watched a dozen thoughts move through them—a woman's tally of risk, a woman's memory of harm, a woman's need to see if a man was speaking because the wind had picked up or because the season had changed.

"I was thinkin' of leaving," she said at last. "Not because I wanted to. Because I thought maybe I should. This isn't the life you meant to have. I didn't want to sit in a home I borrowed and watch it sour in your eyes once the danger passed and habit set in. I didn't want to be loved out of duty."

"It isn't duty," he said. "Duty's standin' a fence in sleet because a hinge broke and there's no time for coffee. Duty's feedin' a man I don't like because the Lord said feed him anyway. This has duty in it—any good thing does. But it isn't made out of it." He let himself smile because if he didn't, the words would get heavy. "This is the other kind. The kind that teaches a man what comfrey smells like hot out of water. The kind that keeps me lawful when my temper wants to climb the fence and go hunting. The kind that ties a man to a porch step like it's the only right place to be."

Her mouth trembled, then steadied. "I'm scared it won't stay," she said. "Not just you—me. Fear's driven my team a long time. Sometimes it still reaches for the reins."

"Fear can ride," he said. "It just doesn't drive." He stepped closer, slow enough for her to lift a hand if she needed space. She didn't. The sheet shifted, and suddenly nothing stood between them but a string of pins and work already done. "I can't promise storms don't come. I can promise I know how to set a beam so the roof holds when they do. And I won't be fool enough to let the first calm day make me careless."

She glanced toward the house; he knew what she was counting. Not dollars. A kind of currency other people don't see: how many nights he had risen when Junie fussed without being asked; how many times he'd checked her bandage and not used the touch for anything the hour wasn't ready to bear; how many tempers he had tied off and set outside because she didn't need to trip over them. He could feel her laying that beside the old sums that had taught her caution.

"What would we be?" she asked. "Not on paper—we've got paper. What would we be in a year? Five?"

"We'd be the quiet kind," he said, the picture coming easier than breath. "The kind where folks quit sayin' our names separate because they don't know how. You'd have a garden in the south patch; I'd pretend not to eat the first tomatoes before you brought 'em in. Junie would climb everything a body can set a foot on; I'd carry her down a hundred times and still set her on a horse when she can hold the horn. We'd go before Judge Markell and see to the adoption proper so no one from any place can reach for that child without our say-so. I'll put her name in the family Bible not as 'kin' but as mine. And we'll ask the preacher to bless what we've already started—not for show, but so the town knows which way to face when they say our names to God."

Something let go in her shoulders he hadn't even seen she was holding. Not a collapse. A yielding, like leather oiled right and giving under a thumb.

"I don't know how to stop running and start staying without trippin' now and then," she said. "If I give my word, will you give me time to keep learnin'?"

"I'll give you my word and my time both," he said. "And my brothers will give you more advice than any woman asked for." He let a grin up into his face because Eli would. "Eli's itching to build a cradle to prove he can make somethin' that holds still. Jesse'll draw a household budget like it's a treaty. Rhett'll teach Junie to spit apple seeds farther than's decent. Tom'll pretend he hates all of it and sleep on the porch to hear you breathe. None of that is duty. That's just how this place loves."

Her hand went to her mouth—only to give it something to do while her eyes filled. She lowered it and stepped in. He didn't take more than she offered. She set her palm on his chest, light as a moth landing, right over the place that had learned to ache around her.

"Say it again," she whispered.

"I love you," he said, and it felt like a good weight set on the proper post—the kind that tells a man the whole frame will sit true.

She rose the inch she needed and set her mouth to his. Not grabbed. Not stolen. Placed. His hat brim bumped a clothespin and sent it clicking along the line; down in the shade, Junie made a testing sound as if she'd copy what she'd heard and then thought better and whacked the rattle on her knee.

He kissed back with the same plainness he'd used for the words—no flourish, all promise. When they parted, the world hadn't changed its color. It had come into focus the way a field does when a cloud moves on.

"I'll stay," she said. No embroidery on it. "Not because I'm scared. Because I'm choosing it."

"Good," he answered, because if he said more, he'd say something that deserved a church, and he didn't have one handy. "We'll go to town tomorrow. Minnie will make too much of it. We'll find the clerk and learn what paper needs drawing so Junie belongs where she already lives."

"Minnie will cry," she warned, laughing a little, the sound coming from somewhere clean. "Then scold me for not telling her first."

"Eli will say he knew all along."

"He didn't," she said, and that made them both laugh like children with a secret.

A cloud shouldered the sun for a breath and moved on. The sheet between them lifted and bellied and fell, as if bowing out of the way at last. Junie had worked one sock free and was chewing it like a biscuit. Maisie scooped her up, pins rattling on their string, and snugged the sock where it belonged with the practiced patience of a woman who had set a child's world right three hundred times.

"Come on," she said, turning toward the porch. "You've been on that leg long enough. Sit while I fetch the comfrey."

He followed. On the steps, he paused and looked out across what was theirs—bells quiet, flags still, cottonwoods making that soft wind-speech like a river too far to see.

"Wes?" she asked, half-turned.

"Just thinkin' how a thing can be held," he said. "With wire and posts. With law and names. With a woman's yes."

She ducked her head at that, and the small smile it hid was worth every mile he'd walked to reach it.

Inside, Jesse's pencil rode a last line and stopped. He looked up at their faces and didn't ask a single fool thing. "Good," he said simply, as if checking a column that had waited too long to be marked. Eli leaned in the back door with a rooster under his arm and an admission on his face.

"I'm not keepin' that bird in the house," Maisie told him.

"It's a present," Eli protested, but his eyes had gone to her hand still near Wes's shirt. "Fine," he amended. "A present for outside."

Rhett called from the yard that the bell had chimed once, no more—just the wind or Harlan Tate on the north trail. Tom, on his slow circuit, lifted a hand and let it fall without breaking step. The house breathed.

That evening, with the last of the wash taken down and the day's heat banked in the stove, Wes sat while Maisie laid the hot cloth to his wound. He didn't grit it out to make a show; he let the hurt pass through and leave, because that's what hurt does when you don't grab it. She tied the new bandage clean and snug.

"You know," she said, eyes on her work, voice easy, "when I first came, I couldn't picture any day that didn't feel like hiding."

"I remember."

"Today didn't," she said. "Not even before you came to the line. The house felt...watched over. Like a church does when no one's in it but God."

He set his palm over hers where it rested on his thigh, not pressing—just laying it there so the thank-you didn't have to carry words. Junie squeaked from the cradle. Maisie stood to fetch her; his fingers caught a thread at her hem and let it go, the way a man does when he remembers he doesn't have to hold tight to keep a thing.

Outside, the mule bell gave one mild note and quit. Not warning, not omen. Just a simple sound in a yard that had learned again what quiet meant. He breathed with the house—

the good kind, end-of-day—and when he looked at his wife, he didn't feel something slipping away.

For the first time in a long time, he felt a thing staying.

Epilogue

Five Years Later

Five years laid themselves over the Calder place like good seasons stacked one on another. Fences held, grass came on, calves dropped sure. Where the north run once wore bells as warning, one old mule bell still hung low out of habit and luck; most days it rang only when a breeze decided to say its piece. Sheriff Lane had long since taken Zeke Blackwell and Roy Danner out of the county—first to the judge, then farther east on matters that didn't belong to this land. Folks quit speaking their names. The ranch breathed easier.

The house had grown like a family grows—first a lean-to that turned honest into a pantry, then a room off the back with windows facing south, then a porch roof run long to fit more chairs. The table stretched to keep up. So did the laughter.

Junie—Juniper Calder—was six and ran like wind with her hair flying, hatchet-straight part ruined before noon. She'd take a doll gently and tuck it in a box, then follow Tom on a fence walk, small hand in his and the other hand full of questions.

"Why's that post deeper than the rest? How come the wire sings sometimes and not others? If I step quiet, will the quail forget me?" Tom answered what she asked and what she meant, steady as all the years in his bones. He claimed she wore him out; he checked her boots before supper like a proud uncle checks a colt's hooves.

Maisie watched and felt the old fear—thin as thread, hardly there now—go slack. This place had taken Junie in and named her, not with speeches but with chores and nicknames and a place on every wagon plank that needed a small set of knees.

There were two more voices in the house now. Thomas Calder, four last month, shadowed Wes with a wooden hammer Eli had carved from a scrap of oak. He fixed what didn't need fixing, tapped chair legs, and muttered, "Hold still," to things that weren't moving. He had Wes's quiet brow and Maisie's stubborn mouth. When he climbed into Wes's lap at day's end, he fit under that big hand like he'd been made for the space.

Ivy Calder, round and fierce at one year, announced herself on every breath. If the house went quiet, she filled it. If the yard laughed, she outdid it. She'd been talking since before she had teeth; now she held court from the kitchen floor and issued orders in a language only she understood, and everyone obeyed.

Eli and Minnie had a little girl with hair the color of new wheat and eyes like her mother's. Some days, she and Junie disappeared into the cottonwood stand with a rope and a basket, returning with stories and grass stains and a gosling once, which Minnie pretended to scold and then kept in a washtub three days. Eli claimed he came "to check the gate" most afternoons. He came for pie and for the way his daughter sat in his hat and grinned like she'd stolen a sun.

Jesse ran the books like a riverboat captain runs a channel—reading shallows, minding bends, never panicking when something floated bad-mannered downstream. He kept a second ledger for orders Maisie sent with Minnie—salves and teas and little packets of seeds tied with the same yellow and orange strings as the old jars on the shelf. Rhett had traded half his fire for patience and put the other half to good use; he still took night watches when it was called for, but now he came in at daybreak and poured his coffee without waking the baby. He made Junie her first slingshot and taught Thomas to spit watermelon seeds farther than any decent person should, and then showed both how to say "sorry" when Mrs. Lyle's porch took a blackened shower.

Maisie wrote letters now—the kind that kept a ranch tied to town without string. Orders to the mercantile, thanks to neighbors who brought news, proper notes for the schoolmistress about a book Junie had taken a shine to and carried home under her dress because she didn't know how to ask. She liked the way her hand looked on a page with this name at the bottom: *Maisie Ward Calder.* The *Ward* stayed for the girl who had run alone. The *Calder* fit the woman who didn't.

They had stood two springs back in Judge Markell's office, Junie in her best boots, Wes with his hat held in both hands. Minnie had witnessed; the judge had cleared his throat too much and read the paper aloud anyway. When he said, "from this day," Junie had tugged his sleeve and said, "From before," and he smiled and signed. The preacher had blessed them on a Sunday with no fuss—just a hand on three heads and a verse about a house planted by water.

Maisie still kept Ivy close. The silver thimble lived in a little tin on a high shelf until Junie asked to learn a plain stitch. Then it came down and found its place on a new finger. Once a year, on the day Ivy had gone, Maisie took the children to the cottonwoods and told a clean, short story: their aunt had been brave, and God had been kind, and love had made a small road through a big dark and brought them here. Wes came at the end and set his hand at the small of her back in the old way, the way that said "I see you" without making a show.

On this afternoon in late summer, the light lay gold across everything that wanted it. Laundry ran along the line from one cottonwood to the next. Steam yesterday; sun today. Minnie had brought over a pie to "celebrate nothing at all," which was every excuse Minnie needed. The men were scattered to their tasks: Tom and Rhett fixing a hinge at the tack room; Jesse checking weights against the ledger; Eli teaching Thomas to respect a hammer without fearing it. Junie balanced on the top rail by the south lot, knees smudged, hair ribbon gone, telling a yearling all the advice she had gathered in six long years. Clara bellowed at a chicken twice her size and won the argument by force of personality.

Maisie stood on the back step a breath and filled her eyes. The yard wasn't pretty in the way city magazines might have liked; it was beautiful in the way a thing is when it fits itself: a pail turned sun-caught, a dog asleep in the shadow of a trough, a man's hat hung on a nail in exactly the one place he reached for it. The breeze made the old mule bell clink once and give up.

She moved inside to the kitchen and took down the yellow and orange strings from their hook. She'd learned to keep string as careful as coin. A woman could tie up most needs with the right length. Clara crawled under the table to beat a spoon against the leg. The sound set a rhythm. Maisie tied three bundles of dried comfrey and two of marigold, breathed the clean, bitter scent, and smiled. Ivy had left her these particular colors—one for knit, one for bloom. They had mended more than an ankle.

Wes came in as the kettle started up—mud on his boots, shirt stuck to him at the neck, hair pushed back by a hand that had likely wiped sweat and then forgotten. He had lines at the corners of his eyes he didn't have five years ago. Maisie thought she'd earned each one and wished for forty more.

"Tom says the east gate needs a new latch," he said, setting his hat on its peg, which he did now without thinking. "Says the old one's got more memory than sense."

"I'll write it on Jesse's list," she answered, wiping her hands. "Pie's on the sideboard. Minnie said it's to celebrate nothin' at all."

"That's worth celebratin'," he said, cutting a piece with the kind of care he gave to everything that didn't look important to other folks and matters most for that very reason. He handed her the first plate without needing to be told. It was a small thing; it always felt like more.

"Junie wants to ride the fence with Tom after supper," she said. "Says she's learned the difference between a nick and a bite."

Wes took a bite, nodded appreciation, then the father's measure. "She can go to the willow and back. No farther. Tom'll fuss. He does it because he likes fussin'."

"He likes her," Maisie said. "He likes us." She meant the whole circle of them and the way love had settled in without clamor.

Wes set his plate down and took a breath like a man who has learned prayer fits best when it's short. "You happy?" he asked—not like a man scared of the answer, but like one who wanted to hear what he already knew said out loud so it could join the air between them.

"Down to my bones," she said. "Are you?"

He looked at her as if the question were a gate he opened and walked through. "I am," he said simply. "It's a work kind of happy, not a leisure kind. But I always trusted the work kind more." He wiped crumbs from his thumb and watched her over the edge of his hand. "You still think about the day you meant to go?"

"Sometimes," she said, because the truth wore better than anything else. "It feels like it happened to someone I knew once. And then I look at this—" she gestured with the string tied around her fingers, the kitchen, the noise under the table, his hat on that peg— "and I can't imagine the step I'd have had to take to miss it."

Clara tipped herself out from under the table and set both hands on Wes's boot. "Up," she commanded.

"That's a new word," Wes observed, then obeyed his smallest general and set her on his arm like a sack of flour made of feathers. She patted his cheek with approval, then grabbed for his pie. He surrendered the crust and pretended to be put out.

"Tonight," he said to Maisie over Clara's curls, "when the children are in their proper places and no one is robbin' me of my supper, we'll sit the porch. I want to tell you something I haven't said right yet."

She felt the old, happy skip in her chest—the one that had first come on a porch at night when the moon put a line on the floor and a baby cried at the wrong time and the right promise had waited. "All right," she said, making her voice steady because a woman ought to meet joy without wobbling if she could manage it. "I'll hold you to it."

They ate standing, a bite here and there between interruptions. Wes went back out with Thomas to set eyes on the latch Tom had mentioned. Eli's laugh carried from the front yard where he'd turned a "gate check" into a game of horseshoes with Jesse, who swore he didn't care and then cared very much. Minnie scolded that the horseshoes were too near her new herb bed and then set a wager of two scones and a jar of quince jam. Rhett came through the kitchen with a paint can and Clara's spoon tucked behind his ear like a brush, kissed Maisie's temple in passing, and pretended not to notice when she took the spoon back.

Supper came and went with the slow, content racket of a house that knew itself. After, Tom set Junie on the top rail and pointed out a bite mark on the far wire, not from men but from a mule with a taste for mischief. "You can tell because it's ragged," he said, making the word important and sending her off to sleep with a new piece of knowledge in her pocket. Minnie carried her girl home over her shoulder like a sack of flour that would talk all the way and sleep by the time she crossed her own porch. The sky let go of its last light, reluctant and then all at once.

When the house settled to the breaths Maisie loved best—children deep, men quiet, the stove ticking as it banked—Wes took two mugs and went to the porch. She followed. The cottonwoods talked in the small voice they use for people who listen. A whip-poor-will called once and quit, satisfied someone had heard.

They sat where the rail still remembered an almost-kiss. He set the mugs down and turned his hat in his hands, then made himself stop. He had outgrown fidgeting when words mattered; he was learning to speak them plain and let them land how they would.

"I've said I love you," he began. "Likely I'll say it crooked most days—by fetchin' wood before you ask and takin' a baby when you don't mean to let go. But I want to give you the other thing too. The one I didn't have before."

She waited, heart steady.

"Joy," he said. "Not the loud kind. The kind that sits down in a man and lets him rest even when he's moving. I had duty and I trusted it. I still do. But you—" he let the word be what it was— "you've made joy a piece of my work. I thought a life was something to hold together with both hands and your teeth. Turns out it's also something that holds you."

She felt it strike true and sweet in the center of her. "You give me that too," she said. "I just didn't have a name for it when it started."

He smiled, easy. "We can call it what it is now. We've earned that."

Junie's window sat open a hand's width; a little square of lamplight lay on the yard like a promise that could be picked up any time they needed it. The mule bell ticked, no more than a token sound. Somewhere out beyond the willow, a calf bawled once and a cow answered, and the whole of it—land, house, people—felt to Maisie like a chord in tune.

"Remember the prayer you said once?" she asked after a while. "Short and plain. You thought I was asleep."

Wes's mouth kicked at one corner. "Lord, keep them. I'll do my part."

"That one," she said. "Seems to me He has."

"And we have," Wes answered, no boast in it.

She leaned her shoulder into his and let the quiet do what it did best. When he turned his head, she met him. The kiss wasn't for promise this time. It was thanks.

Behind them, Clara stirred and settled. On the far fenceline, a night rider from Harlan Tate's place tipped his hat and kept going. In the morning, there would be eggs to gather and letters to send, a hinge to mend, and a quilt to turn. Fear still lived in the world; it just didn't live in this house.

Maisie set her hand on the rail and felt the old wood warm under her palm, the way a rail keeps the day's sun after dark. A woman could measure a life by what held heat like that.

"Come inside," she said at last. "Tomorrow's got its own list."

"Always will," he said, rising with her.

They went in and drew the door to. The latch fell home with the satisfaction of a thing made right and kept that way. Outside, the bell didn't ring. It didn't need to.

THE END

Also by Ava Winters

Thank you for reading **"Their Colorado Promise"**!

I hope it brought a little warmth to your day! If you enjoyed it, you might also like some of my other favorites:

My latest Amazon bestsellers:

#1 Their Nebraska Marriage Deal

#2 Risking Love in Nevada

#3 A Forever Home With Her Mountain Man

#4 Love's Journey Across the Oregon Trail

#5 The Rancher's Trial Bride

You can also find *all* of my stories here:
https://go.avawinters.com/bc-authorpage

Thank you for letting me keep doing what I love—it means the world to me! ♥️

Printed in Dunstable, United Kingdom